OF DOUBT

To Robin

SEA OF DOUBT

THE GREATEST STORY EVER SOLD

Jeremy D. Holden

Thanks for the wonderful endorsement

— Jerry

Clean Publishing
Raleigh

Published by Clean Publishing
6601 Six Forks Road, Suite 400
Raleigh, NC 27615

ISBN 978-0-9978970-0-5

Cover and Interior Design: Scott Scaggs
Editor: Cynthia Zigmund

Printed in the United States of America.

To Natalie, my extraordinary wife, whose courage, brilliance, and radiance takes my breath away every day that I'm blessed to share with her.

"He's not the Messiah, he's a very naughty boy."
—Terry Jones in *Monty Python's Life of Brian*

1

You know who was big on fishing? Jesus. Jesus was all about fish and fishing.

I don't know my Bible all that well, but there was the miracle of the loaves and fish, where Jesus fed 5,000 people who had come to hear him speak. With just five loaves of bread and two fish! Then there was the fact that he liked to surround himself with fisherman, notably most of his disciples. And of course, he was a fan of using fishing metaphors like, "Follow me and I will make you fishers of men." I was never quite sure about the translation of that phrase, "fishers of men." It didn't seem like proper English to me.

I have no idea why these thoughts are going through my head at this moment, but, then again, perhaps it's because I'm feeling that this might be the ideal time for Jesus to show up and perform a miracle, as it looks like I'm very seriously buggered. I don't mean that literally, just in the way the English use it to mean utterly screwed, entirely fucked, and totally up shit creek without a paddle.

How could I have been so stupid as to find myself in this situation? Then again, how was I to know that Lula was in fact psychotic? As far as manservants go, he seemed more Agador Spartacus from *The Birdcage* than Luca Brasi from *The Godfather.*

In normal circumstances, being on a fishing boat would seem like the perfect way to clear my head and begin to make sense of everything I'd learned over the past week about Sebastian, Amelia, and of course Baptiste himself.

But this isn't about Lula going rogue; he's acting on his master's orders. How could I have misread Baptiste that badly? The fact that I don't know is illustrative of just how far out of my depth I've gotten over these past weeks and months.

And so here I sit on the floor of this twenty-four-foot Cobra fishing boat. I mention the make of boat because I'm focusing on the logo in order to try and regain full consciousness. The last thing I remember was looking into the empty glass of my Bloody Mary as Baptiste said, "Sleep well, my friend," and there you have it, the rambling semiconscious mind of an aging ad man.

My arms are tied behind my back, and from what I can see the rope is then attached to what looks like some kind of heavy mooring buoy. It must weigh one hundred pounds, so Lula clearly intends to drown me when we reach the appropriate distance from shore. I've been conscious for about ten minutes now, enough time at least to get my bearings, and I think I may even have made some progress in loosening the ropes that bind me, but not enough to free myself yet.

I've fished here in the Florida Keys a handful of times, and for some reason, perhaps the vibrant blue tinge to the water or the feeling of the wave resistance against the boat, makes me think we're on the Atlantic side versus the Gulf side. Not that it really matters where I'm drowned, of course. But yes, it must be the Atlantic side, as he'd want to drop me at a depth of at least thirty feet. And I remember that on the Gulf side, every mile you go out equals an extra foot of depth—and Lula would want to reach the preferred depth for drowning me quickly in order to make it back to the dock before it gets completely dark.

I seem calm, even to myself. But I'm actually not brave, not at all, so this must be the lingering effect of whatever I was drugged with. Nevertheless, I can feel the panic and terror rising within me. Strangely, it's less about the fact that I'm about to die, and more to do with the manner of my ending. I'll admit that I'm not "accustomed to pain," as Frankenstein's monster once opined, and I'm wondering how he'll finish me before he dumps me over the side of the boat.

No chance of an overly elaborate death, where he leaves me with a sporting chance of freeing myself. No, he will likely just shoot me or cut my throat and then tip me over the edge. That said, I remember him being awfully finicky about mess on his boat when we went fishing together with Baptiste a few weeks ago, so he won't want my blood or my brains spewing out everywhere. No, he'll likely just knock me out and then cut my wrists on the way over to attract the sharks.

Bollocks, I think I'm going to soil myself. Are these ropes feeling looser, or is it my imagination? I can't let these be my last thoughts on this mortal plane. No, I must focus on Mara, Charlie and Jess. I wonder if they'll be okay? Of course they'll be okay—eventually. I know this from losing my father in my teens. The thing is, that while the pain never truly leaves you, time is the healer that allows you to carry on. I know that I am truly loved, and I love in return with all that I am, so I have that to take with me, which is all that anyone can really ask for at the end. And there is nothing you can do to take *that* from me, Lula, you cocksucker.

I can't actually see him from where I'm slumped down, nor can he see me thankfully, but now and again I can catch a glimpse of his disproportionately large feet. It's probably those feet that made me think of Agador Spartacus as he tripped while answering the door for Senator Keeley and his family. And I realize that I'm still wearing the windbreaker that Mara hates, and now she'll have to identify me in this crusty old thing.

I need to stop letting these random thoughts enter my head and focus on the visceral experience of being on the water. I can feel the spray on my face, so fresh and salty tasting on my lips. The brightness of the sun gleaming off the endless waters that surround the Florida Keys. God, I love the vibrant blue color of the sea here.

Growing up on the southern coast of England, I never saw ocean that color until we went on a family vacation to Greece. Corfu, I think it was, yes, and we took a boat trip to Paxos and its uninhabited sister island Antipaxos, and that's where I first saw water that color. And I swam in it and unconsciously stored that memory away, only for it to resurface at this of all times.

I suppose I get the consolation of having a few moments of reflection before my death, and at least I'll be able to expire in these pure waters I've become so enamored with. Who am I kidding? It's no consolation at all. Oh, and there is Lula's bloody great foot again. I don't know what a mass murdering fuckhead is supposed to look like, but it's not this clown.

Lula's just a freak. He must be six-foot-five and he stoops, and he has those bloody great feet and a sort of ungainly yet oddly graceful way of moving. He also gives you the sense that he has inhuman strength, so even if I could magically free myself from these ropes, I'd still likely be screwed. Not that I want to give the impression I'm a total wimp. I played rugby at school until I got injured, and I try to stay in good shape for a man in his early fifties. But I'm realistic enough to know that even if I managed to free myself from these ropes, I'm no match for a bastard like this who has a practiced penchant for violence and mayhem.

And then there is his face. It seems to be entirely at odds with the rest of him, as it resonates kindness and gentleness, almost like a crippled puppy that wants your love. It's that face that is his unbeatable advantage. It draws you in and says, "This man is your friend and poses you no threat." And then he drugs you and binds you and weights down your legs to mercilessly drown you. While no doubt maintaining that sweet, sickly smile.

Baptiste said Lula had been with him since they were forced to flee to the United States from Cuba toward the end of the revolution in the late fifties, when Lula was just a boy. Lula was the son of his father's manservant, or whatever he did for him, and Lula stayed with the younger Baptiste and eventually took on the same role.

I'd guess he's probably ten years younger than Baptiste, so maybe in his early sixties, but he seems somehow ageless. What turned him into this creature, I wonder, and how many others has he killed? Perhaps he keeps some kind of perverse souvenir when he kills someone? Maybe he'll cut off one of my fingers—or worse. I guess I'll find out soon enough. Jesus, there I go again, letting my mind wander off into awfulness instead of savoring these last precious moments of life.

But now the engine is slowing, and I can feel Lula gradually bringing the boat to a stop as he places it into neutral. And I haven't been able to loosen these ropes enough, and there are those gargantuan feet coming toward me. And I can't see his face in the glare, but I can see he has a wrench in his hand. So this is it then, my whole life isn't flashing before my eyes, but I know that I love you, Mara, Charlie and Jess. And I'm sorry I didn't do more with this life and for each of you. But what I did and what I was, it was all for you, my loves. I am, I was, Mal Thomas.

2

In order to put the previously relayed events in context, I need to go back in time and tell you a little about myself, so you can begin to understand how I came to this perilous moment.

You now know that my name is Mal Thomas, although in actuality I was christened John Malachi Thomas. And if you grew up in England as I did, you will know that John Thomas was, and is, a truly disastrous name. I was called John after my mother's father, and Malachi after my father's best friend, who was also chosen as my godfather, but none of that excuses the cruel lapse in my parents' judgment in naming me after a common term for the male appendage.

I discovered how the rest of the world felt about my name on my first day at the preparatory boarding school my parents had chosen for me, when each of the new boys' names were called out at morning assembly, and the entire gathering, including teachers, descended into fits of uncontrollable guffaws, heaving, and whimpering in their collective rapture at my distress.

After that, I tried to ride it out for a couple of weeks, but my encounters with other boys quickly came to follow a predictable pattern. They'd ask me my name, I'd forcefully tell them, and then they'd proceed to laugh in my face, at which point I'd punch them as hard as I could in the nose or in the stomach. Or occasionally, for variety's sake, I'd knee them in the testicles. If they remained upright after my initial assault, a lengthy melee would then ensue until a teacher happened upon us, breaking up the fight and dispersing the inevitable circle of boys that are drawn to a fight.

Therefore, it came as no surprise when I was summoned to the headmaster's study in order to explain my seemingly endless series of battles. After detailing the recurring cycle of violence, he enquired irritably, "Don't you have another name, Thomas?" as if I'd intentionally selected a name that was liable to be an ongoing source of conflict for me, and a disruption for him.

When I told him I did have a middle name, and that it was Malachi, he said, "I see. Well, that won't help, will it? How do you feel about Mal, instead?" I told him I thought that was fine. And so it was that at the age of seven, my name was casually changed by my junior school headmaster. And through that I learned a valuable lesson about the darker side of human nature, inasmuch as people and particularly small people, that is to say children, will seize upon anything they find to be a weakness or a difference in another, and exploit it to the fullest degree in order to inflict maximum pain and misery, simply to get a rise or a laugh.

When I explained all this to my mother on a "privileged weekend," when I was allowed to go home for one night—even then it amused me that being allowed to go home for a single night at age seven was considered a privilege—she seemed genuinely clueless about the whole John Thomas being slang for penis issue.

On the other hand, she seemed quite offended that the headmaster should consider Malachi to be an unsuitable alternative, and blustered on to my aunt, who was visiting at the time, about how shocking it was that anti-Semitism was still rampant in this day and age.

When I enquired what anti-Semitism was, I was subjected to a rambling and at the same time extremely graphic description of the Nazi treatment of the Jews in death camps like Auschwitz, which traumatized me to such an extent that I couldn't sleep that night for fear of Hitler's SS dragging me away at any moment and turning me into a bar of soap.

I was actually quite relieved to have my privileged weekend come to an end and return to the relative safety of school. I shan't belabor these early life experiences any more than to say that, until I reconnected with Baptiste less than a year ago, I was under the impression that no one in the continental United States was aware of my birth name. And I certainly couldn't have imagined that anyone would have placed significance on its original Hebrew meaning. You see, I changed my name officially to simply Mal Thomas when I became an American citizen some twenty-four years ago.

You might conclude from this that I had a somewhat elitist upbringing in England, and you'd be correct. It wasn't *Downton Abbey* or anything like that, but by the standards of most people, my parents led a comfortable upper-middle-class existence, from which I, as their only child, benefited in terms of getting all that I needed, and much of what I wanted. Both my parents had come from what they labeled as working-class families, and they had advanced up the societal ladder to a point of relative affluence that my grandparents could only have dreamt of.

My father sold commercial real estate until his death—just a couple of days after my sixteenth birthday—and my mother, being the independent women that she considered herself to be, also worked outside the home, at a nearby three-star hotel where she organized trips and events for the guests. As far as I could tell, she acted in the manner of a concierge, although they would never have dreamed of bestowing that title on a woman in those less enlightened days.

My private education was the result of their labors and specifically a trust fund that my father had established before his untimely death, and it was an endless source of social pride for them both to be able to say that I attended Marlborough College in the county of Wiltshire, which was, and still is, considered one of the premier public schools in England.

Of course, one of the reasons it's talked about today is because the Duchess of Cambridge, formerly Kate Middleton, attended the school. And by public school what is meant is a private school, which makes absolutely no sense to my American friends—nor should it.

It was during my first year at Marlborough when I experienced a life-threatening event on the rugby field in a match against a visiting school team that was on tour from Cape Town, South Africa. My American friends like to boast how physical "football" is in the States, but they haven't played rugby, where when the ball goes to ground, rather than the referee stopping the game, a "ruck" ensues instead.

During a ruck, when there are various bodies on the ground fighting to retrieve the ball, and it used to be permissible to use your boot to try and ruck the ball out of the melee, in order to regain possession. Unfortunately for me, a particularly burly opposition player mistook my head for the ball and proceeded to ruck it with his boot, with near fatal consequences.

Although I knew little about it then, as I was in a coma for almost a week after the accident, a metal boot stud that was quite legal at that time had actually punctured my skull. The trauma occurred on the left side of my occipital lobe, resulting in internal bleeding at the base of my brain and causing the temporary displacement of my pineal gland. The pineal gland is a small, pine cone shaped gland located near the center of the brain that can affect your sleep patterns, and which some cultures have referred to, rather intriguingly, as the "third eye."

The specifics of this meant very little to me, and I just recall thinking it was kind of heroic that I was going to have a metal plate inserted onto my skull. That the metal they would be using was titanium—the same stuff they used on the space shuttle—as well as the fact that the lead character on my favorite TV show, *Knight Rider*, had had the same surgery, gave it an undoubted cool factor.

The craniotomy entailed a small plate of about three millimeters long being inserted, in order to secure the bone flap to my skull. It was then secured into place with several tiny screws, leaving a rather freaky set of bumps at the base of my head. The cool factor quickly wore off, however, when I experienced problems with my vision, as well as dizziness and nausea for several months after, and according to my mother I sometimes complained about hearing voices and sounds that would keep me awake at night.

Eventually, I was able to go back to school, with a somewhat more fatalistic outlook on life. I did well both academically and on the sports field, particularly as a footballing center forward, although my rugby playing days were over. I was even invited to try out for the prestigious Arsenal Football Club Academy, although my lifelong support of their North London rivals Tottenham Hotspur made that a nonstarter.

When it came time for me to choose a university, it was recommended that I apply for Oxford, much to my mother's social euphoria. However, I was to disappoint her gravely, as I'd heard about something called the Morehead Scholarship that would allow those privileged few that were selected, to study abroad in the United States.

And bugger me, again please don't take that statement literally, if I wasn't awarded a scholarship or a "full ride" as I now speak of it, to the University of North Carolina at Chapel Hill. And there I fell head over heels in love with America, with North Carolina, with the South, and with my Mara. And I have remained hopelessly in love with all of them, but most especially with Mara.

I remember vividly the first time I laid eyes on the campus at Chapel Hill. It was also the first time I saw Mara, and I was instantly smitten with both of them. Is there anything sexier in this world than watching a vision of loveliness playing Frisbee?

I freely admit that I am and have always been a boob man. I'm magnetically drawn to a splendid pair of breasts in the same way most dogs are drawn to squirrels.

When I spy a perfect pair, it can literally stop me in my tracks, as it did that day when I laid eyes upon the last pair of exquisitely formed and perfectly sized jubblies, bosoms, or Bristol's, that I would willingly ever touch or caress again.

Beyond these obvious assets, about which I shall say no more, Mara had, and still has today, a number of striking physical features that combine to form her magnificent totality. She has piercing blue eyes and short, dark, vital-looking hair, as if she just stepped out of an orgasm-inducing Herbal Essence commercial. Her petite waist and frame projected a natural fitness and coordination and of course served to emphasize the feature I've agreed not to mention again.

She also has disproportionately small hands and feet, neither of which, it must be said, were serving her well in the Frisbee contest. But the upside of her failures to catch the pink disc were a series of smiles that entirely took my breath away in the way they combined authenticity with simple joy and utter sexiness. She was, and still is, quite perfect.

I watched Mara and several of her friends play Frisbee for almost an hour, apparently without having been observed engaging in my lechery, and then I did the unthinkable for an Englishman and approached her uninvited to introduce myself.

It's been my experience that when it comes to women and business, a British accent is invariably a fine asset to possess in most parts of the United States, and particularly in the South for some reason. It buys you instant credibility, creating the impression that you are intelligent, which is nonsense since, in relative terms, Britain produces just as many beer-swilling imbeciles as America does. In any event, it can give you an initial advantage in some conversations, as it apparently did with Mara, and I blatantly exploited it.

I discovered that she was born and raised in North Carolina, having spent her youth in nearby Oxford, North Carolina. It's always been interesting to me how many towns and cities in the United States are named after places in England. As a favorite comedian of mine once observed, "Amazing coincidence how the Pilgrim Fathers left from Plymouth and also landed in Plymouth!"

Whether this was due to a lack of imagination in naming or whether it was about a desire to recreate the homeland, I'm not sure. In any case, comparing and contrasting Birmingham with Birmingham, Boston with Boston or Southampton with Southampton has often proved to be a pleasant distraction on a business trip.

Although Mara was a freshman like myself, her North Carolina roots meant she already knew the campus very well, and she offered to show me around. I took this as a good sign, and she proceeded to do so for the next two hours. Naturally, I failed to register any of the useful landmarks she pointed out, like the Old Well, Silent Sam or the Morehead Planetarium, which was named after my scholarship benefactor, as I was, in truth, way too busy falling hopelessly in love with her.

I don't believe in love at first sight. I think it's actually a sort of post-rationalized lust. I do believe, however, that when we meet someone who will be significant in our lives, we intuitively recognize them—often unconsciously but sometimes consciously. Whether that's the part of our brain that American psychologist William James suggested we aren't using, or whether it's the Zen notion of past life recognition, I've no idea. But still I knew with certainty that Mara would be central to my existence the moment I laid eyes on her.

For some reason, I'd decided I wanted to go to college in the United States, but I had absolutely no idea what I wanted to study, let alone what I wanted to do with my life. Mara on the other hand seemed to have a blueprint she'd been working from since the age of about ten. She was going to get her undergraduate degree in engineering at Carolina, then do postgraduate studies at NC State's School of Design in order to become an architect.

That's what she imagined, what she planned, and what she made happen. What she hadn't planned for, however, was yours truly. But as long as I didn't interfere with the career blueprint, she seemed happy to include me in the script. And so I started courting her, and I've never stopped.

The weekend after she graduated near the top of her class with honors, we got married under glorious Carolina blue skies at the charmingly renovated Fearrington House and grounds, with several hundred members of Mara's extended family in attendance, along with my mum and a couple of old mates from Marlborough.

I think my mother had been dreading the trip and having to socialize with a gaggle of uncouth Americans, but she seemed genuinely taken with the warmth of her southern welcome and the beauty of the surroundings. It was the first of many visits she would make over the years, becoming quite acclimated to our American way of life. (You know when a Brit has been here a while, because they use the word acclimated instead of acclimatized.)

I also managed to graduate toward the top of my class with a bachelor's degree in communications and business. And rather than wanting to do post-graduate studies, I was ready to turn the world of advertising on its head. One of the unexplained results of my traumatic head injury was that it seemed to shift me from someone who was a left-brain logical and analytical thinker to someone that was more right brain wired. As a result, the creative problem-solving dimension that existed in advertising held far greater appeal to me than the world of finance or international business.

Looking back, I don't know how Mara and I dealt with the long periods apart that our careers have demanded while remaining together and sane. Or maybe it was because of those long periods apart that we've been so happy.

The only job I ever had in North Carolina—where Mara and I chose to make our home—was my first job out of school, at a small advertising agency based in Raleigh, and I stayed there and learned the basics of the business while Mara finished school.

Once she'd finally received her master's in architecture, we decided that if we were going to have a professional adventure, we'd better get on and do it before any kids showed up. And so I sought and landed a job with a bigger agency in London called CREATIF. Mara fully intended to come with me until out of the blue, she was offered her first job—in North Carolina.

As it turned out, an associate professor at NC State had been very impressed with Mara when he'd taught her in several classes there. So much so that as soon as she graduated, he'd offered her a position at the startup architectural practice he and his partner had named Bright Lines—simply because they thought it sounded cool.

The name of the company seemed to offer a sign, since Bright happened to be Mara's maiden name. And in the years that followed, it proved to be quite apt, since she ended up owning the company and turning it into one of the most respected practices in the state, with offices in Raleigh, Greensboro, and Charlotte, achieving a national reputation in the process.

The other thing that stopped Mara from coming to London with me was the not insignificant and most definitely unplanned event of her becoming pregnant with our first child, Charlie. Prior to this terrifying yet wonderful news, Mara and I had decided that I should take the job in London, convincing ourselves that we'd find a way to deal with a transatlantic commute. It's amazing how optimistically delusional you can be in your mid-twenties. As a result, I'd been in London for precisely a week when I got the news about the impending arrival of Charlie Thomas.

I immediately went to see my boss and was amazed that instead of accepting my resignation with appropriate irritation, he instead offered to transfer me to CREATIF's New York office—effective that moment. Apparently it had been their intention all along to train me in London for a year or so and then send me back to the United States to help kick-start their fledging New York satellite office.

I naturally agreed and was at the same time introduced to an American guy from Connecticut named Oliver, who would be transferring to the New York office at the same time as me. Once again, I intuitively knew this was someone who would play a formative role in my life, although, in this case, I can say with absolute certainty that I didn't find Oliver Melville Grouse III to be in the least bit attractive.

So it was that precisely ten days after arriving in London to start my new job with CREATIF, I found myself heading back stateside with my new friend Oliver, of whom I shall speak more of at length later, while contemplating the daunting prospect of becoming a father for the first time. Although it was not ideal that I should be working in New York while Mara would be home in North Carolina, it was a damn sight better than commuting between London and the United States, and of course domestic air travel was hardly the dehumanizing experience then that it has become since 9/11.

I would take the short flight home to Raleigh most weekends, and if I needed to work on a pitch and had to remain in the city, Mara would fly up, and we'd share delightfully cosmopolitan weekends in New York on a budget—visiting art galleries, seeing off-Broadway shows, and discovering a host of niche restaurants that served dishes from exotic parts of the world I'd yet to visit.

CREATIF's tiny offices were on Fifteenth and Ninth, just across the street from the now-burgeoning Chelsea Market. I rented a one-bedroom apartment in the Village that I shared with Oliver, and we alternated weeks sleeping on the couch. Twenty years later, I now own that apartment, and our daughter,

Jess, is happily embedded there, as she recently secured a much sought-after internship at *Wired* magazine.

I've spent almost my entire career at CREATIF, and I'm proud of what we've accomplished from our humble beginnings in New York. CREATIF, as the name signals, was founded in Paris almost a century ago, not long after World War I, by a flamboyant Frenchman named Pascal Renoir. Renoir had what was considered at the time to be the quite radical notion that advertising should be emotional in nature, rather than purely transactional. CREATIF's early work for companies like Paris Match and Moët & Chandon made customers feel something at a visceral level, and a new genre of advertising was born, the principles of which continue to guide the industry today.

When I joined CREATIF in New York, it was a little upstart French agency that had the temerity to believe it could take on the titans of the U.S. advertising industry—companies like J. Walter Thompson, Leo Burnett and Doyle Dane Bernbach. It quickly became evident to Oliver and me that we were the only people in the New York office who weren't intent on coasting. We had drunk the CREATIF Kool-Aid in London, or, in my case, slammed it down like a shot, and we were determined to make our mark.

We formed a triumvirate with a splendidly foulmouthed yet undeniably brilliant young Aussie copywriter named Delilah Bishop—known as Del for short—and together we went out and pitched every piece of business that the rest of our lethargic agency didn't want to touch. And eventually we won one, thanks in large part to Mara.

Through her Lamaze classes, Mara had become friendly with a couple that had started their own brewery in Chapel Hill, selling what they termed "craft beer" out of the back of a bright red and black, beat-up old Volkswagen Beetle. They'd named the beer Lady Bug—after the car—and it had established a cult-like following in what we call the Triangle, the area formed by the near proximity of the cities of Raleigh, Chapel Hill, and Durham. So much so that they'd had to stop making the beer at home and had bought a warehouse on the outskirts of Durham and converted it into a brewery.

The couple, Nash and Rebecca, had no concept of how to market their products, so I became their unpaid marketing director on the weekends and enlisted Oliver and Del to create low- or no-cost promotions to help fuel their growth. And grow they most certainly did. Was it the beer? Well, it was an easy-to-drink pale ale, and the cute stubby bottle and crude Lady Bug label provided instant badge appeal. But what really drove its success was the fact that women and their boyfriends both felt comfortable drinking it. That and the fact that it showed up at the right place and the right time at the dawn of the craft brew movement in the United States.

When a year later Nash and Rebecca received an offer from the beer and spirits division of the global corporation BAPTIST to buy a controlling interest in Lady Bug, they agreed to do so with several provisos, the first being that BAPTIST hire CREATIF as their agency, with Oliver, Del and myself forming the nucleus of the brand team. Surprisingly, they agreed. We had won our first account and, more importantly, we had established a foothold for CREATIF into BAPTIST, which would later prove to be a springboard for all of our careers. And twenty years later, through a myriad of circumstances, it would bring me to the moment of reckoning with that motherfucker Lula.

Today, those early, heady days at CREATIF seem a lifetime away. I resigned from the company less than a year ago, after twenty-plus years spent building the business in America, for reasons I will expand upon in due course. I will simply say that my partnership with Oliver, the most important professional partnership of my life, became strained to the point that it ultimately fractured. And we could no longer coexist at the company we built together for fear that I might at any given moment drive the nearest weighty object into the top of his skull.

Anyway, I'm over it. I really am. I've had an amazing career. I've worked with some of the biggest companies and most famous brands in the world. I helped build CREATIF into one of the strongest agencies in the United States, as a result the second-largest agency network in the world, and BAPTIST into America's largest corporation.

I've won every available creative, strategic, and business award that the industry has to offer. Hell, I even won an Oscar for a documentary I helped write and produce, detailing how communications and branding helped build BAPTIST into the monolith it's become. I've sat on a dozen boards, made a bucket-load of money and now, at age fifty-one, I get to kick back and enjoy spending quality time with Mara, particularly since we have just recently become empty nesters.

We moved our main home from Raleigh to Boone in the Blue Ridge Mountains of North Carolina, because Mara and I love everything about being up there—especially the opportunity it allows us to fly-fish, hike, and ski. Mara has great leadership and talent in place in each of the regional offices of Bright Lines, and as chairman she remains fully engaged without having to deal with too much day-to-day client stuff.

I've also been keeping my hand in by working with an old client at a paper company who recently came to me with a new line of products called Wipez, a type of moist flushable bathroom wipes. It's actually proven to be a fascinating window into the bathroom habits of the average American. I really had no idea that about a third of all adults admit to using a moistened paper towel when they are taking a dump! "How do they get a wet wipe in the stall?" you may be asking. You'll wish you hadn't when I tell you that one in every three people dunk their toilet tissue in the water bowl when they are doing clean up!

The interruptive vibration of my iPhone broke my concentration, and I looked down to see that the caller ID spelled out OMG. I paused for a moment to take a full breath, then pressed the accept key.

"Mal, it's Oliver. We need to talk," said the voice at the other end of the phone.

3

"It's been too long, old friend."

"Not nearly long enough, you floating pile of malodorous flotsam. Jesus, you've got a nerve calling me Oliver. Just what in the name of all that's good and decent do you want anyway?"

"Nice to speak with you too, Mal, and as you can probably imagine I wouldn't be making this call if it wasn't absolutely necessary."

"You've got one minute then, as I've got to be somewhere. So make it quick."

"Okay, Mal. Baptiste called me. He has a very large and very secretive assignment that he wants to give us."

"Good for you, Oliver, but you'll recall that I don't work for CREATIF anymore, as *we* are no longer partners after that fucking disgraceful bullshit you pulled."

"I'm aware of that, Mal. But could we please just put our differences to one side for a moment? Baptiste had one important condition."

"I'm listening."

"We only get the business if you will lead it."

"And you no doubt explained, Oliver, that this wasn't going to be possible, as I no longer work for CREATIF, ever since you chose to stick a red-hot poker up my ass and jiggle it about."

"That's certainly put an image in my mind that I won't be able to shake for a while, Mal. Yes, of course I reminded him of the fact that you had left the company. And he was well aware of that, but still doesn't give a shit. Basically, it's up to me, to us rather, to find a way to patch up our differences or some other agency gets this account."

"And I should care, because ... ?"

"You should care because you were instrumental in building this agency. You hired most of the people here with me. And whatever you say, after twenty-plus years, you're still emotionally invested in our success. And winning this will pay a lot of salaries and provide bonuses for a bunch of good people that you care about."

"You total bastard. Every time I think I'm out, they pull me back in." (A favorite line from one of my favorite trilogies, *The Godfather.*)

"I've missed your movie analogies among other things, Mal. And I deeply regret the way things went down. I need to give Baptiste an answer in the next day or so. So please think about it, and let me know your decision."

"In order to make a decision, I'll need to speak to Baptiste directly to understand what all this is about."

"Of course. So you'll at least think about it?"

"And even if I were to decide to take on this assignment, there would be one condition."

"Here it comes."

"I would lead this without any interference from fucking Oliver Melville Grouse, and I would handpick my team from current as well as ex-agency folks."

"Agreed."

"By the way, do you know where Del is at the moment?"

"Last time we spoke, she came into my office, tipped my chair over, and started pounding me on the head with my own shoe. Seems she blamed me for you leaving."

"Everybody blamed you for my leaving. That's because it was your fault, you inbred cretin."

"Yes, well, I haven't seen her since. I did hear a rumor she was headed for Sydney to spend some quality time in the old country, but she won't stay away from New York for too long."

"If I do this, you know she's a deal-breaker. Could your gargantuan and yet ever so brittle ego cope with us working in close proximity again, both resonating unfiltered loathing toward you?"

"As I said at the beginning, I wouldn't be reaching out unless it was essential, and that goes for Del, too."

"Right then. I've got to go and tell Mara about how you came groveling back to me for help, and how I could have been abusive, but that I'm much too classy for that."

"She's been married to you long enough to know that's bullshit. How is your distinctly better half, by the way? Sick of having you and your acerbic wit hanging around the house every day?"

"Mara's great, but stop behaving as if you and I still have the basis of a cordial relationship, Oliver. Because we fucking don't. And after what you did, we never will again. Just tell Baptiste I'll be calling him to arrange a meeting in the next day or so."

"All right, Mal. I'll tell him. And again, I'm so sorry that things went the way they did."

I hit the off button and sat there in a mild state shock for a moment. After the last time we spoke and my exit from CREATIF, there was no way Oliver would have called me if it hadn't been absolutely necessary. So this business about Baptiste giving the agency the assignment only if I ran it must be true.

But why would he make that proviso? It wasn't as though he and I had been especially close, or that our relationship had extended beyond mere professional courtesy.

Let me pause for a moment to try and see how I can best describe Oliver Melville Grouse. I will say that when OMG became a verbal and texting staple for twelve-year-old girls about ten years ago, it created a deep reservoir of pleasure for Del and I, as Oliver never ceased to rise to the bait. She could work "like OMG, OMG" into virtually any sentence, and the exasperated look on his face never got old.

To help explain the dynamic that existed between the three of us, I should mention for the uninitiated that in any ad agency, there are brand teams that have three central players.

First, there is the account leader, whose job it is to sound like he understands and actually cares how the clients make money, take them out for dinner from time to time, kiss his or her ass frequently, and call to let them know when we're pissed or when we've fucked something up. That's extremely harsh and untrue, actually, because the best account leaders are seriously smart business consultants whom their clients come to depend upon completely.

That was Oliver's role, and in truth he was one of the best I'd ever seen. Clients loved him, he made the agency money, and Del and I supported him when Paris needed to appoint a new CEO for CREATIF New York, because he'd always supported us and helped us do great work.

Second, there is the creative director, who actually dreams up the advertising that you still see in commercials, but whose job increasingly centers around seeding ideas through social media sites like Facebook, Twitter and Instagram that people pick up and share. This saves the advertiser the inconvenience of having to use their own money to buy media, like print, TV, radio, and billboards.

The digital revolution changed advertising completely, yet had very little impact on the way Del conceived and developed ideas. She had always refused to come up with concepts within the confines of a TV commercial or a print ad, much to the frustration of some of our clients. So it was completely natural for her to imagine how something should live across any medium and be shared and tweaked by whoever liked it.

Del was always a little rough around the edges, to say the very least, but she had a genius for cutting through to the core of an idea, and she had zero tolerance for bullshit. She kept me honest, and Oliver on Prozac.

Last but not least, I trust, is the strategy lead or planning director, which was always my role. A planner is traditionally the one that actually ventures out and speaks to the public and wades through a ton of research in order to figure out how a brand should be positioned in the marketplace. Then they write a brief for the creative folks to develop the ideas from and stay involved to make sure the work remains relevant.

There's a lot of serious pontification involved in being a planner. You have to be able to strike a professorial pose as needed, and a Henry V-style beard and a British accent also definitely help. In my case, I only did this at home, as I mostly spent my time in the office acting as a referee between Oliver and Del. I used the insights I'd gleaned from research and conversations with the people who actually bought the products as a form of tiebreaker between Oliver's literal business perspective and Del's impassionate creative viewpoint.

I remember reading how the Beatles success was due in part to the fact that they'd accumulated some 10,000 hours of practice on stage before their breakthrough performance on *The Ed Sullivan Show*. I don't know that Oliver, Del and I had put in that many hours pitching together in those early days at CREATIF, but it can't have been far off. We certainly had our own roles down pat and could finish each other's sentences, and Oliver and Del even managed to channel their simmering disdain for each other into something that resembled sibling banter.

It would be nigh impossible however to mistake Oliver and Del for siblings, even before Del opened her mouth and revealed a pronounced Aussie accent. For as long as I'd known Oliver, he had battled his weight. A mop of blonde hair that looked almost bleached sat atop his six-foot-two-inch, overfed schoolboy frame which, when combined with his unfortunate propensity to appear breathless most of the time, gave the general impression of someone old beyond their years who'd allowed themselves to go to seed.

The impression conveyed by Oliver's appearance was squarely at odds with the fact that he was extremely active, playing basketball, cycling, and working out religiously whenever he traveled on business. Oliver didn't smoke, and I never saw him eat to excess or in an overly inebriated state, so I'd concluded long ago that his swollen and rather unshapely appearance was the result of challenging genetics rather than lifestyle.

When Oliver spoke, it was in stark contrast to his enlarged and seemingly out of control appearance. Oliver's manner of speech could best be described as both considered and very precise. I can count on one hand in twenty years the number of times I heard him raise his voice or say something that you didn't sense he'd practiced and prepared carefully in his own mind first. I learned that this effect was entirely cultivated, as Oliver had battled a severe stutter through his early years, eventually overcoming it and leaving an ingrained belief within him that he could overcome any obstacle with hard work and discipline.

Like myself, Oliver had received a privileged upbringing and attended the Salisbury School in Connecticut, thereby following in the footsteps of the first and the second OMGs. But unlike myself, Oliver came from old money and was set to receive a substantial inheritance upon the death of his father. We both knew what it meant to be an only child and to be loved unconditionally while at the same time carry the family hopes and aspirations on your shoulders.

Oliver was an easy target in the manner of Louis Winthorpe III in *Trading Places,* and in much the same way people anticipated his demise with an unhealthy sense of glee. But Oliver wasn't so easy to knock down. He was highly intelligent, resilient and driven, and would do whatever it took to keep himself and his team on top. I recall him repeating the unofficial family mantra to me on various occasions where we faced some adversity, namely that "A grouse only shows himself when the hunter is distracted!" And for most of my time at CREATIF, I benefited mightily from our partnership and his unconditional support, until I fell victim to his well-honed survival instinct.

Del was everything Oliver was not. Female, Australian, creative, free-spirited, instinctual, spontaneous, and extremely petite in build, weighing in at about a hundred pounds and standing less than five feet tall, Del wasn't book smart, but she was street smart. She was and is one of the feistiest and most formidable people I've ever met, and if one attribute described her best, it is moxie.

Del loved advertising, New York, sushi, Metallica, and women, probably in that order. In the time we worked together, she had a seemingly endless stream of girlfriends and yet didn't seem to have a discernible preferred body type. I was introduced to women with an infinite variety of looks, ethnicities, and sizes. Blonde, dark, grey, flat-chested, big-breasted, fat, thin, and anywhere in the middle. I asked her once what all of them had in common, and she answered simply, "Each of them in their different ways was an exquisite fuck." And there you have it!

On reflection I think I functioned as their Goldilocks' baby bear. A little shorter and trimmer than Oliver, a little less loud and abrasive than Del, I was the glue that held these opposites together, because they most assuredly didn't attract. Standing between Oliver and Del, no one quite realized I was actually a big guy, or that I was being dismissive of an idea, or that I could be temperamental or passionate or linear. Unless I set my hair on fire and ran around the office naked while making parrot noises, no one would ever think I was the extreme one of the bunch.

And yet there was one thing I'd always been able to do that set me apart from Oliver and Del. I may not have had Oliver's business acumen or Del's creative instincts, but I could see the connection between things more quickly than anyone and make a powerful argument about how they should fit together. I think if I hadn't become an ad man, I'd have had a pretty good career as a trial lawyer, because I think quickly on my feet, I can be mighty persuasive, and I'd probably see the importance of a piece of testimony before my rival counsel.

In a business like advertising, originality is revered utterly. But I've increasingly come to question how much of what we do is truly original anymore. An idea we've never seen before might come along every ten years or so, and that becomes the benchmark for us to reach for and mostly fail to do so on a daily basis. In most successful ad agencies, as is the case within entertainment and even literature, much of what is produced isn't so much original as it is distinctive in its construction and packaging.

I had this discussion with Del one time, and I remember her using words like moronic, Neanderthal, pussy and Judas quite often. Yet her colorfully adorned counterpoints couldn't dissuade me from the belief that the bulk of our creative endeavor today centers around how we mash established ideas and concepts together to form something that feels new rather than creating something that actually *is* new.

But perhaps this has always been the case. Maybe that's how Monet and Cézanne felt at the apex of the Impressionist movement, although not Van Gogh, I'm certain. Striving for absolute originality can cost you an arm, a leg, or perhaps an ear. Or, even more tragically, your life.

So it was that this oddly balanced and extremely driven triumvirate took it upon itself to turn a tiny beer account into a relationship that would span the length and breadth of the monolith BAPTIST corporation, making us all rich in the process.

Alfredo Baptiste had been nineteen years old in 1959 when his family was forced to flee Cuba, and his father and brother were killed in the process. He therefore grew up quickly, as he was required to take over the reins of the family rum business and re-establish it on American soil.

From the single brand of Baptiste rum, Alfredo first built a powerhouse beer, wine and spirits company that included in its stable of brands Notch vodka from Norway, Cardigan gin from England, and Iona blended whisky from Scotland, to name a few. Using that platform, he looked to diversify over the next several decades, successfully extending BAPTIST into seemingly every key area of American business and industry including cable television, cellphones and infrastructure, energy, airlines, automotive, software and technology, banking and financial services, health care, mining, industrials, education, and utilities.

Sometimes the BAPTIST brand was front and center, but more often than not, it was the acknowledged power behind a company, and on the board.

After securing the tiny Lady Bug account, we made it our mission to find out everything we could about the reach and nature of BAPTIST companies and brands in order to position ourselves to win as much business as possible within the corporation. And after helping to secure growth of 200 percent for Lady Bug in its first year under the new ownership, we were invited to pitch for the Notch business, which had fallen behind Absolut as the leading imported vodka. We won the account and helped secure a turnaround that saw Notch reclaim the top spot with a dramatic and sustained sales increase.

We pitched and won four more beer and spirit brands from the BAPTIST stable, and our sibling CREATIF agencies in London, Paris, Rio, and Shanghai were able to ride our coattails to win the respective accounts in their markets. As a result, Oliver, Del, and I were promoted to positions where together we effectively controlled the agency in New York. Oliver became CEO. I took over as president and head of strategy, while Del assumed the role of chief creative officer.

We moved to larger offices precisely one block away, at the other end of Chelsea Market, into the top floor of a converted warehouse building on the Hudson River, where at night I could watch the sun going down behind Lady Liberty. We got a hell of a deal because Notch's corporate offices were on the ground floor, and BAPTIST executives liked the idea of their agency being conveniently located, allowing them to be at their beck and call, day and night.

The previous tenant had been a gaming company that had created a very nontraditional workspace that felt like a series of connected playrooms. We kept many of their ideas and decorative treatments in place, creating a feeling for any client or potential hire that CREATIF was a true creative destination.

Both Del's office and mine were on the side of the building that got the best light in the evening. This made sense, as many of our creative and strategy folks didn't wander into work until around ten but stayed late into the evening after the "suits" had gone home, when the agency was quiet and they could think and ideate.

Oliver's account teams, and our finance and tech support groups, occupied the other side of the building, which got the morning light. And although in one sense it created a division between the suits and the creative folks, the daily competitive banter and teasing that went on actually seemed to fuel a common culture rather than leave us feeling divided.

For all our apparent success within one division of BAPTIST, it was just the tip of the iceberg. First we were invited to pitch for their rapidly growing cellphone account, Yelo, which amazingly we won against stiff competition from Saatchi & Saatchi New York, as well as a surging young agency from Portland, Oregon, called Weiden+Kennedy, who helped turn Nike into a world-beater.

That success led to our being invited to pitch for the JetRider business, the airline for which BAPTIST had recently acquired a majority stake. This proved to be the first time I actually met Alfredo Baptiste in person, and I remember our first encounter quite clearly.

Somehow he had crept into the back of the briefing room unseen while we were busy asking the JetRider marketing team questions about the assignment, trying to learn anything that would give us an edge in the pitch. From the back of the room, a deep, Latin American voice suddenly inquired, "Oliver Grouse and Mal Thomas, which of you is which?"

We both looked up, and it dawned on us that this was the great man, the recluse, the source of numerous legends, and to many quite simply the most fascinating man in the world. We got up and introduced ourselves, trying not to act like starstruck teenagers meeting a favorite music idol for the first time.

He continued, "Your team at CREATIF has been winning quite a lot of our business recently. My various marketing teams seem to think highly of you." To which Oliver and I tried to appear humble in thanking him for his kind words and praising his staff, while gushing internally at the apparent esteem with which people at the companies of BAPTIST seemingly now held us.

The JetRider marketing team appeared equally shell-shocked, having clearly had no idea that Baptiste was in residence, let alone planned to crash their meeting.

Then he turned to me and asked pointedly, "Is advertising the only area where you apply your talents, Mr. Thomas, or do you have other interests?"

I was so taken aback that I just stood there for a moment, processing the question, while Oliver gazed at me, willing for a smart answer to escape my lips. After a moment of awkward silence, I responded, "My passion lies in decoding what makes people want to join a movement, or a cause, or adopt a brand, and the often illogical basis for the decisions they make. Advertising is therefore just one of many avenues that interest me."

He stood and studied me for a moment and then replied with only "Good," while nodding, before turning and leaving the room.

Afterward, Oliver praised me for thinking of something smart to say, but I felt embarrassed that I hadn't delivered a moment of inspired brilliance, and had instead provided what seemed like the kind of contrived response you might give as a conference panelist, which is probably where it had come from.

However, later that day we got an extraordinary call from the marketing director at JetRider informing us that his team had decided to take the unprecedented step of canceling the competitive review. They instead had decided to simply hand us the business!

Whether this was due to the influence of Baptiste himself, we never learned, but I've long suspected that the JetRider team was so awed by the appearance of the great man and impressed that he chose to personally introduce himself to us that they decided that it would be a smart career move to simply give us the account.

I am recalling all this as I type in the number of his executive assistant, having agreed with Mara that I should at least explore this to the point of a conversation with Baptiste himself.

"I'd like to speak with Mr. Baptiste, please. This is Mal Thomas, and I believe he may be expecting my call," I said.

"Of course, Mr. Thomas. Actually, Mr. Baptiste asked me to tell you that he would prefer to meet with you and your team in person here in Miami. If it would be convenient, he would like to send one of our company jets to pick you up on Wednesday at 8 a.m. Is Raleigh-Durham still your nearest airport?" his executive assistant inquired.

I remember making a garbled acceptance along the lines of that being "quite convenient," and thinking it gave me several days to pull a team together and locate Del. I pressed the off button and then turned to Mara with a wide-eyed expression on my face and said, "Wednesday at 8 a.m. He's sending a plane to RDU and wants to know if that would be convenient. What the fuck is going on?"

4

It's about a three-hour drive from Boone to Raleigh, and since my flight was leaving at 8 a.m., Mara and I had decided to travel the evening before and stay at our apartment in town.

When we decided to sell our house in Raleigh and move to the mountains, we'd wanted to keep a place there in order to stay connected with friends, as well as being able to have a more urban experience when we felt the need for it. Having the apartment also meant that Mara had somewhere to base herself when she was working out of Bright Lines' Raleigh office. She planned to do this on Wednesday and Thursday, and then we'd drive back together when I got home from Miami.

I remember the first time I visited downtown Raleigh. It felt like the city was closed. Today, by New York or London standards, it's still relatively sedentary. But through an urban revitalization project, it's become a vibrant small city metropolis with a plethora of eating options, great live music, comedy clubs, art galleries, and shopping. It even has an annual bluegrass music festival that takes over the city in early October and sees it brimming with life, color, craft beer, and sound.

I was never much of a fan of its sibling folk music when I lived in England, but the bluegrass scene has a strangely compelling combination of roots, dirt, soul, and authenticity about it that makes you want to fling on a dusty one-piece and go find a hayloft to make out in.

In fact, the downtown area came to life to such an extent in the last few years that it's become almost too noisy at night for an old fart like me, particularly on the weekends, with an ever-growing list of bars and restaurants playing music into the wee hours. So much so, that when choosing the area for our apartment, we opted for the fast-growing midtown area of the city, locally known as North Hills, which has also seen rapid growth over the past decade.

I said my goodbyes to Mara, which I must say I find increasingly difficult to do as we've become accustomed to never being apart these last months, and headed to the airport early as I'd promised to meet the CREATIF folks who were flying in from New York. We'd agreed that I'd meet them and take them over to the area of the airport allocated for private planes, and I'd had confirmation earlier that a BAPTIST jet was waiting to fly us down to Miami.

I'd had a difficult task tracking Del down but had finally done so the day before, and was relieved to find she was back in New York and seemingly ready to roll. After attempting to beat Oliver to death with his shoe, she'd walked out of CREATIF after twenty years without looking back, and she didn't plan to return anytime soon.

She'd decided she needed some time away and booked a flight to Sydney that same night to fly the next day. After catching up with her aged parents and four of her five brothers, which goes some way to explaining her rugged combativeness, she told me she'd rented an SUV, bought some camping gear, and gone on a walkabout.

I've never been to Australia, but based on Del's description of the people, the cities, and the beaches, I had been planning to go perhaps for a month so that Mara and I could also try to visit New Zealand as part of the same trip. However, when I explained to Del that my understanding of the term "walkabout" was that it literally meant a journey on foot through the Australian Outback living in the traditional aboriginal way, she confirmed that was in fact what she had done for almost a month.

There are a number of reasons why I can say with absolute certainty that I'd rather have a couple of my toenails pulled than to go on a walkabout in the Australian Outback. First, there are more deadly snakes in Australia than in any other country on Earth, and most of them can be found in the Outback. In fact, the five most venomous snakes in the world are all Australian, little beauties like the Black Tiger snake and the Inland Taipan snake, which is also known as the "fierce snake," suggesting that it must be really very fierce indeed having earned that title against some pretty stiff competition.

If sleeping out under the stars with these darling creatures doesn't dissuade you, perhaps the sight of a Huntsman spider, the second-largest spider in the world at about a foot across—roughly the size of a hubcap—will. The Huntsman would have the top spot worldwide were it not for the splendidly named Goliath birdeater tarantula from the northern area of South America.

And if that doesn't curb any final instinct to visit, how about being set upon by a rabid kangaroo, stung to death by a swarm of killer bees or bitten by any one of the numerous types of scorpion you're likely to encounter? Then of course, if you are fortunate enough to make it back to civilization alive, you might come across the unusually aggressive Sydney funnel-web spider. And we haven't even touched on the distinct possibility of being bitten in half by a great white shark if you're foolish enough to swim in the ocean over there.

In order to avoid fueling my anxiety-ridden imagination any further, I didn't probe too much on the details of Del's walk-about and instead moved the conversation subtly onto the next destination of her extended sabbatical, namely Phuket, the island paradise that is one of Thailand's southern provinces.

Apparently Del fell in love with a Canadian woman named Elaine, who she met there while recovering from her walk-about, and she informed me of her plans to make a permanent move to Vancouver, where Elaine lived, at some point in the near future. However, when I asked if she'd therefore finally decided to become monogamous, she owned up to having slept with an old girlfriend "a couple of times" since she'd been back in New York.

I made a note not to plan a trip to British Columbia anytime soon to celebrate their nuptials. The passion with which Del denigrates her adopted city of New York tells you where her heart really lies and why I strongly doubt she'll ever leave. In fact, it took some persuading to get her to fly down to Miami with me in order to figure out what this assignment was all about, so we could decide whether we wanted to do it or not.

Her one condition for considering it was that she wouldn't have to see or speak to, let alone work alongside Oliver ever again, declaring, "If I ever lay eyes on that fat fucker OMG again I'm not going to hit him with his shoes, I'm going to shove those sodding Florsheims all the way up there where the sun don't shine." And I believe she meant it.

After I parked the car and walked into the terminal, the team was there waiting for me. It would be hard to imagine coming across a more physically incompatible and seemingly random collection of individuals. The first one I spotted was Massimo. When it comes to getting older, there isn't a ton to get excited about, but I strongly believe that one of the highlights is in finding a younger person who adopts you as their mentor.

Massimo Tesi came to CREATIF about ten years ago, straight out of college, and I originally met with him simply because he was a Tar Heel and, like me, had been a Morehead Scholar. He'd had a humble upbringing on the beautiful yet relatively isolated Italian island of Sardinia. But through his own perseverance, extraordinary intellect, and uncanny emotional intelligence, he'd been offered a place at the prestigious St. Stephens School in Rome. He'd excelled there and subsequently followed the same academic path to Chapel Hill that I had more than a decade earlier.

To be a great strategic planner in the advertising business, first and foremost you have to be fascinated by the human condition. That doesn't mean you have to actually like people, simply that you possess an intuitive understanding of what makes them tick. Massimo had more natural intuition than any planner I'd ever had working for me, and in his case it came from a genuine love of people.

He wanted to understand them, crawl under their skin and into their consciousness, and discover what they believed and why. He was the best I'd ever seen at being able to draw out someone's hidden emotional motivation, no matter how illogical their viewpoint might be.

I had never probed too deeply in trying to understand what Massimo's upbringing had been like in Sardinia, but it was clear that his family had endured some hardship, and that his relationship with his father in particular had been strained. I recall him saying that his father had been a taxi driver and that he would sometimes join him on the night shifts around the town of Oristano where they lived.

Massimo could never understand why his father wanted him to join him on those evenings, as he mostly seemed to ignore him for hours on end. And his father appeared to resent it when Massimo was able to effortlessly strike up conversations with the passengers with a level of comfort that he never could manage. It was in this way that Massimo discovered he had a way of putting people at ease. And that once they felt they had a natural rapport, they would tell him virtually anything and reveal any secret.

It became an enduring source of pain for Massimo that the one person he couldn't seem to put at ease and comfortably engage with was his father, and perhaps that went some way to explaining why he came to view me as more than simply a boss and a mentor, but someone more akin to a surrogate father.

To have someone see you as their mentor or even a father figure, particularly someone with Massimo's talent and charisma, is a rare privilege. And I had felt honored to have him working with me for more than a decade. I knew how hard it would be for him when I left CREATIF, and I had intentionally chosen not to reach out to him much after leaving in order to give him his space in taking over my role at the agency.

At least that was what I convinced myself of when, in fact, I had various swirling emotions in relation to *leaving* Massimo, all of which were, of course, illogical. I felt guilty at having left my protégé when I truly had no choice but to do so. And at the same time, I felt resentful of the fact that he'd taken over my position when in actuality it was the last thing he would have chosen to do. Little wonder that I'd taken the easy way out and opted to keep my distance.

After Del, Massimo was the first one on the list of people I'd sent to Oliver. But now that we were here together, I wondered if it would be difficult for him working with me after six months of leading the strategy team himself, given the unspoken but acknowledged depth and nature of our relationship.

To say that Massimo was good looking didn't begin to do him justice. To women, he was gorgeous, irresistible, an Adonis. To give you a movie image to work from, think Agent Stone in *The Untouchables,* only taller and with more foppish hair, a modern, tight-cut suit, and a beaming smile that revealed a set of perfect gleaming white teeth, and you had the jaw-dropping idol that was Massimo Tesi.

It would be absurd to suggest that he didn't know the impression that he had on women, and even Del said that if one man could make her switch teams, it would be Massimo. But to his credit, he never acknowledged and seldom used his appearance overtly to gain favor. As a result, people didn't resent his physical perfection in the way that beautiful people are often scorned and derided behind their backs.

Knowing Massimo, I shouldn't have worried for a moment that he'd find our reunion and working together again awkward, because as soon as he saw me, his face lit up, and he came rushing over to give me one of his all-enveloping patented hugs. He pulled back and grinned at me as a child might in having rediscovered a much-loved and long-lost toy and said, "It's so good to see you, Mal, I can't tell you how everyone has missed you. You look so relaxed."

"Stop humping him, Massimo. And in any case, he doesn't look relaxed, just bloody fat," came the gruff Aussie voice from behind him that I knew and loved so well, as Del stepped between us and kissed me full on mouth.

"Let's get out of here and go raid the minibar in that luxury jet, shall we, Malteser?" Del went on, using the pet name she had for me that was actually a delicious chocolate-covered malt ball candy brand from England.

"Where are the others?" I inquired.

"Tish went to the lounge to make a call and try and print something, and Elliot went to take a shit," replied Del with her usual tact.

At that moment, Elliot appeared behind Massimo and waved as he made his way over to us with Tish Farrow in tow. Elliot Johansen was and would always be Oliver's man. And while I knew he would report everything straight back to him, I nevertheless trusted him and had found him to be both ethical and tactful in all of our dealings.

Elliot was that guy you forgot almost as soon as you'd met him, and even now I struggle to describe anything distinctive about his appearance. Medium brown hair, medium height, medium build, medium dark brown eyes, dressed Banana Republic business casual, and wearing classic dark-rimmed prescription glasses. As if to throw us a bone in providing some physical feature of note, Elliot had a soul patch that he kept playing with nervously, like the facial hair equivalent of worry beads.

Elliot was a Midwestern man and rightly proud of it. Previous generations of his family had emigrated from somewhere in Scandinavia that no one seemed to be quite sure of anymore, and he'd grown up in Champaign, Illinois, before heading to Michigan State. I liked him, in part, because in a business of egos, he was almost egoless. And although we didn't have a ton in common, and his allegiance to Oliver had created a subtle yet discernible gap between us, we had always managed to fall back on discussing Spartan versus Tar Heel basketball prospects during March Madness. Since I'd decided I needed one of Oliver's guys with me, Elliot was by far the best choice.

As Elliot walked up, he leaned in for an unconvincing man-hug, shoulder-bump type of greeting, cracked a half smile, and said, "Mal, it's good to see you. I appreciate you involving me in this, whatever *this* turns out to be. It's exciting."

"Let's see if we're all still feeling excited after Alfredo the Great has told us about the latest acquisition that he wants us to sell. Might be a new shuttle service to Mars? He already owns a piece of everything on Earth worth having, so maybe we're going off planet this time," quipped Del.

Tish Farrow, my chosen account manager from Elliot's crew for whatever *this* was, stepped forward at that moment and shook my hand with an endearing formality, saying, "Mal, it's so good to see you again. I hope you're well and I'm very excited to be part of the team for this project." To which Del sighed audibly at the nauseating respect being afforded me, while I proceeded to pull Tish into a proper hug in an effort to counteract the false formalities.

Coming to the realization that to any attractive young woman you are basically just an old geezer, old enough to be their dad at a stretch, comes as quite a surprise to most men in their late forties and early fifties. I think it's because the last time an unknown female checked us out sticks in the mind so clearly that it tricks our consciousness into thinking that it just happened yesterday, thereby creating a deluded sense of our own attractiveness.

I wouldn't describe Tish as being beautiful in the classic sense, but she was extremely attractive, and you often heard people, including Mara, describe her using terms like "endearing" and "resonating a kind of goodness." Tish grew up in upstate New York, somewhere very cold and close to Rochester as far as I can recall, and then went to Syracuse, where she had planned to be a sportscaster before falling prey to the unexpected lure of advertising.

I remember having a conversation about her being a New England Patriots fan versus a Bills fan, and she being quite adamant about only backing consistent winners—that and the fact that she'd had a childhood crush on the Patriots' star quarterback. Well, that aged me right there, as I still see him as a young guy.

Tish was African-American, although her ethnicity wasn't immediately obvious upon meeting her for the first time. She possessed an athletic build, and I seem to recall she competed in triathlons, but without question her most noticeable feature were her eyes. They were huge, they were the color of a perfect emerald, and according to Del, "You just wanted to dive into them and get good and messed up."

Tish had moved up the ranks at CREATIF quickly, in part because people soon realized that if you needed to get Del to do or sign something quickly, you only needed to send Tish over to ask her to do it. Much to Del's disappointment, however, Tish wasn't gay, and as far as I knew had lived with a longtime boyfriend in Brooklyn for several years. She was smart, she seemed to stifle any drama and, most of all, she made Elliot seem more interesting whenever she worked with him. He seemed to recognize this and therefore partnered with her as much as possible.

Perhaps the quality that most distinguished Tish, however, was an apparent willingness to see and believe the best in people. While this may be a common characteristic in a teacher or a nurse, in an advertising professional, that kind of optimism and hopefulness about your fellow man is often sadly lacking, at least in my experience. This was certainly the quality that drew her to Del, as Del knew it to be lacking in herself.

Del had told me that at one time she'd gone out for drinks with Tish after a photo shoot and had gained insight into an event that had shaped her personality and her outlook while still a young girl. Seemingly Tish had been the victim of a sexual assault by a star member of her high school football team, but because the boy in question was a top NFL prospect, the incident had been hushed up with the tacit acceptance of Tish's family. Her parents had been assured that Tish would receive a very favorable recommendation from the school in relation to her application to Syracuse, if everyone would be prepared to "move beyond this unfortunate misunderstanding."

Instead of letting this painful event and the related injustice define her, causing her to become untrusting or introverted as it might understandably impact others, Tish had made a conscious decision to go the opposite way. She had determined to present an eternally positive façade to the world, while looking for the best in everyone. Her faith had been central to her being able to cope with the trauma of the assault and ultimately to rise above it.

This experience however had had an impact on Tish's readiness to experiment in her relationships, which helped to explain why she'd been dating the same boyfriend since college and why she appeared to be a little naïve when Del and others at the agency were discussing their sex lives. Del had told me that she honestly believed it had been months before Tish had cottoned onto the fact that she was even gay, a topic that Del had never been reticent to discuss.

Although I didn't at that point know Tish very well, it was apparent that her positive aura almost to the point of appearing naïve, inevitably separated her from her often cynically minded colleagues, and it made people want to be in her presence more so than others.

Tish was nobody's fool, however, and while she may have conditioned herself to trust people, if you ultimately played her false she would let you have it, as I saw a couple of colleagues and even a client discover on occasion.

Everyone having now assembled, the A-team and I headed out to the car to take the short drive over to the private area of the airport.

5

I've got a thing about little planes, and I've been that way for as long as I can remember. I don't like turbulence, and it's been my experience that the smaller the plane, the more of it you can feel. I've often wondered whether it has anything to do with the metal plate in my head which, contrary to popular belief as well as the comedic wishes of Del, has yet to set off a metal detector at an airport.

Whenever I was flying into LaGuardia from Raleigh, I'd pick my flights based on whichever airline was flying a larger plane. You can't say any of this was logical, as a small plane has a greater chance of landing safely if it experiences a mechanical problem than a larger jet, but then fear is invariably illogical, a reflection of something that has become lodged in your psyche from earlier in your life, or even from a past life, if you believe in that stuff.

In fact, Mara suggested that my fear might be a lingering past-life experience where I'd suffered a traumatic event on a plane, but I'm doubtful about reincarnation to say the least. Have you ever noticed that when some celebrity claims to have been hypnotized and then regressed back to a past life, they were invariably a princess from ancient Egypt or something of that ilk rather than, say, a taxidermist from Queens?

Mr. Baptiste, however, didn't so much send a small jet to pick us up as a flying version of the Napoleon Suite at the Paris Las Vegas Hotel. As I nibbled on warm almonds and sipped my iced tea, I surveyed the brochure for the Bombardier Global 7000 while taking in my surroundings. Apparently the Bombardier 7000 is one of the most popular and sought after private jets in the world among the one percent of the one percent who can afford one. Our jet had four separate living areas and a dining table that sat six, as well as massive panoramic windows which I wasn't quite so keen on as they gave the impression that I was floating without support at 20,000 feet.

Before boarding, we were met by the pilot and our cabin assistant, who doubled as the co-pilot, and I was certainly the only one amused by the fact that their names were Terry and June, harkening back to a ludicrous 1970s British sitcom of the same name. As we entered the cabin, Elliot whistled, Tish shook her head in mild amazement, and Del sat down next to me and said, "This is a bit over the top, isn't it? Just what the hell is he trying to butter us up for with the royal treatment?"

I had been asking myself the same thing, as I'd previously gone to a hundred meetings around the world both with and for BAPTIST in the past, and no one had ever sent a private jet for me before, let alone one as lavish as this. But then again, this was the first time I'd personally been summoned by the great man himself, so perhaps this was just his normal way of operating.

I had asked Elliot to brief us on the status of all the BAPTIST accounts at CREATIF, as well as on any and all BAPTIST news and activity that might relate to what we were being summoned to discuss.

Elliot and Tish sat across from Del and I, and he pulled out his tablet and began filling us in. "Because it would take far longer than we have on this short flight down to Miami, I've asked Tish to only brief you on the most active account stuff. And when we've gone through that, I'll tell you what we know about rumors of potential mergers, acquisitions, and anything else of note about BAPTIST the company, as well as Baptiste the man," explained Elliot.

Tish then proceeded to go business by business in detailing what BAPTIST had been spending agency time on—as well as their money promoting—over the past six months since I'd left the agency. There was the creation of a new online bank under BAPTIST Financial and a new collection of single malt whiskey brands under BAPTIST Beers, Wine & Spirits (as well as a craft beer extension). There was a corporate push to fuel positive dialogue in the mainstream energy community—around undersea wind farms—in advance of a major investment BAPTIST Energy planned to make. There was also a campaign to launch expanded services in Asia Pacific for JetRider.

Lastly, BAPTIST had dipped a toe into their enormous pool of capital, an amount that would allow them to acquire half of the Fortune 100 companies, if they so chose, and to take a majority share in Medican, the largest hospital and care facility organization in the United States. The name would now disappear and simply be folded under BAPTIST Health.

In truth, from my experience of past BAPTIST account activity at the agency, this seemed like a fairly typical cycle, and nothing stood out to me that was likely to be the obvious catalyst for this meeting or that warranted our celebrity treatment on the Bombardier.

"And what's going on with Baptiste himself that I need to be aware of?" I inquired, after Tish had finished her briefing.

"You mean beyond the death of his wife?" Elliot replied.

"Wait, Sylvia Baptiste died? When was this?" I asked.

"Really, Mal, you didn't know that? I heard about it in the Australian fucking outback! What, have you been living under a rock in the mountains for the past six months? She died just days after you and I told The Famous Grouse to shove it," Del said.

"Wow, you're kidding me. I had no idea. Guess I've been more disconnected than I realized. Baptiste must be devastated. They were married for what, fifty years and completely inseparable. Poor man, they never had any children either. What's the word on how he's dealing with it?" I asked.

"Well, that's the thing, Mal. No one knows, as he's not been seen out in public since the funeral. He hasn't even been glimpsed going into a BAPTIST office. There is even speculation in the tabloids that he died of a broken heart and the company is keeping it quiet. So far it hasn't affected the share price, but if he stays holed up, things could spiral downward quickly," Elliot said.

"Jesus. And yet he's seeing us. If the press got wind of the fact we'd been summoned, they'd be all over this," I said.

"They most definitely would. And I think we need to be prepared for the fact that he may be a little, how shall I say this, *off* when we meet him," Massimo added.

"You mean nuts, Massimo. Look, I know he's paid our wages along with half of the Western world's for a couple of decades, but I've always thought he was a little off. To be frank, I'll be happy if he's just a little off, cause I'm afraid this will have sent him totally over the edge, and he may be all over the place like a mad woman's breakfast," said Del.

"Well, that certainly paints a picture," chuckled Massimo.

Just then, Terry informed us that we would be landing in ten minutes. So I sat back in my seat, closed my eyes as I always do when a plane is going up or down, and reflected on what I knew about Baptiste the man, and how the death of his wife would likely have affected him.

This was a man that one could truly say had lived the length and the breadth of his life. He had known tragedy and despair at an early age, following the deaths of his father and brother. Not a tremendous amount was known for sure about the details surrounding their deaths, although one unauthorized biography had claimed definitively that they had been caught and murdered by Castro's forces while attempting to flee the country on a plane laden with family heirlooms and important business documents.

I remember the release of the book setting off a feeding frenzy in the blogosphere, with various conspiracy theorists and the great uninformed, asserting that Baptiste's father had secretly been a CIA informant who was privy to confidential information concerning America's role and influence in Cuba, and that the U.S. government had made certain promises to him in the unlikely event that the rebels won.

The speculation went on that Baptiste's father knew too much, and in the confusion during the overthrow of the regime, the CIA took the opportunity to eliminate any potential embarrassment. No proof of this wild theory had ever been offered up to the best of my knowledge, and it seemed exactly like the kind of exotic fiction that often sprung up in relation to Baptiste.

Certainly he had never graced it with a comment publicly, which was how he dealt with most of the invented stories that surrounded him and BAPTIST. People seemed to want to paint him as being mysterious and daring, and his reclusive nature and lack of public comments only served to fuel the mythology.

In any event, the young Alfredo would have been too busy to dwell on the death of his father and brother, as he was thrust into the role as head of the Baptiste family, as well as president of BAPTIST, from the tender age of nineteen.

How he found the strength and the wisdom to survive in a country that must have been largely alien to him and translate the legacy of a relatively small business into the biggest corporation the world has yet seen with the largest market cap in history was the stuff of legend. No wonder the world was waiting and watching for the great man to resurface. If ever a company was too big to fail, too big even to teeter, it was BAPTIST.

I looked down through the plane's panoramic window, saw the sun glistening on the water off the Miami shoreline, and realized we were now in final descent into MIA. I remembered the one time I'd met Sylvia Baptiste, the love of Alfredo's life, and smiled at the recollection.

The folks at JetRider had invited us to the annual BAPTIST symposium that was being held that year in Chicago. The symposium was an opportunity for all the executive leadership teams of the BAPTIST companies in the United States to mingle and kick back. As was his preference, Baptiste had flown in early on the final day to shake hands, be seen and give the closing address. I saw him speak on several occasions, and while he wasn't a great orator, his presence and singularity of purpose always created a sense of awe for his corporate disciples.

For the first time I could recall, Baptiste had brought Sylvia with him to the event. She was waiting as he left the platform, and they embraced warmly and exchanged a few words. Then they made their way through the crowd while his executives and their spouses formed an informal line in order to shake his hand, in much the same manner as members of Congress do with the President after the State of the Union address, but with far more genuine warmth in this case.

Oliver and I positioned ourselves toward the back of the line, more with the hope of being seen rather than actually engaging him. But as it turned out, both he and Sylvia passed directly by us, and we were able to shake hands and offer congratulations.

She was an attractive older woman, by then in her mid-sixties, and by far her most distinguished attribute was the fact that she was content to age gracefully without surgery, cosmetics or radical dieting. She looked, well, normal, and to my eyes, all the more beautiful for it. She resonated a quiet intelligence and genuine curiosity as well as kindness, and she clung to Baptiste with a devotion that suggested both a deep affection and an evident discomfort in being in this very public forum.

Sylvia's parents had been first-generation immigrants from Argentina, and legend has it that Baptiste had met her during his first week in the United States when she served him in the campus coffee shop at the University of Miami, where she was studying to earn her bachelor's degree in Latin American history. Baptiste was on campus with a view to enrolling in some classes, and the story is that the mere sight of her convinced him to spend enough time at Coral Gables to ultimately gain his degree in business and economics. She was destined to be his first and only love.

Baptiste paused as he walked by us, and he said to Sylvia, "This is Mr. Grouse and Mr. Thomas from our advertising agency, my dear. They were responsible for the commercial you didn't like." On hearing this, I attempted to shuffle surreptitiously behind Oliver without success as Sylvia then spoke, saying "Oh, yes, it was the commercial for original Baptiste Rum I saw at Christmas. It was too sexual, Mr. Thomas. It isn't necessary to sell our oldest brand that carries our family name using innuendo. We have a rich and interesting heritage, and our rum is the finest in the world. Perhaps you can make a commercial that shows these qualities instead?"

She smiled then, as if to show that there was no malice or threat in her comments, merely an expression of her opinion and that it was up to us to either act on it or not. Since she had addressed me personally, I nodded and replied, "I'm sorry you thought we missed the mark, Mrs. Baptiste, and I hate that you felt the commercial wasn't in keeping with the family name and heritage. We will consider what you have said and revisit our strategy." With that, she nodded and they moved on. After which, I remember looking at Oliver and saying, "OMG, OMG." To which he replied, "No shit."

As soon as the plane landed, we quickly disembarked and jumped straight into a pair of waiting Cadillac Escalades that would take us to BAPTIST's corporate headquarters. I've got to say, if I had the kind of money that would allow me to avoid flying commercial with all the terminal bullshit that entails today, I'd do it in a heartbeat, even though I'm afraid of small planes. As the Buddhists believe, flying is harmful to the soul because it's unnatural, so I figure you owe it to your soul to minimize the damage and go private if you've got the cash.

The Brickell district of Miami overlooks the historic central business district, and more than a decade ago it became the most exclusive financial center in the city, and one of the most important districts in the entire United States. The area got its name from Mary Brickell, who oversaw the construction of a series of lavish mansions along Brickell Avenue in the early 1900s, only to see those gradually replaced with skyscrapers that were built from the 1970s onward.

Today, the only residential mansion that exists lies *within* the largest and most imposing skyscraper at the northern end of

the Brickell skyline. BAPTIST Tower has majestic views of the
Miami River, and while Baptiste's empire boasts offices in practically every major city on the planet, Brickell is mission central
for the business empire, in large part because it is from here that
the great man himself operates.

I had heard that the top floor of BAPTIST Tower housed his
private residence. It was said to be a palatial mansion on a single
floor, towering above his corporate headquarters. No one got to
see it, and I had no expectation of doing so today or any other
day, for that matter. The building had sixty-eight floors, and after
signing in, we were told to take the elevator to the sixty-seventh
where we would be received by one of Mr. Baptiste's executive
assistants, as only Baptiste occupied the sixty-eighth floor.

Oliver had told me previously that Baptiste had an executive
assistant for every major business segment: finance, aeronautics,
energy, automotive, and so on. And that he also had an assistant
for non-BAPTIST private events and issues. Elliot and I had a list
of who was who, so that whichever assistant met us, we figured
that was probably the industry segment he planned to discuss.

When the elevator opened, a well-dressed woman in her
mid-forties wearing a claret-colored pantsuit with matching
high heels greeted us, introducing herself as Gloria. I glanced at
Elliot, who was looking a tad disappointed.

The sixty-seventh floor was an exquisite study in how to use
glass in a corporate setting to create a sense of clinical power
and beauty. If the interior designer who had been selected to
create the great man's private offices had stolen their inspiration
from somewhere, I guessed it would have to have been from the
Icehotel in Jukkäsjarvi, which I'd been lucky enough to visit one
time when Mara and I had vacationed in Sweden. In truth, it was
a vision of minimalist elegance, and I wished Mara could have

been there. I vowed to myself to ask Baptiste if he'd allow me to take some shots on my iPhone.

We were taken to a large conference room that took the glass sculpture theme of the overall interior to new heights, and were asked if we'd like anything to drink other than the mineral water which was already in the room. I noted that the brand of bottled water was VEEN from Finland, with its distinctive indented bottle, that many people consider the purest in the world. Elliot leaned over to me and said, "Gloria is Baptiste's executive assistant for private affairs, Mal, so we're still clueless, I'm afraid."

Gloria surprised me at that point by asking that I follow her, as Mr. Baptiste had requested that he and I first have a private word. I raised my eyebrows as I glanced at Del, and she made a discreet movement with her hand and wrist indicating that I was a wanker, which is a colloquial English term for one who masturbates excessively.

I was led into a smaller room that was clearly designed for more informal conversations, as there were only three chairs and a coffee table. And again, quite strikingly, every object in the room either was or appeared to be made out of glass, including the chairs themselves.

When Gloria left, I sat down, expecting the chair to be rather uncomfortable. But quite the opposite was true, as it seemed to have been designed to perfectly support my spine. I poured myself a glass of VEEN and waited for Alfredo Baptiste to join me.

6

Just a few minutes later, the door opened, and Baptiste entered and moved to shake my hand. He looked much the same as I last remembered seeing him, perhaps a few more bags around the eyes, but there had been no dramatic shift in his appearance. For a man in his early seventies, he had a strong-looking frame, with his chest still pushed out, appearing every inch the champion amateur boxer he'd been in his youth in Cuba.

It was true he did look a bit like the guy they cast in those Dos Equis commercials for "the most interesting man in the world," with his salt-and-pepper hair and full beard. However, Baptiste was much taller, perhaps six feet two inches, and he was slimmer and certainly better groomed.

He was dressed simply in a pressed white shirt, casual brown pants and brown leather shoes, but each of the items he wore was beautifully hand-tailored and fitted his body precisely.

"I see you have something to drink," he said as he poured himself a glass of water and sat down across from me.

"I appreciate you coming here to meet with me and bringing your team. I was sorry to hear that you had left CREATIF, but it seems that your differences with Mr. Grouse were not entirely insurmountable," he said, with just a hint of a smile on his face.

"I'm happy to be here, Mr. Baptiste, and I want to say how truly sorry I was to learn of the passing of your wife. I would have written at the time but, in truth, I had rather cut myself off from the world these last few months," I said.

"Thank you for saying that, Mal, if I may call you that, and I trust you will call me Alfredo. Sylvia is with the angels now, she was my angel here on earth, and I owe everything to her. My life will forever have a void at the center until we are together again," he said, with the resigned sorrow of one who has lost a great love. I contemplated for a moment the idea of calling this man by his first name and felt myself twitch a little uneasily at the informality.

"But enough of Sylvia or I shan't be in a fit state to discuss the reason that I brought you here," he said, although I quickly interjected, "Yes, and many thanks for sending your plane to pick us up. It's very impressive."

He nodded and said, "You've worked with many of my businesses, but we don't know each other well, Mal. So you may be wondering why I asked Mr. Grouse to arrange for you specifically to work on this assignment."

"Well, yes, there has been some secrecy it seems, and both my team and I are eager to hear how we can be of assistance, um, Alfredo," I said as his name awkwardly escaped my lips.

"You may be surprised to learn that I know quite a bit more about you than you might imagine, Mal. Let me explain how and why," he said. I gave a curious smile in response and waited for him to continue, and all the while an intuitive sense of unease started to creep over me.

"You and I have more in common than you might realize. We both lost our fathers at a young age and became the great hope for our family. We both made our way in countries that were not of our birth. We have both been agnostic most of our lives." As he said this I began to feel really uncomfortable, as I couldn't imagine how or why he would know about my religious beliefs.

At the same time, I was surprised to hear him describe himself as agnostic. I had always assumed he was a Christian, as I suspected the rest of the world did. Certainly his surname and the name of the company had been sending false signals.

"It may surprise you to know that I've watched you and I've studied your work for a number of years, Mal. Or I should say more accurately that I've had people do so and report back to me. It's clear that you have a gift for understanding what drives and motivates people, but you don't like people, do you? I suppose it comes from being forced to survive away from your family at a very early age among those born into privilege, and there is no group more ruthless than those who've been given a silver spoon. It's because they perceive that they have so much to lose." I could feel my face reddening and I adjusted my seating position with some difficulty in the spine-clinging glass chair.

He continued, "And yet, from a tender age, your parents placed you among them at a prestigious English boarding school, and you learned to assimilate and appear to be one of them. But all the while you felt like an outsider, and that continued to be your way of being into adulthood." He didn't seek any acknowledgment of what he was saying, as he clearly felt he was stating fact rather than opinion.

"And so you were an outsider as a child who learned to doubt rather than taking anything on faith and trust, and you are still a doubter. For all your successes and all your self-assurance, your darkest secret and greatest fear is that you don't truly believe in anything. I know these words are hard to hear, particularly from someone you don't know, but I say them because in order for you to assist me in what I must do, we must be open with one another. And you must learn to have true faith again, Mal, as you once did as a child," said Baptiste.

I felt my discomfort and embarrassment at what he had said turning to anger at the brazen nature of his assumptions, and I found myself responding in a tone that I suspect the great man wasn't used to hearing. "Mr. Baptiste, Alfredo, setting aside for a moment the fact that I don't believe that any of these things you've said about me are true, how in the world could you possibly presume to know them, or to know me? We've only met a handful of times, and we've never exchanged more than a few polite words. Who are these people that you say you've had studying me? Did you plant people at CREATIF, or did you have some private investigator doubling as a shrink spying on me at home?" I responded.

"Mal, I knew this would be very difficult for you, as it was for me. However, you must believe me when I say my intention is not to offend you, but rather to enlist you in an endeavor that will make everything I've done and achieved to this point seem as nothing. CREATIF has played an important role in building BAPTIST into the force it has become today. Did you imagine I wouldn't want to know everything I could about those largely responsible for building the image of my company? From the earliest time you became involved with BAPTIST through the acquisition of the Lady Bug craft beer, we've studied and monitored you and Mr. Grouse, as well as Ms. Bishop. She's becoming quite agitated waiting for news by now, don't you think?" he asked rhetorically.

"She will, but please explain why you are telling me this now. And let's not pretend it's about my appropriateness as a business associate. These things that you say you know about me are deeply personal in nature. Please tell me now why I am here, what it is that you want from me, and why you needed me to bring a team of expert marketers here from CREATIF, which I'm beginning to suspect was just a smoke screen in case the press got wind of our visit," I said, with the growing agitation of one who has been blindsided and is fighting to regain the initiative by proving that he's figured something out, although he hasn't.

"Very well. But before I tell you about the assignment, I recognize that your reluctance to take things on faith will be a great barrier to you on the journey we are about to embark on, so I need you to promise me that you will try to withhold judgment. Believe it or not, Mal, your instinct to question and doubt is one of the chief reasons I chose you for this. If you of all people can come to believe absolutely in what we are offering people, if you can come to have true faith, then I'll know we have a chance of persuading others," said Baptiste.

"Okay, sure, I promise. And, yes, I'll admit that I am intrigued to hear what this is really all about," I said, with a mix of irony in my voice as well as a genuine curiosity for what was coming next.

"Thank you, then we have taken the first step without you flying back home to your mountain perch. Now you are ready to meet someone who has changed my life, and I believe will change yours and many others," said Baptiste as he motioned to me to stand and walk with him.

I followed Baptiste through the offices to an elevator that led to his private residence. I noticed my hands were clammy and my heart rate was elevated, whether at the prospect of entering his private sanctuary or, more likely, at hearing what was at the center of all this. As we exited the elevator, Baptiste took off down a long corridor that led to a glass spiral staircase. As we walked, I glanced from one side to the other where there were a series of charcoal and pencil drawings displayed, showing various sketches relating to what I imagined was a final masterwork. I noticed the signatures all read Picasso and was not the least bit surprised.

We climbed the spiral staircase up several flights to a door at the top, and as Baptiste opened it, I squinted to avoid the sudden bright glare of sunlight. We walked out onto a rooftop paradise at the top of BAPTIST Tower. To my left was an Olympic-size infinity style swimming pool that created the illusion of water flowing over the edge of the building. Beside the pool was a size-able modern structure, equivalent in scale to a small single-floor family house, which was entirely open at the front, creating the effect of a massive gazebo. To my right was a tennis court that butted up against a thirty-foot upraised platform on which sat the largest helicopter I'd seen outside of a military base.

As we approached the open house beside the pool—it was much too large to simply call it a pool house—I noticed a young man sitting with his feet dangling in the water and wearing a white T-shirt with the single word, "Miami," written on it; the kind you might find in any tourist shop in the city. He also wore a pair of plain blue, knee-length swimming shorts.

He was quite simply the most beautiful person I'd ever seen, male or female. It was impossible to say what his ethnicity was. He had the appearance of one of those models that fashion houses covet because they look like a universal citizen of the world, forged from a melting pot that contained every type of culture. Seeing him up close, he looked to be in his early twenties; his skin color was medium brown and appeared entirely natural, rather than the result of artificial tanning.

His hair was golden brown with flecks of blonde and was naturally wavy, providing the kind of unkempt look that people would pay a stylist a fortune to re-create. His facial features were pronounced, especially his lips, and yet he appeared to be perfectly proportioned. His eyes were the purest azure I had ever seen. His physique was fit and defined without being overly muscled, and as he stood up to greet us, I guessed he was about six foot tall.

As we were walking over to meet him, I'd started to speculate just who this beautiful young man could be. Certainly Baptiste hadn't brought me to Miami just to meet his pool boy, unless he'd completely lost the plot, which to be honest I was starting to be concerned about after the conversation downstairs. Baptiste had no children, unless ... but, no, that would have come out in the media before now.

I wondered if he could be a nephew or a friend of the family, but then he smiled at me, and I forgot what I was thinking. This was a man who children would follow home in the manner of the Pied Piper. I was still processing all this when Baptiste signaled for the young man and me to sit down at the table under the gazebo next to the pool. I moved to shake his hand and I introduced myself, to which he simply smiled at me without reciprocation.

Then Baptiste introduced us, saying, "Mal, this is Sebastian. He is my adopted son. He is special. Actually, he is unique. Sebastian, this is Mal. He is our friend; he is here to help us." Still, Sebastian didn't speak and continued to smile at us, and I started to wonder exactly what Baptiste meant by special.

Then Baptiste said something that would change everything. "Mal, I've considered many times how best to say this, and there is really no way to make it easier for you to accept, so I'll just be direct. Sebastian is the one whose coming was foretold, he is the Son of Man, the Messiah."

I stared at Baptiste for a moment, and then I turned and looked at Sebastian who was still smiling at me with those piercing blue eyes. I was searching for some visual proof of this ridiculous assertion, I guess. I resisted the instinct to run and throw myself into the pool in order to wake myself up, and while trying to compose myself, I said, "I'm sorry, Alfredo, but did you just say that Sebastian is the Messiah?"

"Yes, Mal, I did. He has come again," replied Baptiste.

"I'm sorry, Alfredo, but I don't know how to respond to that. In fact, I can't even conceive of what you are saying to me," I said.

"I'm sure this is the last thing you expected to hear this morning, particularly from someone who claims to have been agnostic for much of his life, but I need to explain to you how it is that the three of us come to be here together at this moment.

"You see, a few weeks after Sylvia died, an old man named Aaron came to see me. He told me there was a young man living in poverty in the favelas of Rio that I needed to find and bring home to live with me, adopting him as my own son," said Baptiste.

He went on, "He told me the boy's name was Sebastian and that he had the mark of the holy lance, and that it was God's will that I raise him as my own and keep him safe. He told me that the boy was the Messiah returned to us. He told me that I was John the Baptist reborn, the one chosen to pave the way for his coming, and that I was to use all of my wealth and power to ensure that his message was heard throughout this cynical and divided world.

"He told me that I would need help and that I should enlist a man called Thomas. I couldn't think of anyone I knew named

Thomas, and then I remembered you from our various assignments with CREATIF, so I did a little digging. You've only introduced yourself as Mal Thomas, but you were christened John Malachi Thomas, weren't you? Malachi, it means 'the messenger' in Hebrew, and Thomas was one of Jesus' disciples who doubted him at first, and then went out to spread word of his coming.

"It is you I'm supposed to enlist, Mal. You're the one who must help us persuade the world of who and what Sebastian is. You will understand their doubts, because you'll share them, as I can see you do now. And through that understanding, you'll help people come to believe in him.

"Mal, everything you've experienced in life has led up to this moment. You were born to do this for him, for mankind, and you must find a way to embrace your true faith once more," Baptiste concluded.

Through all this, Sebastian simply continued smiling and staring at us both as if he hadn't really been listening to any of it; that he was thinking about something else entirely.

I needed a moment to compose myself, but in the absence of anything well considered, I said, "Well, Alfredo, that is without question the most extraordinary thing I've ever heard. And you'll understand if I say that I don't quite know how to respond at this moment. I need some time to process all this. That said, I feel I must ask, at the risk offending you, whether you are feeling quite well, and whether you've spoken to anyone about this, perhaps a doctor or several doctors?"

In truth, I realized that I was dancing very close to suggesting that one of the most powerful men on earth was, in fact, delusional. And I knew that I needed to proceed with caution.

I continued, "I mean no disrespect by saying this, but this man, Aaron, comes to you soon after the death of your wife and tells you this fantastic story. Isn't it possible that he was exploiting your grief and vulnerability at that most difficult of times? Although to what end I can't imagine."

"I don't blame you for thinking that, Mal. And, yes, I can assure you that I retain all of my faculties. As we talk more over the days and weeks to come, I'm confident that you will see that Aaron was telling the truth and that this is all quite real, rather than the delusions of a grieving old man," said Baptiste with a wry smile.

"And now I think it's time that we heard from Sebastian, don't you?" he said.

7

I turned my attention toward Sebastian and said, "Sebastian, do you mind if I ask you a couple of questions? Although I'm not entirely sure where to begin." What I'd really liked to have asked him was whether he could do anything to prove he was who Baptiste claimed he was. For example, turn all the VEEN water in the building into wine like his alleged previous incarnation, that sort of thing.

Sebastian stared back at me, and I couldn't tell if he'd understood me, but somehow I sensed he'd heard me. Baptiste responded for him, saying, "Of course you can ask him questions, Mal. But I'm afraid Sebastian won't respond verbally as he is mute. However, you can send him a text, as that is the way we communicate most often. He's also quite active on various social media sites, Twitter in particular he seems to like, and he actually has several hundred followers."

I looked from Baptiste to Sebastian and back to Baptiste again for any glimmer that I had missed one the most elaborate pranks ever played, but I saw nothing in their expressions. I took a big gulp of air before speaking, because I knew I was in severe danger of having the tension and surreal nature of this situation cause me to bust out laughing at this latest twist.

"Sebastian is mute you say, but I can text him, or send him a tweet? At the risk of stating the obvious, how then do you imagine that he'll be able to persuade the world that he is who you say his is, let alone engage people in his message?"

I said this, but what I was actually thinking was, "Mr. Baptiste, Alfredo, if it's a doubter you're looking for, you came to the right man. I don't believe a word of this fucking nonsense, and at the risk of offending you, in the words of *Blackadder,* 'I can see you're as mad as a mongoose, so I'll bid you a good day, sir.'"

"In the past, I'll admit that it might have been impossible for Sebastian to be heard, but in today's social media-driven world, with your expertise, and that of your colleagues waiting downstairs, I know you'll find a way for his message to be heard and to cut through," Baptiste responded.

My internal monologue was working overtime now, probably as a coping mechanism, and I found myself constructing a comedic riff in my head along the lines of, "So let me get this straight. An unknown old man comes to see you out of the blue and tells you to adopt a poor young Brazilian guy who just happens to be the new Messiah. Minor problem being that he won't actually be able to tell anyone anything or do any preaching per se because it turns out he's mute. But on the upside, he sure is good-looking, and he does love to tweet.

"Oh, and the reason you've been enlisted is because your surname happens to be Baptiste—you know, like John the Baptist—and it's got nothing to do with the fact that you're a gazillionaire. Oh, and he tells you to enlist a guy named Thomas, after the doubting disciple Thomas, and I'm the only one you know, so you pick me. Just one question then, if everyone here is enlisted primarily because their names match a biblical figure, shouldn't Sebastian be called Jesus or some close derivative?" said the exasperated little voice inside my head.

What actually came out of my mouth, however, was, "Alfredo, can you please tell me how this Aaron managed to convince you of the truth of what he was saying; that Sebastian is who he claims he is?"

Alfredo explained, "At first, I refused to even see Aaron, assuming he was someone that wanted to exploit my fragile state of mind after Sylvia's death, but then he wrote to me and told me things about my life that no one could possibly know, and how my various experiences had led me to this one moment where I was most needed.

"Your journey is harder in some ways, Mal, because you cannot be convinced of the truth in the same way that I was. Your path to true faith must inevitably be more tortured, because only by assuaging your own doubt will you learn how to do so for others, and you'll have to start with your own team. And, incidentally, it is time we rejoined them, or they will start to think I've done away with you," said Baptiste, with a wry smile that I was reassured to see.

"Is there nothing you can tell me at this time to help me begin to overcome my skepticism, or to use in persuading my team, including, ultimately, Oliver, that we should move forward and be involved with this?" I almost pleaded with him.

He looked at me sympathetically and said, "All right, one of the things Aaron wrote in his letter was about an incident that took place over twenty years ago in Buenos Aires while I was there completing the takeover of a company. For the first and only time in my marriage to Sylvia, I'm deeply ashamed to admit that I was unfaithful to her. It happened one time only, and I have carried the disgrace of having betrayed my beloved wife all these years. Sylvia never knew of it, I'm certain, and neither did anyone else, as I've never spoken of it until now."

"I'm honored that you would share this with me, Alfredo, and you have my word that I will not repeat it, but perhaps this Aaron heard the story from the woman in question," I suggested, while pondering that Aaron's purpose had been blackmail, and that there was much more to this than Baptiste was telling me.

"I considered that possibility but ultimately dismissed it because I'm certain that if he had known her, then he would have come forward long before now," he responded.

"And Sebastian, he was alone in the world when you found him?" I asked.

"Basically yes, although we made inquiries and learned that he has or had a sister who seemed to have vanished some years before. Sebastian confirmed her existence, and that her name was Amelia, but he hasn't seen or heard from her in many years, and I fear that the all too brutal existence in the favelas may have taken her."

"Thank you," I said, and I meant it. I wouldn't have expected him to have trusted me with information of such a sensitive and personal nature, and it helped convince me at least of his sincerity in wanting me to believe him. I went on, "I'll need some time to process this—about twenty years!" I quipped, and he smiled back at me.

"Of course, although you'll need to make a decision a little sooner than that. And now you can see why I wanted to talk to you alone. You need time to decide how to tell your colleagues about this, and most especially Ms. Bishop, I would imagine," he said.

Then, after pausing for a moment, he continued, "There is one more thing I will tell you before we go back to the others.

When we finally found Sebastian begging for food on the streets of Rio, he had a crumpled piece of paper in his hand. When he saw me for the first time, he seemed to recognize me and handed the paper to me. On it was written the words, 'She is at peace now, and she forgives you,'" said Baptiste, and I noticed tears beginning to well up in the corners of his eyes.

Almost immediately, he regained his composure and motioned for us to stand. I turned for a moment to smile at Sebastian and said to him and Baptiste, "Would it be all right if I asked Sebastian one question now?" Baptiste looked at Sebastian, and the beautiful young man smiled and nodded. And so I said simply, "Sebastian, are you who Mr. Baptiste has said you are? Do you believe you are the Son of Man, the Messiah?"

He fixed me with those piercing blue eyes, and gave a single nod.

We left him with his feet dangling in the pool again, and headed back down the way we had come to rejoin the team. When I entered the glass boardroom, they all rose as one and Del practically shouted, "Mal, where in the name of Jesus fucking Christ have you been?" at the exact moment that Baptiste came into the room behind me.

"Oh, bollocks," said Del without quite realizing she had said it, and the rest of the group just froze where they stood at the great man's appearance. With that wry smile that I'd started to become accustomed to, Baptiste surveyed them and said, "Ms. Bishop, it's good to see you again. I'm sorry to have kept you all waiting, but Mal and I just had a very productive conversation which I'm sure he's going to want to fill you all in on as soon as possible.

"Thanks to all of you for coming down here at short notice. Mal, you have this room for as long as you need it, and then

Gloria will see you out. Please let her know what time you'd like the plane ready to leave. Mal, call me once you've talked to the team and conferred with Mr. Grouse. Ms. Bishop and Mr. Johansen, as well as Ms. Farrow and Mr. Tesi, I believe. Good day and have a pleasant flight." Then he looked at me with a knowing glint in his eyes, nodded to the team, and left the room.

They all stood there in stunned silence for a moment, and then Tish spoke, "He knew my name. I can't believe I just met Alfredo Baptiste, and he knew my name."

The spell having been lifted, Del and Elliot moved toward me, and Elliot said, "Mal, what was that all about? Where have you been with him? We are all desperate to know what's going on." To which Massimo added tactfully, "He's not dead then." Noticing my complexion for the first time, Del said, "Are you all right, Malteser? You look like you've just had your balls forcibly shaved."

I turned to them and said, "I've just had the most utterly surreal hour of my life. I'm going to tell you everything I just learned, I promise, but not here."

"Why, are you afraid the room is bugged? 'Cause I have an app on my phone that can probably find it," said Tish helpfully. "No, because I need a bloody Grey Goose vodka tonic before I try to download everything."

"Thank fuck, I'm as dry as a camel's titty," said Del.

We informed Gloria that we were going to meet off-site and would call Terry and June an hour before we were ready to take off. We took the BAPTIST cars that were waiting for us to Blackbird Ordinary and sat out in the backyard area next to their famous edible wall, where they grow fresh herbs and flowers.

Once I had a drink in my hand, I began to tell the team what had transpired. I started at the beginning, gave them the fullest possible account, and watched their facial expressions as they went through a range of emotions similar to those I'd experienced, including scorn, confusion, amazement, and ultimately a sense of fear at what was being laid in front of them.

The only thing I held back was what Aaron had told Baptiste about his liaison in Buenos Aires and what was written on the piece of paper in Sebastian's hand when they found him. Although I was tempted to break my promise and share this with them, I knew better.

I hadn't expected Del in particular to be able to keep from interrupting me, but she knew me well enough to know that I needed to purge myself completely, so she let me spew out the information.

When I'd finished, I sat back and let them talk it out among themselves. In truth, they reacted much as I had, although in Del's case with predictably far more colorful language. She stated on a couple of occasions that she needed to fly straight back to the relative sanity of New York and forget all about this, which was a sentiment I strongly empathized with. After the initial wave of reactions and well into our fifth round of drinks on an empty stomach, I finally spoke again in a state of building intoxication.

"I've had time to reflect while seated on my mountain perch these past months, and it's become clear to me that the thing people are almost always crap at is getting outside their own heads. It's why people seem shocked when they discover that they've gotten fat. Instead of taking a frequent look in the mirror, they are too busy judging someone else, and they don't realize that the extra cookie or doughnut was one of tens of thousands they'd snarfed down over years, causing them to turn into a bucket of lard. Do you see my point?" I slurred out as a stream of incoherent consciousness. When it comes to drinking, I've always been a bit of a lightweight.

To which Del responded, "I think I speak for us all, Mal, when I say no, and what the fuck are you blathering on about?"

I tried again, saying, "Okay, look, I'm a persuader. I persuade people to do or try things they otherwise might not want to. And if I'm honest, I do it because it makes me feels good about my ability to do it, and on some deeper level, because it makes me feel powerful. But I've been doing it so long, and let me say rather successfully, that as soon as I hear about a new assignment, I start mentally searching my experience archive for a template to apply.

"I pull out the correct persuasion file, and I use it in cookie-cutter fashion. And it works ninety-nine times out of a hundred, but it leaves me feeling like a fraud, like I've trotted out a tired for-mulaic solution, instead of using my God-given talents to think of something completely fresh. That's why I had been feeling so burned out before I left CREATIF. It wasn't because I'd been working too hard, or that I'd had too many disappointments, or that I couldn't stand the sight of Oliver any more ... well, it was that last one a bit. It was because I'd become so predictable that I could no longer see the potential for something truly original."

"Well, I'm sure we all appreciate your honesty, Mal, you sad, old tosser. But what has that got to do with the royally fucked-up situation we're talking about now?" asked Del.

"It's like this, Delilah. Say what you like about this surreal assignment but one thing you must admit is that it's unlike any-thing you've ever been challenged with before, or will be again, and it has the potential to change everything and change us in the process. All the communication challenges, all the advertis-ing campaigns that have gone before will pale by comparison.

We would be like the team who worked on the Obama '08 presidential campaign, except in our case the candidate would actually *be* divine!" I laughed a little at my own joke, proving that I was getting both punchy and drunk.

"I cannot believe you're actually considering this," said Del. "All the fresh air you've been getting, mixed with alcohol, must have addled your already damaged brain. Don't you see, that's the problem, Malteser. He's not the bloody Messiah. In fact, listening to you talk, he's probably just some good-looking special ed kid, that Baptiste has plucked from squalor because he's grieving for his wife and has become delusional.

"Look, about ninety percent of people on this planet believe in some kind of deity, and we'll be practicing the greatest hoax in human history on them. I've only ever once refused to work on something for ethical reasons," Del added. At which moment, Tish asked, "What was that?"

"South African orange juice back in the eighties, when Mandela was still locked up and the apartheid system was still in place," Del answered. "But other than that, I've happily sold booze, smokes and any number of cholesterol-raising processed foods, because I always believed that people had a choice and they can choose to say no.

"I remember being lectured by a friend on the nature of addiction after we'd finished a campaign for a Las Vegas casino, but in the end it didn't stop me thinking that people should just exercise their free will. If they chose to screw up their lives gambling or getting shit-faced, who was I to screw with that or judge them? And after all, if I didn't advertise it, someone less talented would," said Del.

"Not the most humanitarian viewpoint I've ever heard, Del, but I'm tracking with you," chimed in Elliot from the bleachers.

Del continued, "But this, messing with people's religious beliefs, this takes it to another level, Mal. We wouldn't be any different from one of those fucking TV evangelists trading on the poor and uneducated to fleece them out of their hard-earned cash for the promise of everlasting salvation.

"Like most religious messages, it's all driven by guilt. You know, you've sinned, repent, and pay up, and you'll go to heaven. It's the same as the bloody jihadists telling impressionable boys to go and kill people without asking questions. Oh, and when you get to heaven, you'll get seventy-two virgins. Duh, sorry for the mistranslation, that was actually seventy-two white raisins, dickhead!

"Not only would we be charlatans, what scares me most is that by shaking the belief trees, we'd dislodge all the crazies who stopped listening to logic a long time ago. They would go after anyone in an instant to defend their zealot-like beliefs, and let's not forget they would also come after the messenger. They'd come after us and maybe even our families. Have you thought about that, Mal?" said Del as she concluded her monologue.

"I hadn't, but I am now thanks," I said, sobering up after Del's splash of reality.

For the first time in a while, Massimo chimed in: "Let's say we could do this anonymously, and let's say we committed not to use guilt as a driver in our work. And to your point, Del, if we don't do this, Baptiste will find someone who will. Isn't this what we secretly yearn for when we are shilling toilet tissue, suppositories, and laundry detergent? The chance to use our collective talents to elevate something with real meaning and substance.

"This is why agencies do political advertising, because they want to be part of something beyond mere profit; they want to make a mark in society. Well, tell me, what could create a greater or more lasting mark than bringing word of the new Messiah to the world? And I promise you, that isn't my Catholic upbringing speaking, it's the ambitious part of me that is both excited and terrified by this challenge."

"That's the kind of smart, reasoned yet emotional pitch I'd expect from a planner who happens to be Italian and Catholic, but at the risk of repeating myself, there's one big-ass problem, Massimo. In the famous line from Monty Python's *The Life of Brian*, 'He's not the Messiah, he's a very naughty boy,'" Del said. And we all cracked up, breaking the kind of tension that builds up when drunk advertising people start discussing religion and morality.

"So what I'm hearing, Del, is that what it all comes down to is the fact that you don't believe he's the Messiah, which is fair enough because you've only got my word to go on, and I haven't exactly tried to convince you that he is. But what if you did believe it, would you want to do this then?"

"That's a ridiculous hypothetical, Mal, because I can't even conceive of the possibility that he might be who Baptiste says he is."

"Well, yes, the whole situation is ridiculous, nuts, otherworldly in fact. But say it was true, Del, would you?" asked Massimo, repeating my question.

"Okay, in the totally preposterous scenario where I'm certain that he's the Messiah and we have carte blanche to figure out how to persuade the world of it, and unlimited piles of cash to do it with, in that farcical situation, perhaps I might conceivably want to do it," Del said between clenched teeth.

"Well, all right then, I feel the same way, and apparently so does Massimo, which makes the next step pretty straightforward. We have to find a way to communicate with Sebastian without Baptiste being present, so we can be sure of who he is or who he almost certainly isn't.

"I can call Baptiste and ask him to arrange for us to meet with Sebastian so that we can interview him alone. He knows I'll have my hands full getting you guys on board to say the least, so I'm sure he'll agree to it." My mildly drunk colleagues nodded their agreement in unison.

"Well, I must say I'm glad we haven't rejected this out of hand, because there is the small matter that Baptiste implied he'd be prepared to spend an obscene amount of money on this. And much as I hate to interrupt this moral debate with talk of compensation, we all know that's what Oliver will be thinking.

"And if we say no, he'll try and persuade Baptiste to use another CREATIF team, probably one with a conveniently named Thomas in the mix, and the moral debate will be over. Which reminds me, I'm supposed to call him soon to report on the meeting. What would you like me to tell him, Mal?" asked Elliot.

"Hold that thought, Elliot," I said as I pulled out my phone and dialed the private number that Baptiste had given me, and he picked up instantly. I explained our request, and he immediately agreed. However, it turned out that he and Sebastian were now back at his house in Marathon, so he suggested we stay in Miami that evening and he'd send his helicopter back to pick us up from BAPTIST Tower in the morning.

Seconds after I hit the off key, Gloria called, having apparently just spoken to Baptiste. She confirmed that we needed to be back at their offices by eight a.m. to catch our ride. She also informed me that she had booked rooms for us all at the Four Seasons in Brickell, a splendid perk of BAPTIST now owning a controlling stake in the holding company.

After I thanked her and we hung up, I told the team that we couldn't all travel down there in the morning, as the helicopter only took six passengers, and two BAPTIST employees also needed to be shuttled to Marathon on the same flight. We agreed that Del, Massimo, Tish and I would go to Marathon while Elliot would return to New York to give Oliver a download in person. That way, the four of us would be able to take the BAPTIST jet home once we were done in Marathon.

We took the car to the Four Seasons, and then I made my excuses, as I just wanted to get to my room and call Mara. I needed her to tell me I was doing the right thing in pursuing this for at least another day, even if she didn't think I was.

8

Massimo, Del, Tish, and I were met by Gloria when we arrived back at BAPTIST Tower and were shown through the same corridor and out onto the rooftop where the helicopter was waiting to take us to Marathon. We were introduced to the two BAPTIST executives who were flying down with us, and we quickly got on board and began to take advantage of the abundance of luxury that Baptiste's helicopter had to offer.

Given the presence of the two executives, we weren't able to discuss today's interview with Sebastian, and so I just settled in to enjoy the short trip down to Marathon. I'd flown in normal helicopters before, but when the S92 began to rise, I could feel this was going to be an entirely different type of flying experience. I say "feel" because, of course, I had my eyes closed for takeoff.

As we lifted smoothly, swiftly, and remarkably quietly over the Miami skyline, heading out toward the Keys, I remember wondering what living this way all the time would do to a person. Roman generals had it right when they were granted a triumph, in that they had to have a slave alongside them in their chariot, whispering, "Remember, you are not a God, you are mortal."

How could you stay grounded when you were continuously rising above everyone else, literally and figuratively? I chuckled to myself, as I used "literally" in an appropriate context, recalling that one of Mara's pet peeves was when someone, usually Charlie or Jess, used literally in the wrong context. They would say things like, "It literally blew my mind," to which my normally ever-tolerant wife would reply, "Literally you say, that literally happened, did it?" It's the little things that cause you to fall in love over and over again if you are blessed to have a great marriage.

As we left the downtown metropolis of Miami, I could see the narrow ribbon of land that is the Florida Keys ahead of us. From the air, the Keys have always put me in mind of some great American maritime construction project, akin to the Great Wall of China, and similarly visible from space. I'd imagined it being built to keep some prehistoric sea monster from easily traversing between the waters of the Atlantic and the Gulf. It's little wonder that so many movies have been filmed down here.

The bridge itself begins just beyond Marathon Key, and having fished down here before with Charlie on a couple of occasions, I recognized it as we began our descent. Marathon has a small airfield to cater to private planes, and there was seemingly a special area on the field set aside to accommodate Baptiste's monster helicopter. As we came quietly and gracefully to a landing after no more than fifty minutes of flight time, I looked across at Del, Massimo, and Tish and could tell that, like me, they were thinking they could get used to this treatment.

As we exited the helicopter, a tall man in his sixties wearing a tailored suit with a white, open-neck shirt approached us and introduced himself as Lula, Baptiste's chauffeur and aide. As he led us toward an oversized silver Ford Excursion, I noted his disproportionately outsized feet that gave him a rather penguin-like appearance.

He explained that Baptiste's house was just minutes away and offered us cold water before heading out. On the short drive to the house, he shared that he'd been with Mr. Baptiste since he'd first arrived from Cuba and that he did many things for him, including driving, helping to keep the estate up and cooking, as well as fishing with the great man. I instinctively took a liking to him, demonstrating that my instincts about people aren't always razor sharp.

In comparison to some of the extraordinarily ostentatious thirty to forty million-dollar homes you might see in Laguna Beach, California, say, Baptiste's house was a bargain, probably costing just a tenth of the price. Nevertheless, it stood out like a beacon of affluence in the relatively modest community of Marathon, an equidistant two-hour drive from Miami as well as Hemingway's Key West.

Unlike Key West, it doesn't boast progressive, artistic, and LGBT communities. Nor does it have an historic appeal dating back to having been claimed at various times by Cuba and Great Britain, before becoming part of Florida and the United States. It also lacks the tourist anchor associated with Hemingway, all of which has helped to fuel Key West's growth in the past twenty years in particular, supported by a growing international airport.

In many ways, Marathon's greatest attraction for visitors is its relative seclusion and lack of development. That and the fact that there is arguably no better place to fish in the United States, in large measure due to its proximity to the Gulf Stream. When fishing from Marathon on the Atlantic side, you can be out catching sailfish or tuna within forty minutes of leaving the dock. And if you should tire of pulling in one set of fish in the morning, you can shift over to the Gulf side and fish off the reefs and the wrecks for dinner, as many of the restaurants in Marathon will cook your catch for you.

The house that Baptiste and Sylvia had built jutted out on a point like a Long Island mansion from *The Great Gatsby*. The house was positioned on several one-acre lots, had an eight-foot fenced perimeter and a gated entryway, as well as an old Chicago-style brick driveway. The overall design of the exterior was Mediterranean, with an abundance of archways housing numerous balconies.

This was their real home: Sylvia had decorated it and land-scaped the property with a Cuban flavor that was suggestive of Baptiste's childhood home, yet it also had a progressively open Floridian feel to it.

The views out to sea and across to the nearest strip of land were sumptuous as seen from the requisite infinity pool, and from every room in the house for that matter. At the end of the boat ramp sat a surprisingly modest twin-engine twenty-four-foot-long Cobra fishing boat.

I was to learn that some of Baptiste's warmest memories from childhood involved days spent fishing in a nearly identical boat with his father and elder brother, and that he felt most con-nected to them when out on the water.

As you followed the buoys out to sea for a day's fishing, accompanied by an occasional school of flying fish, it became apparent that Baptiste had secured for himself one of the finest locations that the Keys had to offer.

As we came up the driveway, I was surprised to see that Baptiste himself had come out to greet us, and that Sebastian was standing beside him. The two executives who had flown in with us were doing a double take at this welcoming party, and they glanced at us again as if reconsidering an earlier opinion that we weren't much worth bothering with.

As we got out of the van and exchanged pleasantries with the great man, I went to introduce Del, Massimo, and Tish to Sebastian, who smiled and nodded back at their greeting. I noticed Del and Massimo scrutinize him for a moment as if searching for clues, and I also noticed Sebastian holding his gaze with Tish, and vice versa, for a second or two longer than he had done with the others.

With Sebastian in tow, Baptiste showed us into the house and through to an informal dining room cum reading room, with majestic views across the water, and told us to settle in while he had someone bring us a few drinks and snacks. He patted Sebastian on the shoulder, at which point the young man turned and embraced his adopted father, before they exchanged a final glance and he left us. A maid of the house then bustled in, bringing us pitchers of water and iced tea, as well as a plate of various freshly cut fruits.

Once Baptiste had gone, Sebastian seemed to relax a little. He pulled out his iPad and began texting, at which point I received an alert on my phone and a message saying, "Please give me your friends' cell numbers so that we can begin texting." I looked up and showed the message to Del and Massimo, who immediately programmed his number into their phones. Although Sebastian could hear us and gesture his responses, we'd determined to use texting for the interviewing as it was how he preferred to converse, plus we'd have a record of the exchange.

We had agreed that Massimo would take the lead in asking the questions and that Del and I would interject with follow-ups as necessary. Tish sat off to one side, and when Sebastian noticed she hadn't yet stored his number in her phone, he signaled for her to come over and do so. Oh yes, Messiah or not, Sebastian was definitely heterosexual, I concluded.

It might have seemed that we could have just done the whole thing remotely since we were texting each other, but both Massimo and I were experienced in using Neuro-Linguistic Programming to read body language and to employ eye-scanning techniques, to monitor the truth of any responses. And so this most bizarre of interviews got underway.

"Sebastian, it's very nice to meet you. I'd like to ask you a few questions, if that would be all right," said Massimo.

Sebastian nodded, his sweet smile never leaving his face.

"Sebastian, please tell us a little about your life before you came to be with Mr. Baptiste," said Massimo.

"I lived in the favelas with the other children. We made figures from pieces of wood we found, and we sold them," replied Sebastian.

"Where did you sleep, and who looked after you?" asked Massimo.

"On the street. We looked after each other."

"What about your parents?"

"I don't remember my parents."

"Who looked after you when you were very young? Do you remember?"

"Amelia looked after me. She is my sister. She found places for us to sleep and food for us. She taught me to read and write. One day, she went away and never came back, and I was alone. So I joined the other children who lived by the docks, and they helped me. We helped each other."

Out of the corner of my eye, I caught Tish looking at Sebastian with a mixture of compassion and thinly veiled attraction.

"How and when did you learn to read and write English?" asked Massimo.

"Amelia taught me a little before she left me, and Alfredo has helped me improve since I've been here with him. He says that I am a natural and that he is very pleased with my progress."

Massimo continued, "Have you ever been able to speak?"

"Not that I can remember. The doctor who came to see us at Mr. Baptiste's house said I couldn't talk because of a trauma I'd had when I was much younger, but I don't remember that."

"Have you tried to talk?" Massimo continued.

"Yes, but I don't know how. Alfredo says he will find people who can teach me. Rahim also believes I will be able to talk one day," said Sebastian.

"Who is Rahim?" asked Massimo.

"He is my teacher and my friend."

"Did Alfredo bring Rahim here to teach you?"

"No, he has been with me for as long as I can remember. He is very wise and very kind, and I never feel alone because of him."

"Can we also meet with Rahim?"

"I don't see how that would be possible. He doesn't have a body. He only has a voice."

Massimo discreetly looked across at Del and me, and we held each other's gaze for a split second, trying not to let our facial expressions betray what we were all thinking at that moment.

Massimo continued: "Can anyone else hear his voice, like Alfredo, for example."

"No, only me, but I wish other people could, as he says so many things that are wise and make me feel happy."

"So Rahim is a voice in your head, that only you can hear, like an invisible friend?" Del interjected, while adopting a cynical expression.

"Yes, exactly like that," Sebastian replied.

At which point, with a smirk on her face, Del blurted out, "And have you ever had a CAT scan or an MRI?"

Sebastian looked confused and cocked his neck a little, while I angrily shook my head at Del and signaled for Massimo to continue.

"Can you tell us a little about when you first came to Alfredo's home?" asked Massimo.

"Yes, it was a beautiful day and I was with the other children on the street selling the figures I had made when Alfredo and Lula came and asked us our names. When I said my name was Sebastian, they took me for lemonade and asked me if I had a mark on my side, which I do have. I showed it to Alfredo and he was quiet and looked sad but also happy, and then he asked if I'd like to come with him to his house, and I said I would like to."

"Sebastian, do you remember giving Alfredo a piece of paper when you first met him?" I asked, and Massimo and Del both gave me a curious look.

"Yes," replied Sebastian.

"Do you remember what was written on it?" I asked.

"No, I don't, Mal. I'm sorry, is that important?"

"No, that's okay, Sebastian. It doesn't matter."

"Sebastian, may we see the mark on your side?" asked Massimo, continuing his line of questioning.

Sebastian nodded and lifted up his T-shirt enough to reveal a reddish mark on his right side, halfway up his rib cage. At a glance, it could be taken for a wound made by a large knife or a spear. At the sight of the scar, Massimo discreetly crossed himself, and Del and I glanced at each other without making any further gestures. I heard a slight exhalation coming from Tish that I guessed had less to do with the mark and more to do with Sebastian revealing his well-toned midriff.

"Sebastian, when we met yesterday, I asked you if you were the Son of Man, and you nodded. What do you mean when you say that you are the Son of Man?" I figured it was about time we went straight to the heart of it.

"Alfredo says that I am special and that people will want to talk to me and to learn things from me. I didn't have any parents, and everyone helped me in the favelas and took care of me. I belonged to all of them, and they belonged to me. So I feel that I am the son of many people. That is why I say that I am the Son of Man. Do you see, Mal?"

"Yes, I do see, Sebastian, thank you," I said, with a knowing smile and look of understanding on my face.

"And when you say you are the Messiah, what do you mean by that, Sebastian?" said Del.

"That I was their savior, just as they had saved me many times in the favelas."

"I think we've asked you enough questions for today, Sebastian. Del, Massimo, Tish, let's leave it here for now, okay?" I said, and motioned for the others to start moving.

We each went to shake hands with Sebastian. After the others had done so and were moving toward the doorway, Sebastian suddenly leaned forward to give me a hug. And as he did so, just for a moment, time seemed to stand still. I felt a sudden pain in the back of my head and I heard a voice that appeared to emanate from all around Sebastian and yet not from him.

The voice said, quite distinctly, "Look beyond this mortal vessel, my doubting friend."

I pulled back suddenly with a look of fear and confusion on my face which must have seemed unnerving to the others, as Massimo reached forward to steady me. And it was fortunate he did, as I suddenly felt faint and nauseous, as if I might pass out. Massimo held me up, and Del came around to the other side of me to provide support as she asked with real concern in her voice, "Mal, what is it? Are you okay?"

And then the faintness and nausea began to lift, and I looked at them both and said, "I thought I... wait, no it's nothing. I'm fine really. I just need some air, I think."

When I looked at Sebastian, I observed a look of confused curiosity on his face, but I saw nothing to indicate that he had heard what I had.

9

After my moment of dizziness or whatever it was, Massimo and Del insisted that I take some time to rest up before we started our return journey. In the back of my mind were concerns that what I'd experienced was in some way related to the head injury I'd received as a child, but I wasn't ready to go there yet.

Lula intercepted us leaving the interview with Sebastian and, overhearing us talk, suggested I go and get some fresh air on the main veranda of the house. No sooner had I sat down, however, then Baptiste himself came to find me and ask after my health. It seems that word of my episode had spread quickly throughout the house.

I thanked him for his concern and tried to assure him I was fine, but he would have none of it and insisted that I not attempt to travel again that day. He instead suggested all of us should stay in Marathon as his guest for the afternoon and evening and enjoy the sun, ocean breeze and eighty-degree temperatures. It was mid-February and mighty cold in the mountains, and colder still in New York, so we didn't need much persuading.

Baptiste explained that he was planning to go fishing that afternoon and, since he knew I fished, suggested that if I was truly feeling up to it, perhaps we'd all like to join him on the boat. Del declined, saying she preferred to be in the water with the fish and asked if she might borrow a swimsuit and some snorkeling gear, while Tish admitted to getting seasick and would prefer to stay close to the house and get some work done.

And so it was settled that Massimo and I would join the great man and Lula for an unexpected afternoon of fishing. I was secretly quite pleased for the informal time alone with Baptiste, which I hoped would allow me to garner more details about Aaron as well as any vision that he had for getting Sebastian's message out there, whatever that message might be.

Massimo, Del, and I had a few minutes out on the veranda together before our various aquatic activities got underway to talk about our interview with Sebastian and compare notes. Tish should have joined us, but she seemed to have temporarily disappeared.

"So, you're really feeling okay now, Malteser? You had us all worried for a second there," said Del.

"Yes, thanks, nothing to worry about, I assure you. I feel fine now. The thing is, though, and this is going to sound very strange, but I thought I heard something, well actually someone, a voice, as Sebastian leaned in to embrace me. And to be honest, it freaked me out."

"Is that what caused you to feel faint?" Massimo asked me.

"No, I'd already started feeling nauseous, and then I thought I heard this voice," I answered.

"And you are sure it actually wasn't our mute Messiah showing us his true colors?" asked Del.

"Yes, I'm certain it wasn't him. That's the odd thing, you see, the voice seemed to come from nearby him but not actually from him. It was very weird, but then these last twenty-four hours have been so bizarre that I'm probably just losing it and starting to hear things."

"Jesus, Mal, you need to have that old head injury looked at to see if a screw has come loose and is rattling around in there. You're feeling faint and hearing voices all of a sudden. Next you'll be exhibiting weird mental powers like telekinesis and bending spoons with your mind," said Del, without exhibiting a great deal of sympathy.

"So, what did this voice say, and what did it sound like?" asked Massimo, politely ignoring Del, and looking at me with a mixture of curiosity and sympathy.

"I think it said, 'Look beyond the mortal vessel, my doubting friend,' and it sounded like an older man's voice. It was deep, and if I had to guess, I'd say it was Middle Eastern in origin. Nuts, right? I can't quite believe I'm having this conversation."

"Seriously, I believe you think you heard this, Mal, and maybe this was some kind of voice projection from Sebastian. We need to consider the possibility that our Messiah isn't mute after all. Perhaps he isn't the innocent he pretends to be and is actually trying to manipulate us in the way he's already manipulated Baptiste," said Del.

"I can't know what it was for sure. But if it was Sebastian, he's one hell of a ventriloquist, because he made no movement to speak, and the voice sounded like it was from a different era. And it emanated from all around him or behind him. I saw nothing on his face afterwards to suggest he'd even heard the voice, so he'd also have to be a pretty good actor," I answered.

At that, Massimo tried to introduce some logic into the conversation. "Listen, let's consider some scenarios here. We have a secretive billionaire with a cult-like image and following, as well as a legendary ability to make money from almost everything he touches, telling us he's been called upon by God to announce the second coming of the Messiah. We have a young man who is mute that was plucked from the streets of Rio, and whom Baptiste claims is the Messiah.

"There are a number of scenarios here that I suspect we are all considering. First, that this is some elaborate scheme by Baptiste, although to what end we have no idea, and perhaps Sebastian is just a pawn in it. Second, it's still a scheme, but Sebastian is also in on it, and maybe he's a pretty good actor and a ventriloquist as well. Third, Baptiste actually believes all this, but he isn't in his right mind after the death of his wife. And fourth, this is all real, and we can't see it because it seems too incredible to us.

"I agree with your first three scenarios, Massimo, and I'm leaning toward the second myself. But the fourth one, where we get involved in persuading the world that the actual Messiah has returned, seems too incredible. Because, in fact, it bloody is," said Del.

"Is that how you feel, Mal? Should we just eliminate the fourth option because it's too incredible? Because I have to tell you, and please don't laugh at me, being in Sebastian's presence this morning and seeing his scar in the precise position of the Holy Lance, it affected me. His aura, and how shall I put this, it's as if a state of grace surrounds him," said Massimo.

"I'm not laughing, Massimo, but I feel like I need to slap you to bring you back to reality. You understand the human psyche as well as anyone. Surely you must see that this is the power of suggestion combined with Catholic indoctrination from your upbringing that's blinding you to the truth here," Del responded.

"You may be right, Del. Like Mal, this has me very confused. I'm not sure what I think right now. I'm actually terrified of being a part of this, believe me. My mother's reaction alone to my involvement in what she'd probably consider to be the work of Satan makes me want to run away from this," Massimo answered.

"But we're not going to run away from this, any of us," I finally said. "I understand that neither of you wants to even conceive of this right now, and that your instinct, like mine, is to run as far and as fast as possible. However, like me, you both need to know more, because curiosity is both our blessing and our curse."

"None of us can just turn our backs on this, even though we suspect that we only know a fraction of what's going on and that we are probably being manipulated. It's not just the desire to know what's behind all this, it's the fact that we've all spent the last day thinking how to build a communications plan around this event. What's the positioning? What's the creative concept and the connection idea, and how are we going to seed it? Tell me I'm wrong, and we'll head back home right now."

After a pronounced pause, Massimo said, "Yes, you are right. It's an utterly fascinating challenge. Even the possibility of attempting to persuade the world of this has my head spinning with ideas."

Del fixed me with her best squinting-eye scowl and said, "Bollocks, Mal, I hate that you know how to play me. Yes, I've been thinking about how to advertise this, but we are dealing with perhaps the most powerful man on the planet, and we don't have any idea what his game is, and it scares the shit out of me. And I don't scare easily, as you well know."

We looked at each other and nodded, thereby creating an unspoken bond to move forward together, at least for the time being. I knew that Del didn't believe for a second that Sebastian was who he claimed to be and that Massimo was struggling to conceive of the possibility. What I knew at that point was that my curiosity demanded I learn more and that our collective professional instincts were sensing the challenge of a lifetime.

At that moment, Tish appeared and asked what she'd missed. When we explained that we'd made a collective decision to continue with the assignment for the next few days, subject to talking with Oliver, she seemed pleased and even a little relieved.

I asked her where she had disappeared to, and she replied that she'd just been looking around the house and the grounds and had run into Sebastian. When Del said suggestively, "And what exactly did he show you around, Tish?" she glared at her and looked a little flustered.

She then proceeded to change the subject, suggesting that we follow her into the house in order to get settled in our rooms, as she knew where they'd put each of us. We did so, and I glanced at Del, who gave me a look that said this couldn't get any stranger with Tish now apparently being courted by our Messiah.

After I'd freshened up and changed into the T-shirt, shorts, and Sperry's that had been left for me in my room, along with my old windbreaker I'd brought with me—as well as leaving a voice message for Mara, explaining that I would be spending the night in Marathon and that I'd call her later—I headed down to the boat dock to meet up with the others.

After we set off from the dock, following the buoys, it quickly became clear that among his other talents, Lula was an experienced captain. He knew all the right spots around the reef and wrecks, at least on the Gulf side where we'd decided to fish that afternoon because, as he informed us, there was a bit of chop on the Atlantic side.

Our first spot netted a variety of good-sized yellowtail and mangrove snapper, of which we kept the largest for dinner that evening. At our second spot, we mainly hooked Spanish mackerel, although Baptiste pulled in an exquisite dolphin fish.

I've caught mahi mahi before, and the beauty of their coloring is quite breathtaking. And seeing the color drain from them before my eyes as they are kept out of the water has actually caused me on a couple of occasions to throw a delicious supper back into the ocean.

At the two other spots where Lula anchored the boat, between the four of us, we hooked a nice porgy, a dogfish, a huge amberjack and, rarest of all, a fifty-pound goliath grouper, which is now a protected species. The goliath grouper was formally known as the jewfish, but it seems that political correctness also extends to the fish naming community.

Through most of the afternoon, we'd focused on the fishing and hadn't spoken a great deal other than to signal a catch or encourage one another. Lula had shown great patience in tutoring Massimo, who was an inexperienced fisherman, which had only reinforced my positive impression of him, while Baptiste and I had lost ourselves in the all-consuming distraction of catching fish.

The wind had begun to get up later in the afternoon, and I'd put my old windbreaker on, which in reality acted more like a wind sock, and had made it rather difficult to feel the tug on my line. Mara had been nagging me for ages to replace it with something that didn't act as an air pocket, but I was rather attached to the ancient thing. It put me in mind of those personal survival swim tests I used to take as a boy, where they would require you to make a flotation device out of a random article of clothing, which invariably seemed to be a pair of nylon pajama bottoms.

The intent was that you'd pull them swiftly from behind your head to the front in order to trap the air inside, having previously tied a knot in each leg. I recall that all I could think of while creating this bizarre air pillow was what were the odds of actually finding yourself adrift at sea with a handy pair of nylon pajamas?

As we left the boat, Baptiste walked beside me and said, "I'm sorry, but I won't be able to join you for dinner this evening, as I have a prior engagement, but Escobar, my chef, will prepare the fish in several ways, all of which are quite delicious."

"Thank you, Alfredo, for your hospitality and allowing us to stay at your magnificent home, you really have been too kind and generous," I replied, and I meant it.

"I haven't asked you how your interview with Sebastian went earlier, and, in truth, I don't want to know too much. As I said, you must find you own way in assuaging your doubts and those of your team. All I ask is that you confirm as soon as possible whether you are willing to take on this assignment."

I told him that we were close to making a decision and that we were leaning toward moving ahead with it, but that I wanted to go back to New York and talk it over with Oliver in person before making a final commitment.

He nodded and seemed satisfied, and then he turned to me and asked, "Tell me, did something happen to cause you to feel faint after you'd interviewed Sebastian? Did you perhaps see or hear something?" to which I paused and then simply nodded in response.

Then he shocked me by saying, "Perhaps it was this Rahim that spoke to you?" I paused, not knowing how to reply, and he continued, "I know this seems fantastical to you, but I simply ask that you keep an open mind about what happened. Sebastian has told me all about this Rahim who is as real to him as you or I, and yet he's only ever engaged with Sebastian, until now perhaps."

I didn't know what to say, and so I answered, "I'm trying to keep an open mind," mostly in order to close down a conversation that I wasn't sure I'd ever be ready to have. He nodded and walked away, and I headed up to my room to freshen up, leaving Lula explaining to Massimo how to expertly gut and filet the fish, using a large, razor-sharp knife that he apparently kept strapped to his boot at all times.

Over dinner, we didn't talk about anything that had gone on that morning. Sensing a collective need to unwind, we swapped stories about the afternoon's adventures, while Tish and Massimo got Del and I caught up on the agency news and gossip.

Our freshly caught fish were perfectly cooked for us in several ways, including blackened Cajun, pan-fried, and Escobar's own pineapple and lime recipe. After we'd eaten and said our good nights, I headed up to my room to call Mara.

As I went to close the blinds, I saw Tish standing by the water's edge. She was with Sebastian. As I watched, he pulled her gently toward him by the waist and bent to kiss her, and she responded in kind.

I relayed this and everything else that had gone before today to Mara, who listened to me with customary patience and without making judgments, no matter how strange all of this must have sounded to her. I could tell that she had made the connection to my old head injury, as she knew I would, but to her credit she heard me out instead of simply dismissing the experience I thought I'd had. She asked me several questions that cut to the core and helped me to process what I was thinking and feeling.

She asked me whether I trusted Baptiste, if I thought the voice I'd heard was real or a product of my own imagination, and finally if I thought we could actually be successful if we took on the assignment. I told her I did trust him, that I thought the voice had been real at the time but that now I wasn't so sure, and that I believed we could be successful, and I admitted that I found the possibilities as frightening as they were intriguing.

"Well then, my love, perhaps it doesn't matter that you doubt who Sebastian is. What matters is that Baptiste believes in him, that you believe in Baptiste, and that you know you can do this," replied Mara. And as usual, she was right.

I didn't tell her about the pain at the back of my head or about having felt dizzy when I thought I'd heard the voice earlier, as I knew she'd remind me that I'd had two similar dizzy spells in the last few months, both most likely caused by lingering stress, according to Dr. Phillips. She'd also have reminded me that I had chosen to ignore the doctor's advice in having a precautionary MRI just to make sure there wasn't any connection to my old head injury. No, I wasn't going to open that can of worms tonight, but I made a commitment to myself to schedule a neurology appointment and an MRI once all this was over.

Before we'd retired that evening, Gloria had called me to say that Baptiste had instructed her to have the plane sent to Marathon so the team could all fly back to New York directly. As a result, I'd told Mara to head back up to the mountains the next day without me, and that I'd be home in a day or so.

Say what you like, Alfredo Baptiste knew how to treat the people who worked for him, and I was starting to better understand how he managed to inspire such loyalty, and in our case to step into the abyss.

10

It was a little after nine the following morning when Terry lifted the Bombardier 7000 off the ground, and I opened my eyes for a split-second to see the vibrant blue waters of the Keys pass into the distance behind us. I had determined to spend most of the flight trying to talk Del into coming back into the agency with me when we landed, in order to meet and hopefully reach an understanding with Oliver.

I needed her ideas, and I knew that they would only come if Del was back in the middle of a creative team, where energy flowed and she was able to feed off of other talented minds. I didn't know if she'd gotten as far as to make any professional plans after CREATIF, but I hoped that she didn't intend to become a freelancer, as I knew it wouldn't suit her work style or her temperament.

It took less than two hours before we landed at Teterboro Airport, with our route taking us in over Brooklyn rather than past the Manhattan skyline, and I was always happy to avoid the dehumanizing misery of landing at LaGuardia. In any case, flying into the city still created a sense of melancholy for me, ever since I had done so a week after 9/11, seeing for myself the devastation wrought by a handful of misguided religious zealots.

After we talked, Del had agreed to at least come into the agency with me so she could greet her old friends in the creative department, but she still wanted nothing to do with Oliver. That was probably a good thing for today at least, I decided, as my own reunion with the infamous Grouse was likely to create enough tension.

We left the plane and thanked the now quite familiar Terry and June, and passed through some rudimentary checks in a matter of seconds and straight into our waiting limo. It really is amazing how minimal the security checks are for private aircraft passengers in the United States today, considering the TSA routinely seems to give sweet and frail looking old ladies full cavity searches as they step off commercial flights.

As the car pulled up an hour later outside the offices of CREATIF on Fifteenth and Ninth, I looked across at Del and said, "Here we go then, I'm glad I don't have to do this alone." At which point, Massimo said, "You two are crazy. Don't you know how much people have missed you both and how excited they are going to be to see you two?"

Tish nodded in agreement, to which Del responded, "That's bollocks, Massimo, and you know it. A week is an eternity in this business, and after six months, they'll look at us like extras from *The Walking Dead*." "We'll see" was all Massimo said, grinning.

As we walked into the ground floor open reception area, I looked up to the circle of bleachers above us on the first level— Del and I had been insistent they were included in the original building remodel—which created a space for the agency to hold its town hall meetings and larger gatherings. The agency had grown to about 300 people by the time we'd left, and the space had become almost too cramped to accommodate everyone.

I did a double take as I realized the bleachers were completely full of people, just as the applause and whistles broke out! Massimo and Tish had clearly been warned about this reception and had hastily become invisible, while Del and I stood there looking up in stunned silence as they cheered us. I will admit that I felt a tear welling at the corner of my eye, and I think it was less about the emotion I was feeling for myself at that moment and more the look on Del's face.

The Teflon Aussie who had a tongue that could cut like a knife through butter, and wore a virtual coat of armor, looked like a six-year-old ballerina accepting the applause of her parents after her first recital. It was the first and only time I ever saw a look of wide-eyed innocence on the face of Delilah Bishop. And then, in an instant, that look of innocence changed to the face of a predator as she heard Oliver's voice ring out.

"Folks, the two people who did more to help grow this agency than anyone, who represented the heart, soul, and brains of the company for two decades, have come back to us for a visit. When they left here, we didn't have a chance to show how much we cared about them and how grateful we were for all they had done, and so I'd like you to take this opportunity to give them our fullest show of appreciation. Mal Thomas and Del Bishop, everyone."

As Oliver finished, the whole agency erupted into one more effusive burst of applause and cheering, and I smiled up at them and nodded warmly, while Del just kept staring at Oliver. I won't say it didn't mean a lot, it did, and I was deeply moved, but it didn't change the reckoning that Oliver and I needed to have, and we both knew it.

As the noise subsided, old friends from her creative team enveloped Del, while my former peers also surrounded me, and I shook hands and was patted on the back, all the while keeping my eye on Oliver as I edged my way steadily toward his office. When I reached the door, Oliver's secretary, Melanie, welcomed me with a hug and said, "It's great to see you, Mal. It hasn't been the same here without you, but please don't kill him."

I smiled back at her and said, "Hi, Mel. I'll try not to." Then I moved into the office as she shut the door behind me, and I sat down in the seating area where Oliver was waiting for me.

"You look good, put on a bit of weight, but overall you look like those eternal dark circles around your eyes have lightened by a half shade," said Oliver.

"You look just the same as when we last spoke in this office and you fired me, I seem to recall, which I deemed a tad unfair since I'd put your talentless fat ass in that seat, bailed you out of numerous tough spots, and earned you a fucking fortune, you ungrateful inbred buffoon," I retorted, having decided not to bother too much with verbal foreplay.

"Good, I'm glad we get to clear the air without dancing around it. You know that you left me no choice, Mal. As CEO, if I hadn't fired you after you sent an email to everyone in the agency detailing my professional as well as my sexual shortcomings, I couldn't have continued in the job."

I'll admit that he did have a point there, but it didn't stop me from responding: "Nor should you have continued in the job after you lost us the biggest pitch in the agency's history by first attempting to bribe the client into giving us the business, then by attempting to blackmail her with those disgusting and dubious pictures you'd dug up from one of the fucking cesspools you frequent. We had the business won, we had the right strategy and the best creative idea and their team on our side. We just had to pull off the final meeting with the board, and we'd have had it in the bag, you witless cretin, and you know it!"

"You know that isn't true, Mal. Elliot had it on good authority that our competitors BMBO had given Denise, their chief marketing officer, a sweetener, so the deck was loaded against us. You know how it works on these mega accounts; it's never about the work and the idea, it's about who gets what they want. And Denise was there to be bought."

"Except, of course, she wasn't, was she? No, in fact she was deeply offended by your attempt to bribe her and proceeded to cut us then and there in the hallway. And then, of course, you followed her into the women's restroom, and we ended up getting ejected from the building by security guards," I reminded him.

"It didn't happen like that, and in any case she misunderstood my intention."

"Just as she later misunderstood why you had sent her explicit pictures you'd somehow purloined of her fucking a no-name, talentless singer, whose turgid songs she'd been forcing their incumbent agency to use in commercials for months."

"I'll admit with hindsight it was a mistake playing that card at that moment," said Oliver.

"Oh, you think? You hadn't considered the possibility that she might have been gaining a little leverage on you while you were doing the same to her?"

"I knew she was dirty, so I was just playing her at her own game," Oliver responded.

"And then she paid you back in kind, didn't she, genius? You went out on the town in Hong Kong at the CREATIF leaders retreat and were filmed with an underage girl with her mouth around your appendage while another was sitting on your face.

When I learned about all this from Denise, she expected me to confront you and see to it that Paris fired you, but I didn't, did I? No, I stupidly got drunk and wrote that fucking everyone email and hit send, causing you to fire *me*.

"But that wasn't enough, was it. Oliver? You then had to put it about that I'd had a sort of a breakdown, which was the reason we didn't win the Gallant razor account, a win which, by the way, would have crucially helped to balance out our unhealthy reliance on BAPTIST businesses," I concluded.

"If I could take back the things that were said and done then, I would, Mal. I've told you I'm sorry. I know I fucked up big time."

"You made me sick, not figuratively, you understand, but literally. I had some kind of an anxiety attack. My heart rate spiked, and I blacked out for a few hours. I still get dizzy spells that my doctor says are equivalent to a form of trauma suffered by soldiers. I have fucking post-traumatic stress disorder because of you, Oliver."

"And that's all my fault, is it, Mal, and nothing to do with your childhood head injury?"

"Fuck you Oliver," I said, fuming, as I moved to stand up.

"Okay Mal, please, please sit back down. I'm truly sorry, I don't know what else to say."

"Do you know how easy it would have been for me to tell Paris what really happened? But I didn't Oliver, and I'm sure you've wondered why, so let me tell you now. It was not because of our past friendship; it was because I was done with it all, and most of all I was done with you. I really didn't give a fuck anymore. So I made you give me that enormous golden parachute, and left you to sit in the pile of rubble you'd caused.

"I vowed that I wouldn't return, as did Del, and by the way, if you think this conversation is awkward, wait until you meet up with her. I'd hide your shoes if I were you. But here I am, and here we are again, and the circumstances couldn't be more bizarre or unlikely," I said, feeling my anger finally abate somewhat.

"Yes, Elliot gave me the headlines of what Baptiste told you. I mean, is this actually for real? It's totally incredible, the fucking Messiah. If word gets out, it's going to have a massive impact on BAPTIST's share price, just for starters. Everyone is going to assume that he's grief-stricken or off his meds or something. And I hear he's prepared to commit unlimited resources to this; he cannot really be serious, can he?"

"Oh, he's deadly serious," I responded.

"And he wants you to lead this because your name is Thomas?" Oliver stifled a laugh as he said this.

"Also because my Christian name is Malachi, which means the messenger in Hebrew, so he believes I'm the chosen messenger who doubts, like Jesus' famed disciple of the same name. Oh, and he also believes he's John the Baptist reborn!" I said.

"You really can't begin to make this shit up. So are you going to do this with him, with us, again? I know you think I'll find a way to do it anyway, but I won't Mal. I may be flawed, but I'm not stupid. I know we can't do this without you and Del, for that matter. So what's your decision?"

"Assuming it can be done, yes I'll do it. But it will be my way, with the extended team I've chosen reporting only to me, and you will pay me ten percent of the total agency fee for the assignment," I said coldly.

"That's daylight robbery, particularly from someone who two minutes ago was calling me a blackmailer," he retorted, clearly not happy that I held all the cards.

"Which you are, and yes it is, and the size of the fee is mostly out of spite, as you know I don't need the money, and for the pleasure of sticking it to you, of course," I said.

"I have no choice but to agree then," said Oliver.

"I know. Payback's a bitch, isn't it? Elliot will keep you apprised of the plan and the media spend, and your folks can get a contract out to BAPTIST. We should have a project code name for this. I was thinking Project Judas. Seems to work on a couple of levels, don't you think? Oh, and one more thing, you're going to pay Del fifteen grand a week in freelance fees as well," I concluded.

"God, you're such a dick. But I still can't deny I'm glad you're here; it hasn't been the same."

"It's temporary, Oliver. Now, tell me everything I need to know about the business and financial dynamics impacting BAPTIST," I demanded.

"All right, that's a conversation that centers around the departure of Vilas." Oliver then proceeded to tell me what had been going on within the executive team at BAPTIST since my departure.

Victor Vilas was more than Baptiste's protégé; he was the son that the great man never had. Vilas originally came to the United States from the Dominican Republic on a baseball scholarship to the University of Miami. He was a pitching phenom, but sports were not the extent of his abilities. He was highly intelligent and savvy, and he took full advantage of the academic opportunity that Miami offered, studying international business and ultimately receiving a double-major degree.

Vilas first met the great man when he came to watch the Hurricanes standout at Alex Rodriguez Park. Baptiste had been a keen pitcher himself in his schoolboy days in Cuba and had recently purchased the Florida Marlins MLB team as a relaxing pastime. But his real passion was college baseball, and he had played several varsity games himself as a walk-on while studying for his own degree at "the U."

Vilas was going to be a top ten pick in the upcoming MLB draft, and ironically, it looked likely that he would fall to the Marlins. Then, in a pointless end-of-season game, having never had a serious injury in his life, he tore the ulnar collateral ligament in his right elbow, his pitching arm, and he underwent Tommy John surgery.

Although a major injury for a pitcher, recovery is normally assured. But in young Victor Vilas' case, there were serious complications and, tragically, he would never recover fully, and the chance of a career in professional baseball was ripped away from him.

Alfredo Baptiste paid for Vilas' surgery and rehabilitation, and most assumed that he was protecting a future asset of the Marlins. He also paid the fees for Vilas' final year of college, and when it was announced that Victor would never play professionally, the great man hired him straight out of school.

Baptiste clearly saw something, perhaps a part of himself, in Vilas, and acted as his personal mentor as soon as he joined the company. Within ten years, Vilas had risen to become the head of BAPTIST Electronics at the age of just thirty-four.

He took over the reins of BAPTIST Health five years later, after helping the electronics division achieve double-digit growth each year of his tenure. After having a similar impact at the all-important health care division, three years later Vilas took over as CEO of the newly acquired JetRider airline. Finally, at the tender age of forty-three, Vilas was appointed president of BAPTIST North America and was considered by all to be the great man's chosen successor, whenever he decided to step back and move up and into the chairman's role.

Then Sylvia Baptiste died, and within a matter of weeks, Victor Vilas had abruptly left the company. According to a succinct BAPTIST press announcement, it was by "mutual agreement." But of course there was rumor of a major rift, with the timing coming so soon after Sylvia's death seeming to be significant, although no one had any convincing evidence as to what had really happened.

The financial press thought they had their answer when, three months later, it was announced that Vilas had been appointed president of KONG North America—the Chinese multinational that had modeled itself on BAPTIST, and was considered by many to be the company most likely to assume its mantle as the world's most powerful company, should the American monolith's dominance begin to wane. Since taking over at KONG, Vilas hadn't yet made any really significant moves, although the company was rumored to be stockpiling cash for some major acquisition.

I listened as Oliver detailed all this with a growing sense of fascination and perhaps even understanding. Alfredo Baptiste had been, and still was, an extraordinary man, and yet he was also in his early seventies, and over a six-month period, he had lost the love of his life and the man he thought of as a son. Was it any wonder that when Aaron came knocking on his door and presented him with a new purpose to his life and a chance to create a legacy beyond mere business, he'd embraced it?

Or perhaps Sebastian was the reason that Vilas had ultimately decided to leave BAPTIST, fearing for the great man's sanity and the future of the company, and maybe even feeling at a personal level like he'd been somehow replaced. I made a note that I needed to speak with Vilas before all this was done, as it was clear he'd have an interesting perspective, to say the least.

At that moment, there was a knock on the door, and Oliver's assistant, Melanie, came in, looking distinctly harried and, dare I say, even a little frightened. She was about to apologize when Del barged past her and stood there glaring at Oliver. I looked from her to him and back again, and then I got up and headed for the open door before turning back toward Oliver and saying, simply, "Shoes?" I then left them to what promised to be a highly spirited reunion.

11

As I left Oliver's office, I ran into several more folks who said nice things and told me how pleased they were that I was back—and I reiterated I wasn't. Then I saw Liz, my former assistant who now worked for Massimo, and we spent ten minutes catching up. My long-term assistant Linda had retired a year before I'd left the agency, and Liz was fresh out of college when she came to work for me, so it wasn't as if we had a long history together, but she still seemed genuinely pleased to see her old boss, which is always gratifying.

She explained that she'd arranged for Del and me to be situated in *Moonraker*. We'd come up with the idea of naming all of our conference rooms after Bond movies, as defending your favorite James Bond always gave us something to talk about with new prospects and clients. I've always been a Sean Connery guy, but I'll admit that Daniel Craig has run him close, and I know who Mara would vote for.

My plan for the day was that the team and a few extra folks from the agency we wanted to pull into our brainstorming would work to map out the framework for a communications plan, and that we'd then assign tasks moving forward. Simple, right? We only had to devise a way for the entire world to both learn about the arrival of the Messiah and have the lion's share of humanity believe it!

I got situated, and Liz kindly brought me some hot English breakfast tea with a little milk, a remnant from my upbringing in Old Blighty. I never could get a taste for coffee, as much as Starbucks has tried to convert me.

It never ceased to amaze me the ritualistic way in which my traveling colleagues had always sought out a Starbucks for their favorite beverages, as if they'd be unable to adequately perform in a meeting without the hallowed nectar. Watching people place their elaborately rehearsed order always reminds me of the excellent rant in *Curb Your Enthusiasm*, where Larry lambastes customers for failing to recognize that their elaborate orders are basically, "All just variations of coffee and milk."

I looked up when Del entered the room to see if I could find any flecks of blood or gray matter from the head trauma I feared she'd inflicted on Oliver, but she seemed unsullied and actually quite chipper. She said, "I really found it quite cathartic telling the bastard what I thought of him with the knowledge that he couldn't call security this time." I concurred, and we agreed to do what we had to do in order to spend as little time at CREATIF as possible.

Just then, Massimo, Elliot, and Tish walked in, followed by several folks from their respective groups, only one of whom I'd worked with, and most of whom looked younger than my daughter, Jess. Amazing how quickly staff hiring and firing can happen at a New York agency. In some ways, I was relieved they had brought in new starry-eyed recruits, as I feared that when I briefed them on what we'd learned in Florida, more seasoned folks would probably have feigned a bilious attack and left the room never to return.

I spent the first hour laying out everything we knew up to that point and defined the challenge before us, saying, "Okay, guys, some of us have worked together long enough to know the drill and the elements we need to cover. We need to create a movement around Sebastian, someone who doesn't speak and who is unknown to the world at this moment.

"Creating interest in someone who claims to be the new Messiah and who is sponsored by the most powerful man on the planet isn't going to be a problem. Dealing with the chorus of abuse from naysayers and zealots from all sides of the religious divide is where this will get interesting. If we don't find a way to introduce it correctly, this could be over very quickly, in an avalanche of negative publicity. While most of the major religions predict this event, its actual fulfillment challenges everything," I concluded.

Using the labels I'd long adopted, and which were suddenly apt in a way that they'd never been before, we spent the next hour or so profiling the Zealots who would be the first to engage, as well as the all-important Disciples who would ultimately convince the Congregation to follow Sebastian or to reject him. When I had first applied these labels in a marketing context, I'd wanted to borrow from religious nomenclature in order to illustrate the power with which people engaged emotionally with brands. To find myself now using them in this context was ironic, in the truest sense of the word.

Toward the end of our discussion, Massimo said, "In this case, the movement is going to pass through the Zealots to the Disciples and into the Congregation in a single news cycle. As soon as we announce it, everyone that isn't living under a rock or trapped under furniture will hear that Alfredo Baptiste's adopted son, who happens to be mute and looks like a Greek god, is claiming to be the Messiah," and I was in violent agreement with him.

"The first time they see pictures of him is critical. Think Mandela when he walked to freedom after twenty-seven years of captivity, surrounded by mass ranks of his supporters. It looked like the beginning of the unstoppable movement that it became. If that image doesn't do it for you, think *Close Encounters of the Third Kind,* when the chief lanky-limbed alien comes down the steps and makes that welcoming gesture with his arms.

"What we don't need is people seeing Sebastian sitting in the lobby of the Miami Hyatt for the first time, or by the pool in a pair of shorts with his arm around a hot girl," said Del, as she cast a momentary glance toward Tish that probably only I noticed.

"Maybe he needs to appear from the mist in the distance, surrounded by his Disciples, people of all races, genders, and especially different religious denominations. He emerges and then relays his formative message of real substance, which is a problem in its own right, of course, since he can't bloody speak," added Del.

"Perhaps he could play a catchy little tune like the aliens did while mankind has to figure out the meaning," contributed Massimo, unhelpfully. "But seriously, this first contact moment that Del is talking about should be a web video, and we can use our army of social influencers to ensure it goes viral—not that it wouldn't anyway in this case."

"That all makes sense, but what about Baptiste? Do we go public up front about his relationship with Sebastian or leave him out of it? That is Oliver's preference, given the impact this may have on his own image and the collateral effect on BAPTIST's share price, which, of course, affects our ad budgets," said Elliot.

"The reason to use him is that he is universally known and his appearances are so limited these days that anything he says gets instant global attention. People know him as an almost mythical business figure, and he'll bring instant credibility to Sebastian's claim. Although I agree that we don't know the impact this will have on BAPTIST's share price, but that's his problem," replied Massimo.

"I say that, all things considered, we come out with all guns blazing, if you'll forgive the indelicate analogy. Everything Baptiste touches turns to gold, and he's nobody's fool. And that kind of credibility and publicity outweighs everything. We need to create an extraordinary physical and virtual event built around the announcement. I mean, if a basketball player can get ten million viewers by deciding to move from Cleveland to Miami, what kind of audience will the alleged second coming of Christ garner?" asked Del.

"Seriously, we have to hold a one-off type of global webinar, with all the major social platforms primed, so we don't have another Twitter shutdown just as the Messiah's first selfie with the Pope and the U.S. President is going viral," said Massimo, with a slightly tongue-in-cheek tone to his voice.

"I actually love the idea of bizarre selfie-combinations: talk show host Genie Elan, the Pope, a couple of astronauts and Sebastian. Priceless," said Del.

"This might just get a lot weirder than that before we're finished. Let's talk about the most sensitive area of all, namely how various religious leaders will react," I said.

"Well, on the one hand, what could be more powerful than seeing leading figures from the Christian, Muslim, Buddhist, Hindu and Jewish faiths parading together in support of Sebastian? However, the chance of us getting their acceptance of his claim, let alone acknowledging it publicly, is nonexistent," said Massimo.

"Hmm, if I remember correctly, Massimo, the Catholic Church requires proof of three miracles performed before they will grant sainthood. Can you imagine what proof would be required for someone claiming to be the Messiah? What, do we think Sebastian's going to smile and raise his shirt, and tell the Pope about how everyone in the favelas were like parents to him, and the Holy Father is going to just bow down and proclaim him?" added Del.

"Del is quite correct. Counterintuitively, the only way to approach this is to claim absolutely nothing about who Sebastian is at first. We need to fuel a social whispering campaign on a global scale that hangs out there for weeks without any type of response, until it builds to such a point that Baptiste has to say something, and even then his response should be largely ambiguous," I said.

"We can do that, plant seeds in influential social forums, and watch them sprout using our student networks," said Massimo.

"Maybe there is a better way rather than just planting rumors on the blogosphere," said Del, and we all turned toward her expectantly.

She continued, "Think of the Ice Bucket Challenge, which raised millions and created global awareness for ALS. We need something like that at the core of this, something that everyone can participate in. Something that creates a ground-swell of involvement and goodwill before all the naysayers can jump in."

"I love that idea, and I agree that we need something like the Ice Bucket Challenge, but we can't ask the creative teams to come up with ideas until we know what is at the core of Sebastian's message. This is something I started to talk to Baptiste about, but I need time with Sebastian to understand what he really wants to say," I suggested. Del added, "Assuming of course that he does have something to say."

"I'm sure he has something to share with us, and I think as he gets more comfortable with us, he'll open up," Tish interjected, and I noticed she blushed slightly.

"To put it bluntly, if he doesn't have a belief system to share with the world, then neither do we. This isn't like any movement we've created before for a beer, or a candy bar, or a pack of condoms. This is about people's faith in a higher power. It's about selling a creed to live your life by. We don't know what Sebastian believes, but I intend to find that out, one way or another, in the next few days," I said.

"Alright then, Mal, what do you propose as next steps?" I heard a familiar voice asking, and I turned to see that Oliver had crept quietly into the room. At the same time, I noted that Del was giving OMG a disapproving look. At least she didn't seem poised to violently assault him, which I took as a sign of progress.

"Well, let's divide and conquer. Elliot, Del, and Massimo, you guys stay here in New York and start fleshing out the logistics of the launch plan in terms of physical and virtual events, social and traditional media platforms, as well as designing symbols and iconography.

"I'm going to go back home to North Carolina tomorrow and will try and persuade Baptiste to let Sebastian come and stay with me for a few days so that I can elicit from him something resembling a belief system that we can base this movement around.

"Tish, assuming Baptiste agrees to let him come, I'd like you to fly to Marathon so that you can accompany Sebastian back to Boone, and then stay with us and help record everything we learn. If everything goes according to plan, we'll meet back here in New York in a week and update each other on what we've learned and review the communication plan. Sound about right, everybody?"

Everyone indicated to me that they were on board, and as we broke up, I nodded to Oliver to indicate that I'd get back to him. Then I called Tish to one side. "Thanks for agreeing to shepherd Sebastian assuming Baptiste lets him come. In any other scenario, I'd say it's none of my business what goes on in your personal life. But I need to ask you, as it potentially affects this assignment, what is your relationship with him? I couldn't help but notice that there seemed to be a connection between you guys in Marathon," I observed, while trying not to sound judgmental.

"I understand why you needed to ask, Mal, and the simple answer is that we don't have a relationship as such, at least not a physical one. But I'd be lying if I said I wasn't attracted to him, and that the feeling seems to be mutual. I'm also aware of how weird that sounds, given what we are doing and who people say he is. I'm sure this is an added complication that you didn't need, so I'm happy to step back from this assignment if you feel it's created a personal conflict of interest," Tish said.

"Thank you for offering, Tish, and for understanding why I needed to ask. This assignment couldn't be any weirder or more complicated for that matter. On the one hand, you having this connection with him adds another emotional element. On the other hand, if you being around helps Sebastian feel more at ease and able to open up to me, then I'm going to use that to our advantage. That's why I'm asking you to go and get him in Marathon and bring him back to Boone. I wanted to make sure you were comfortable with that, and that we understood one another," I said.

Tish nodded her understanding of what I was suggesting, and said she was happy to proceed on that basis. I agreed I'd let her know when I'd cleared things with Baptiste, and that I'd hope to then see her in Boone in a couple of days.

I then made my way over to Oliver's office to check in with him before I headed out. I knocked and walked in, at which point he looked up, and I noticed a weariness about him, which I assumed was due to the uncomfortable encounters he'd had earlier, first with myself and then with Del.

I explained that I was leaving now, and he acknowledged the wisdom of my plan to get Sebastian to travel to North Carolina so that I could try and draw something useful out of him. He also indicated that he was okay with my plan to have Tish act as nursemaid to Sebastian, which I needed him to do, as she was an employee of CREATIF.

I couldn't resist asking him how it went with Del, and he said simply, "Brutal. That woman has always had a way of making me feel like a piece of dog shit you just picked up on your shoe, and today was the worst of all. Still, at least we have that behind us now, although I shall very soon be needing a stiff drink."

It was probably the degree to which he appeared to be beaten up that made me say, in a conciliatory tone, "Oliver, I should thank you for this morning's welcome reception."

"You built this agency and to have left in the way you both did was … well, I know it wasn't right. Seeing the way everyone reacted to you and having you both back here today, even kicking my ass as you have, made me wish there was a way to repair things permanently. Do you think that might be possible, Mal? It hasn't been the same here without you, or the Tasmanian She-Devil."

"I said thank you, Oliver, and I meant it, but that's all I can manage right now, okay? And in any case, I don't think you can go back, not really," I said.

"Well it's a start," he replied.

"So we are agreed on taking on this one last insane assignment then, on the terms I've stated?" I asked.

"If you're in, I'm in, Mal."

With that, I nodded and left him to walk over to The Standard hotel in order to make a couple of calls to arrange things for the next day and to freshen up for dinner, because I had a date with the beautiful and talented Ms. Jessica Thomas.

12

Since Jess had moved into my old apartment in the Village, I decided to stay at The Standard, which is just around the corner from the CREATIF office. It's not really my cup of tea because it's cool—and I'm not.

The elevator has video running on continuous loop that I gather has something to do with the 1927 film *Metropolis,* which is an epic science fiction film I've yet to see and probably won't, if this elevator experience is anything to go by.

Before a fellow rider told me about the movie connection, I'd assumed it had something to do with *Paradise Lost.* In any case, it's rather disturbing to see Nazis and cherubs mingling intermittently, and you often end up seeing it a couple of times, as the elevator is so dimly lit that you tend to push a button for the wrong floor and therefore have an extended ride.

The thing I find to be invariably true about cool hotels is that the rooms are smaller, the beds are harder and lower to the ground, and it takes an engineering degree to figure out how to turn the lights on, let alone operate the faucets.

However, when you tell people you're staying at The Standard, they usually comment that it's a great hotel, when what they really mean is, "It's cool, and I'm surprised someone as uncool as you is staying there, and not at the Embassy Suites."

I parked myself on the narrow bench seat in my room, designed for someone lithe that practices Bikram hot yoga on a daily basis, and called Mara to give her the update on both my and Del's encounter with Oliver, and to ask if she'd be okay with Sebastian and Tish staying with us for a few days. Of course she was, and I told her I'd be home the next afternoon. She asked me to give Jess a hug and instructed me to feed her up, as according to her mother, "That girl is too busy moving to stop and eat, and otherwise look after herself."

I then called Baptiste to confirm we were formally accepting the assignment and to ask whether Sebastian could stay with us in the mountains, if Tish accompanied him on the trip from Marathon. He seemed genuinely delighted that we'd agreed to move forward and said that he or Gloria would call me back once he'd talked with Sebastian about staying with us.

About ten minutes later, Gloria called me back and confirmed that if Tish made plans to fly commercial to Miami tomorrow, they'd arrange for Sebastian to meet her at the airport, and then they could take the corporate jet to Greensboro, North Carolina, where a car would be waiting to drive them both to our house in Boone. Not too shabby, I thought, as I called Tish and confirmed the plans. Once I'd arranged for my own commercial flight in the morning out of Newark, allowing me to avoid the unspeakable LaGuardia, I headed out to meet Jess.

We had agreed to meet at an unassuming little French restaurant I'd discovered years ago called La Luncheonette, on Tenth Avenue, which looks like nothing from the outside but has an intimate if predictable bistro feel on the inside. But I never came for the décor, I came for the food, which was consistently excellent.

I ordered my staple of beef bourguignon, which is easily the tastiest I've had outside of Paris, while Jess had the duck confit salad, and we both finished off the meal with their signature tarte tatin dessert. It was worth every calorie and allowed me to feel that I'd fed my waif of a daughter, per her mother's instruction.

Jess told me all about her internship, and it turned out she'd been transferred, or rather, leased out permanently by Conde Nast to *Wired* magazine. She'd spent the past week researching tech startups in New York and blinded me with a veritable orgy of technobabble about any number of new companies that were primed to be the next Hatch, Niche or Venmo, which, considering I hadn't really heard of any of these companies that were now set to be upstaged, left me feeling rather ancient.

It still amazes me how you can have two children, both of whom are entirely wonderful and seemingly a perfect blend of you and your spouse, and yet they are so completely different from one another. Jess was our youngest, my little girl, and she was definitely "Type A." She was born with limitless energy and ambition, she has the ability to persuade anyone to do anything, and she has been using this gift unfairly on friends, boyfriends and, of course, her Dad from a very early age.

Because you've changed their diapers, helped them with their homework, and consoled them when they first got their hearts broken, you think you know your kids. But then they grow up and become actual people, and you have to get to know them all over again.

I realized over the course of dinner, as I was relaying what I'd been up to in Florida, and what I'd agreed to do for Baptiste moving forward, that I really didn't know where my daughter stood on the subject of religion or vice versa for that matter. Jess asked me about my religious and spiritual beliefs, and so I told her.

"Well, love, when I say I'm agnostic, what I mean is that I believe there is some kind of existence beyond death that is outside of our understanding, or at least our recollection. I believe that like everything around us, we are made up of energy, and that when we die, that energy leaves the body and goes somewhere. And I believe that the purest form of that energy is love.

"Beyond that, I see little point in speculating. I don't believe in a supreme deity that controls our lives on earth, because I don't believe that any God worthy of worship could be so heartless as to allow the horrors that we see occur every day in the world, and not act to do something to stop them.

"And I don't believe in the Buddhist notion of reincarnation, as I find the idea of living a bad life and being sent back as a honey badger, for example, to be utterly absurd.

"I respect everyone's right to hold the beliefs they do, with the possible exception of the fictional Scientologists, as long as they don't try and impose them on anyone else or try and bring their ideology into the way we govern ourselves, or the way we educate our kids for that matter.

"Your mom and I never tried to impose our beliefs on you or your brother, because we felt it should be something you figured out for yourself in your own time. I hope that whatever you believe now, or you come to believe, that it has love at the center of it, because the older I get, the more I'm certain that true love is the only currency that matters in this life, and that it's the source of the energy we are born with and what we take with us."

I said this, and I was surprised at the clarity of my own thinking and a little apprehensive that I'd shared my own spiritual philosophy with Jess for the first time.

"Wow," said Jess, "Thank you for being prepared to share something so personal, Dad. Instinctively, I feel much the same as you do, I guess, but I can't say I've really formed a clear view yet. And hopefully we've both got plenty of time before we find out what really happens when we die.

"But if you don't mind me asking you, Dad, since you don't believe in God in the biblical sense, how in good conscience can you promote this Sebastian as his son, the Messiah?" she asked.

"No, honey, I don't mind you asking, and I think it's a fair question. I could tell you that I believe in free will and allowing people to make up their own minds, and that I'm just the messenger and it's up to people to decide for themselves, but that isn't entirely how I feel.

"The truth is, that whether you think Jesus was the Son of God or just an extraordinary preacher—remembering that his divinity was only determined at the Council of Nicaea in A.D. 325—his message was one of fellowship and love and he deplored prejudice and division.

"So whomever Sebastian is, if I can use my talents and Baptiste's unlimited resources to bring a message of unity into a world that feels so terribly divided right now, especially along religious lines, then I'm going to try and do so," I said.

Jess nodded and smiled at me, then she got up and went to the restroom, but not before giving her dad a kiss on the forehead, like I'd always done to her as a little girl, just before she went to sleep.

I paid the bill and walked Jess back to the apartment I'd spent so many nights in myself, then kissed her and told her to call her mother more often, and to come home for Easter. I then headed back to The Standard for another ride in the creepy elevator and an uncomfortable night spent sleeping on a hard bed that was too low to the floor.

My journey home the next day was largely hassle-free, as the Midtown Tunnel traffic, as well as the air traffic, conspired for once to deliver me a rare on-time arrival in Raleigh, which of course means thirty minutes late, as the Civil Aviation Authority allow airlines to build a one-hour buffer into their flight time.

It was only when I landed and switched my phone off airplane mode that I realized Mara, as usual, had solved a problem I hadn't yet realized existed. Namely, that I had no car to get me back to Boone. She had left the car at our apartment and hitched a ride with a friend of ours who was heading back up to the mountains at the same time. I took a cab back to our apartment, picked up the car and was on the road within twenty minutes.

If you haven't visited the Blue Ridge Mountains of North Carolina, they are quite unlike anywhere else I've journeyed. In the car, on the way up there, you first start to feel the elevation as you pass through the Yadkin Valley into the foothills, and then the inclines become steeper, and you begin to see slopes full of carefully cultivated Christmas trees, readying themselves for winter.

The first time Mara took me up there was soon after we started dating, and we stayed in a charming place called the Gideon Ridge Inn, in the small town of Blowing Rock. The town is named for the legend of a Native American brave that supposedly threw himself off the cliff, as he feared he couldn't be with the Chickasaw chief's daughter whom he loved. When she arrived at the cliff's edge and realized he'd jumped, she prayed to the Great Spirit who then summoned a huge gust of wind, which promptly blew him back onto the ledge.

Setting the laws of gravity to one side for a moment, it's a charming story, and the romantic aura of the place served Mara and I well in those early days of our courtship.

In fact, it was there in the mountains where we made love for the first time, and we learned that our bodies had been designed to be perfectly intertwined. Until Mara, my various attempts at lovemaking could best be described as spirited rather than expert, but something about her body signaled to me how best to arouse and satisfy her.

That first time we were together, it was as though we had been taken over by a pair of lovers who knew one another so intimately, that they understood with perfect precision how to give and receive the maximum possible pleasure.

If I believed in reincarnation, I would have said we'd made love to each other for eternity and had simply come together again in this lifetime to continue our shared rapture. To find that your lust for the one you love actually intensifies as the years go by is rare, I've been told, and so I consider this one of the most precious gifts I've been given in life.

As I reached the apex of the plateau where we had built the house that Mara designed, I was treated to the everyday majesty of the rolling mountains shrouded in a light mist and creating a tinge of purpled blueness, which gives the mountains their name. I drove toward the illumination of our beautiful three-story house, and as I entered the long driveway through the surrounding pines, I saw my Mara busying herself in the kitchen.

It is difficult for an architect to design for themselves, given that they have to then live with their own choices every day, but I convinced Mara to do so this one time, and she created a masterpiece. The house that we named Owl's Perch sits at the highest point of elevation, with 360-degree views from the highest peak of the ridge across the sweeping valley beneath us.

When we first surveyed the lot, Mara noticed that the cliff that ran down from our ridge had three defined steps, and she used this as the inspiration for her design. The result is that the house appears to be a bulging extension of the natural formation of the cliff, while each level has a breathtaking projected mountain view.

Whether I'm working in my office on the top floor, or waking as the sun fills the bedroom on the second, or dining with friends on our porch as the last of the sun falls away, we receive a constant stream of natural blessings because of her conceptual genius. And since she'd created the exterior design and structure, I played a larger role in decorating the house, adopting a modern minimalist style but with warming accents and features intended to draw your eyes ever upward to the vaulted ceiling that existed on each level of the house.

Owl's Perch is our dream home and, as Mara likes to say, the only way she'll be leaving is when they carry her cold dead bones out on a gurney. Mara came out to greet me, and as I went inside with her, I gratefully took the glass of Pinot Noir that she'd poured for me. I wondered for a moment how it was that I'd ever agreed to get involved in Baptiste's extraordinary escapade if it was going to take me away from this woman, and this place.

Reading my thoughts as usual, Mara said, "So, my love, you're away from me for forty-eight hours and you discover the Messiah is alive and living in the Florida Keys, and then invite him here for the week. Can't say I saw that one coming."

"Neither did I, my love, neither did I," I replied.

I explained that Tish and Sebastian would be arriving sometime tomorrow afternoon, as well as everything else that had happened in greater detail than I'd been able to on the phone. And she listened and shook her head in surprise at the series of bizarre events that had occurred over the past couple of days. I could tell she was caught between understandable incredulity at what I was suggesting, and a desire to be supportive and keep an open mind.

She also informed me that our son Charlie had phoned to say he was planning to come up from Raleigh to see us, as he was meeting up with some old friends from Appalachian State, where he'd studied engineering. Apparently he'd be arriving the day after tomorrow, so we'd have a full house.

Once I'd finished my drink and then another, and given our dogs Wallace and Gromit plenty of heavy petting, Mara suggested we head to bed, and I didn't need a second invitation. I needed to become intimately reacquainted with my wife and ground myself in the exquisite normalcy of our lovemaking before the madness resumed again tomorrow, when I tried to discover what our Messiah really had to say to the world.

13

Mara and I spent the day getting the house in shape for visitors, with the help of Wallace and Gromit, named of course after the splendid Claymation characters in the Aardman Animations movies. We'd had the dogs for about four years now—since they were puppies, when we got them from a rescue shelter in Raleigh.

They were mostly bloodhound with a touch of retriever in the mix, and they were brother and sister, with Gromit being the female and the larger of the two, while Wallace happily followed in his dominant sister's footsteps.

The canine hierarchy was not unlike the human pecking order that existed at Owl's Perch. Strangely enough, Gromit was more attached to me than to Mara, and the reverse was true for Wallace, who enjoyed having two strong females to follow about. When we both had to be away from home at the same time, we had dog sitters come and stay, rather than sending the dogs off to kennels, which was illustrative of the fact that since we became empty nesters, the dogs never had it so good.

Around five o'clock that afternoon, the dogs let us know that Sebastian and Tish had arrived, and we went out to meet the car so that Mara could welcome Tish and be introduced to Sebastian. As they got out of the car, I noticed that their body language seemed like that of a couple. You could tell in the way he opened the door for her and grabbed her bag and never fully took his eyes off her, while she touched his arm protectively to warn him to watch out for the ice, as the dogs busied around them both.

Sebastian came round the side of the car and hugged me warmly, and then did the same to Mara, as if greeting a much loved friend again, rather than the stiff way people typically act when meeting someone for the first time. Tish also gave Mara a hug, and I noticed she gave her a maternal look that said, "He's gorgeous, good for you, girl." I tried to move them inside, but both Wallace and Gromit seemed utterly mesmerized by Sebastian and positioned themselves at either side of him protectively as we walked into the house to show them to their rooms.

After they both had a chance to freshen up and rest for a while, we then officially showed them around the house, amid much cooing from Tish in appreciation of our home. Sebastian was all smiles and seemed very much at ease with us and especially Tish, and we suggested heading out for dinner to a favorite restaurant of ours nearby called Bistro Roca. As we left the house, I actually heard the dogs howling, which, although they are bloodhounds, they'd seldom done before, and I could only imagine it must have had something to do with Sebastian's presence.

As we entered the restaurant, I became aware of people discreetly and even openly staring at us, or to be more accurate, staring at him. Of course he was a strikingly good-looking young man, but that didn't fully explain the draw he had on people. We were seated at the table, and our waitress quickly arrived. She had served Mara and I before, and I recalled she was a student at Appalachian State. She stopped by our table, presumably to offer us some drinks, but then simply stood there and stared at Sebastian, while he smiled back. Eventually, I had to interrupt her frozen gaze by inquiring if she'd perhaps like to take our drink order.

The young girl appeared to wake from a semi-hypnotic state and she trundled off after only having seemed to half catch our order. Meanwhile, Tish was helping Sebastian find his way through what appeared to be more eating choices than he was used to. As we were getting ready to order, a young mother with her husband and their infant child came up to our table and introduced herself to Mara. Apparently, she worked for the real estate office that had sold us the land to build Owl's Perch, and she remembered us.

Of course, this was just an excuse, as neither Mara nor I recalled having seen her before, but it didn't matter, as she just stood there gazing at Sebastian—as did her husband and their young son. Tish eventually broke the awkward silence by asking them how old the boy was, and the husband answered that he was about eighteen months, while never taking his eyes off Sebastian. At that moment, Sebastian reached out to take the child, who went to him without a sound, and proceeded to wrap his arms around his neck.

His parents stood there smiling at them both, and they were then joined by our waitress, who took her place beside them, and they stared contentedly at Sebastian and the boy, who appeared to have instantly fallen asleep in his arms. I looked at Mara and she gave me a quizzical look as if to say, "Well, this is different." I asked our waitress if she'd like to take our order, and the young parents if they'd like their son back. They each seemed reluctant, but they complied nonetheless, and we were able to continue with ordering our food.

After an excellent meal, where I had the Cuban crepe, and overate as usual, we left the restaurant. Tish and I walked slightly ahead of Sebastian and Mara, and I asked her, "Those people, the waitress and the couple with their child, did you experience anything else like that traveling with him from Miami?"

"Yes, it happened with a little boy as we were coming out of the airport in Greensboro, and then with an elderly woman at a gas station we stopped to get drinks at on the way here," she answered.

"It's as if people are put into a trance by the mere sight of him, and to be honest, I know how they feel. Whenever I'm away from him, I feel a sense of sadness, Mal. I'm either in love or I've been bewitched."

"But Tish, don't you have a long-term boyfriend that you live with, if you don't mind me asking?"

"No, we separated about six months ago, so I'm free and single. But I will tell you that I never felt about him the way I feel about Sebastian. The effect he has on me is intoxicating, and it hasn't even become physical between us yet," she said.

We got into the car and drove home, and as we walked through the front door Wallace and Gromit ran to greet Sebastian, completely ignoring their masters. And so it continued for the rest of the evening, until Sebastian went to bed accompanied by two infatuated bloodhounds.

As I lay in bed with Mara, before we turned out the lights, I asked her, "Have you ever seen anything like that love; with children and animals drawn to him like the Pied Piper or something?"

"It's amazing, Mal. It isn't just his looks, although he is quite perfect. There's an aura around him that people want to step inside. I've never seen or felt anything quite like it." And I nodded, as neither had I.

"But you know that doesn't prove he's actually the Messiah, Mal, right? Promise me you'll engage your logical mind, and not allow yourself to believe his undoubted charisma is more than just that," she implored. "I promise," I said, seeking to reassure her.

The next morning, Charles Tristan Thomas, better known as Charlie, our beloved first born, arrived, and I sat him down for one of dad's full English breakfasts, which included bacon, eggs, sausage, beans, and fried potatoes, as well as generous amounts of toast on the side. Of course, in order to be complete, we'd have needed to add black pudding, but Charlie never liked it, so we skipped that.

Charlie is the easiest person to get along with that I've ever encountered. He is quite egoless and without enemies. He's his own man, and trying to get him to do something he doesn't want to do is nigh impossible. But, even so, it never seems to lead him into a confrontation.

I remember, when he was young, asking him endlessly to put his dirty laundry in a basket instead of under the bed, and he steadfastly refused to comply. When I'd finally had enough and confronted him, at age seven, saying, "Charlie, why in the hell are all these clothes under your bed again?" He stood in front of me and said, "I'm really sorry, Dad, but I'm afraid it's just sheer laziness that keeps stopping me from doing it."

I recall having to turn away to stifle my laughter at this charming display of disarming honesty, and that's just a tiny example of Charlie's personality. Honest to a fault, decent to the core, humble, smart and brave. He is truly everything a parent could hope for in a son, and he's now an engineering graduate who plans to spend his life "Building and connecting things, for a living."

I had planned to immediately tell Charlie about Sebastian, but before I had a chance, he told me that Mara had already

JEREMY D. HOLDEN

filled him in on Dad's new unlikely business associate. After he'd finished eating, Tish and Sebastian came back in from their morning walk along the ridge, and I introduced them to Charlie.

Charlie said he was meeting up with his old "App" friends in an hour to go snowboarding up at Sugar Mountain, and he asked if they'd like to go with him. Sebastian indicated that he would and Tish agreed, so we fitted them out with some of our old skiing gear and sent them off in Charlie's beaten-up old Ford Bronco, with instructions to be back by four, so I could spend time with Sebastian before dinner.

This gave me a few hours to catch up on some other work, including the neglected Wipez assignment that had needed to play second fiddle to the new Messiah this past week and now required some attention. When they rolled in at about three, they looked suitably windblown and were laughing together, as if they'd all become fast friends.

I asked Charlie how Sebastian got on and he said brilliantly, and that he loved the guy, although they hadn't done as much skiing as he'd hoped, because all the female members of his group seemed to just want to sit around and look at Sebastian, he grinned.

I wasn't sure exactly what Mara had told Charlie about Sebastian, and so I asked him what he knew and what his impressions were. In his typically understated way, he said, "Mom said there are people claiming he's the Messiah, and that you're trying to get to the bottom of it before agreeing to help. Good luck with that, Dad, and be careful please, because there's a bunch of crazy people out there who aren't going to want to hear that." I smiled and hugged him, and promised I'd try not to do anything rash or stupid. Then I went to find Sebastian.

I asked Sebastian to join me in the office on the third floor of the house, or the top of the perch, as we call it, and Tish came with him, but I asked her to step outside for a while, as I just wanted to spend some time alone with him. I'd prepared a few rather pivotal questions, and I made sure he had his iPad with him to be able to text me his answers.

I began by saying, "Sebastian, there are some important questions that people, fairly or unfairly, are going to ask you, and they will expect you to have an answer to." He nodded to indicate that he had understood me and would try to help.

"I'm texting you the list of questions now, and I'd like you to try and answer them if you are able to." And I sent the text with these five rather big questions:

What happens to us when we die?

Do heaven and hell exist?

Did God make us in His own image, and does He control everything that happens to us on earth?

What is your message for people around the world?

Are you the Messiah, and have you lived among us before?

I noticed that Sebastian was holding a crucifix on a chain in his hand, and I watched as he read the questions while rhythmically rolling the chain between his fingers, causing the crucifix to swing gently. I waited for him to finish the questions, and then he stared at me with a faraway look in his eyes, but still he didn't respond.

Then I felt the same sudden pain I'd experienced before in Marathon as a great sense of heaviness washed over me, and a darkness seemed to engulf me, and then I heard the voice. It was the same voice I had heard before in Marathon, but this time it spoke to me, and somehow we were able to converse.

"You are Malachi, the messenger, and I am Rahim, the empathetic one," the voice said.

In my detached and darkened stupor, I heard myself conversing as I asked him, "Where are you, and how is it that I can hear you? Where is Sebastian?"

"I am here with you, and you can hear me because I will it. Sebastian, as you call him, is here in spirit and is listening to us, but he is silent now," said Rahim.

"I have questions for Sebastian, but I don't think he can answer them. Can you speak for him?" I asked.

"I can answer only those questions that will help people understand one another better, and that will help to build empathy among people, for that is my purpose. This is all they need to know until their lives have run their course.

"I have heard your questions, Malachi, but God cannot be described in the manner you seek. He is evolved beyond the physical and is simply the supreme spirit and the source of purest energy. And when you pass through to this plane of consciousness, you become vitally aware of his energy, just as you become aware of all of us—those you have known, and those you will come to know.

"In this plane, you transition from a permanent state of oneness to rejoining the universal energy, and as you come to experience the shared state of grace, it becomes harder to return, but many will do so, because they must yet grow. That is all I can tell you about this plane of existence, and as much as you can understand now."

And so I asked him, "Who is Sebastian, and what is it that I must communicate, on his or perhaps on your behalf?"

"Sebastian is the seed of all mankind, both for those who live on your plane and for those who stay with me. It is only in the presence of the purest vessel that each side can engage, as we are able to now.

"He is untouched by the thoughts and distractions that blind us to one another, and he has joined you from this place because you need his energy now to push against the forces that are dividing you."

"By the forces that divide us, are you talking about the extremism and intolerance that has surfaced and seems to be growing all around us?" I asked him.

"I am talking about the quality that defines and separates each of you, the capacity for empathy that is my purpose, and that is given fully to us. Empathy is like a mountain stream that mankind drinks from and washes in, and the more you drink from her, the faster it flows.

"There have always been times when the stream flows more slowly as empathy recedes, but with Sebastian's help and yours as well, Messenger, a time is coming when his energy can run through mankind, leaving all of you, as well as us, connected and restored. You see, Malachi, what happens in your plane, echoes in ours," said Rahim.

"The things that you say are incredible, but I don't know how to achieve all this, and I'm worried about what will happen to Sebastian when we tell his story and share his purpose," I said.

"The Messiah's time was short, and his crossing back to our plane was serene. Do not worry for Sebastian, as he is blessed and venerable. And worry not about this great task, Malachi, because you have chosen it for yourself, and have prepared this entire lifetime for it.

"I don't understand, you said that he had already crossed back, but how can that be as he is still here in this plane?" I said.

"Soon enough, you will come to understand all of this and where Sebastian truly resides now, Malachi, but in the meantime, you must know that if you could not have succeeded in this task, then we would not have decided to let you do all this.

"You see, you and I are kindred spirits in the truest sense, and together we have seen and written all of this. Your task, my dear Malachi, is to listen and to find your way through the sea of doubt, and then to believe and become the messenger who persuades others of the truth as only you can. We will talk again soon," he said.

And as the voice faded, the darkness began to lift, and I found myself staring into Mara's concerned face.

I looked across at Sebastian, and I could see that he also seemed to be emerging from a stupor, but whether it was real or a pretense I couldn't tell at that moment. And then I felt myself losing consciousness again.

14

Mara tried to insist that I stay in bed, but I've never been one for daytime napping. When Tish knocked on the door to check on Sebastian and me and received no response, she entered the room and found me apparently passed out and Sebastian in a trance of some kind. Unable to rouse either of us, she sought out Mara, who had tried to revive me with a couple of firm slaps when I finally came out of it.

Afterward, I told Mara everything that had happened and what precisely Rahim had said, or at least what I believed I had heard. While she said she believed me, I could see the concern on her face, and she made me promise to immediately arrange to have the MRI, which I agreed to do the next day, and then to go straight to see the neurologist.

Taking care of this as a priority was Mara's precondition for giving me her blessing to continue with Baptiste's assignment, and while I didn't believe there was anything wrong with me and that the blackout had been caused by the psychic experience I'd had, I knew we both needed this reassurance, and I was happy to oblige.

Months after my childhood surgery, I'd done a little research into my injuries and had discovered with interest that the pineal gland, which in my case had temporarily been displaced in the accident, held a certain fascination in many cultures. Some ancient civilizations referred to it as "the third eye," because of its position at the epicenter of brain, while the philosopher René Descartes believed it to be the "principal seat of the soul." In truth, I needed to know for certain whether what I had experienced twice now was somehow related to my old head injury, as the alternative was completely mind-blowing in a different sense.

I wrote a lengthy email to Del and Massimo, copying Elliot and Oliver, attempting to capture the essential creed that Rahim had communicated to me, although I said that I'd drawn this from my conversation with Sebastian. I felt confident that I could explain what actually happened during my supposed encounter with Rahim to Del and Massimo over a drink, but I wasn't sure that Oliver would be too reassured by the idea that I'd been "briefed" by a spirit from the other side!

In fact, given the importance of this assignment—not only financially based on the numbers they had sent over to Baptiste but also in terms of the agency's relationship with its largest client—I suspected that my casually mentioning "Rahim the empathetic" would probably send Oliver over the edge.

I sent a separate note to Oliver, asking that he use his contacts to try and arrange a meeting for me with Victor Vilas in New York in the next few days. Both Oliver and I had met with Vilas on a couple of occasions in his capacity as president of BAPTIST Health and then later when he'd taken over the reins of JetRider. While I knew that he wouldn't open up to me about the true reason behind his departure from BAPTIST, I hoped I could at least learn how he felt about Baptiste and gauge his frame of mind when he left the company.

Later that day, I heard back from Oliver that he'd been able to secure a thirty-minute meeting for me with Vilas in New

York, but that it had to be the day after tomorrow, as he'd be traveling to Asia that evening and wouldn't be back in the United States for several weeks after that. I also had a cryptic text message from Del saying simply, "Think we've nailed it, come back ASAP to discuss, DX!"

I spoke to Mara, who agreed that I could fly back to New York tomorrow as long as I had the MRI and then saw the neurologist in the morning in Raleigh before leaving in the afternoon. I told Tish my plans, suggesting she accompany Sebastian back to Marathon and then head back to New York. I shouldn't have been shocked when she suggested staying down there to "monitor him," rather than coming back to the office, and so I agreed I'd propose it to Baptiste.

When I spoke to Baptiste to give him an update on the events of the past few days, he surprised me by suggesting that he travel to New York with me the following day to hear the team's initial ideas. And so it was agreed that the next morning I'd drive to Raleigh with Tish and Sebastian, and that Baptiste would arrange for the jet to then pick them up and fly them back to Marathon.

Meanwhile, this would give me a chance to take care of my medical appointments in the morning before the great man himself flew into Raleigh to collect me, and then we'd fly to New York together.

We left early in the morning, well before the sun was up, and while we tried to sneak out quietly, Wallace and Gromit woke Mara up with their pitiful sounding howls at the departure of Sebastian. I'd said my goodbyes to Charlie the night before and reassured him that the "old man" wasn't about to expire anytime soon, and he was the only one that managed to sleep through the dogs' morning misery.

The drive was easy, and I left the two of them at the private section of the airport, where they were greeted by Terry and June. I embraced them both and told Terry I'd see him in few hours when they flew back in with Baptiste to collect me.

After checking in at the radiology department at Duke Raleigh Hospital and making my preferred music selection to negate the pneumatic drill-like sound the MRI machine makes, I took my turn in the cylinder that always put me in mind of Austin Powers being cryogenically frozen. And so, with the Motown music channel playing in my ear, and Mini-Me on my mind, the MRI machine did its work in trying to determine if something untoward was occurring inside my head.

I liked Dr. Badarwi as soon as the first words out of her mouth were, "Well, the good news is that you don't have a tumor or anything like that." She went on to say that, overall, my brain function seemed entirely normal for a person of my age, noting that there were a few indicators of mild cognitive impairment, signaling I may suffer from Alzheimer's dementia later in life.

In short, she saw nothing that would immediately explain my recent dizziness or the blackout I'd suffered and suggested it was possibly due to stress or maybe even a sinus infection. Of course she couldn't rule out the possibility that the symptoms I was experiencing were in some way related to my childhood head injury, but that without further tests, it was impossible to know for sure.

One thing she did comment on from the X-ray she had taken before I'd completed the MRI was that the plate in my skull seemed to be atypically but not dangerously upraised. However, as she had no point of comparison from any earlier X-ray, she couldn't say if that was just how it had settled soon after the original surgery, or if the plate was now beginning to bow outwards slightly. I committed to come back and see her in a month, so that she could determine if there was any change over the next few weeks.

Naturally, I was relieved that there wasn't anything worse wrong with me, but frankly I wasn't surprised, because the conversation I'd had with Rahim had seemed so real to me that I was struggling to believe it could have been a hallucination.

As I was getting ready to leave, Dr. Badarwi stopped me and said, "There is one other thing worth mentioning, and you can take this for what it's worth, but the tests we ran revealed that you have twice the amount of blood flow to the pineal gland in your brain as the average person."

"And what does that indicate?" I asked. "Nothing scientific actually, but some believe it to be a factor in certain people having psychic abilities, if you believe in that sort of thing," she replied.

I considered telling her about the temporary displacement in my pineal gland that had occurred during my head injury, but instead I just smiled politely at her and made my exit. I guess I needed a little time to get my mind around this further indicator that my "third eye" might be getting messages from the other side, and in any case, I was eager to inform my beloved that I didn't in fact have a brain tumor.

After calling Mara and giving her the good news, I checked the time and realized that I needed to be at the airport to meet Baptiste's plane in the next thirty minutes, and so I headed straight there. As I was arriving, I saw the Bombardier 7000, which I was starting to think of as my plane with Terry as my pilot, touching down. The turnaround took less than an hour, and I was soon up in the air sharing a Mojito with Baptiste.

He asked me to relate the events of Sebastian's visit, and I did so with particular emphasis on the strange effect that he seemed to have on humans and animals in sending them into an apparent trance.

I hesitated before telling him about my blackout and supposed encounter with Rahim, but then with a little alcoholic inducement, I decided to go ahead and share everything. He listening intently and asked occasional clarifying questions about our exchange, and then he sat back and said, "Extraordinary. Sebastian has told me about him and shared some of his wisdom with me, but for you to engage with him in this way, Mal, well, this confirms that you are truly the chosen messenger. Believe me when I tell you that this wasn't something that I had ever imagined happening."

We then talked a little about what we would be covering at the agency, and I admitted to being as excited as he was to hear Del's idea.

We landed at Teterboro for the second time that week, and this time we took Baptiste's car into the city. The Bentley Flying Spur is the land-based sibling to the Bombardier 7000, and it was the smoothest and most luxurious automobile I had ever been in. The ride was simply sublime, and I'd never felt so happily detached from the usual Manhattan commuter traffic.

When we arrived at CREATIF, Oliver was waiting in the lobby to greet us, since I'd texted him from the Bentley to inform him we were only a few minutes away. He welcomed Baptiste to the offices for what I realized was the very first time, even though CREATIF had been working closely with a myriad of his companies for over two decades.

As we walked toward Oliver's office, I noticed how smartly dressed everyone appeared to be and how the various examples of work and running videos seemed to have been updated overnight in readiness for the great man's arrival. I wondered to myself whether Baptiste still noticed how everyone and everything was prepared and enhanced for him in the manner of a royal visit and whether it secretly amused him.

Rather than meet in the conference room across a board table, Oliver had arranged his office so that the six of us— Baptiste, Oliver, Del, Elliot, Massimo and myself—sat around a coffee table, creating a more intimate dynamic. They looked to Elliot, who outlined what we proposed to cover in the next hour, and then all eyes turned to me to frame the task and our strategy.

"In essence, the creed Sebastian is sharing can be summed up in one word—empathy," and I paused for a moment to let the word sink in. "In a world that has become divided along religious, political, tribal, and racial lines, people have lost their ability to reach out and put themselves in another person's shoes. The capacity for empathy is perhaps our most distinguishing human quality, and Sebastian can help people find the wisdom and ability to step outside themselves once again."

When I'd finished, Baptiste nodded his agreement and acceptance at what I'd said, which Del took as her cue to speak. She went back to the discussion we'd had in the office earlier in the week concerning the need to create an experience that everyone could participate in, in order to generate a groundswell of goodwill and interest before Sebastian was formally introduced to the world. She used the Ice Bucket Challenge as an example of the type of engaging cultural movement we planned to fuel.

Then Del shared the idea, and I felt the hair on the back of my neck rising as it always does when I hear the perfect creative answer to our strategy. "There is one human gesture above all others that signals empathy to our fellow man. It says I care about you, I understand your pain, I want to help and comfort you, and that I'm like you and love you. It is the quintessential expression of one person's empathy toward another. It is quite simply ... a hug." She paused and then pressed a button on the remote, and a video played on Oliver's widescreen TV.

Against the backdrop of a recently rerecorded version of the classic song "Evergreen," by a young artist I'd never heard of, but who had the voice of an angel, the video showed the power of a hug to comfort, to empathize and to bring people together. I could tell Baptiste was deeply moved, as one of the clips had shown an elderly man hugging his dying wife for the last time before she passed away. Del played the video again to ensure we all received the maximum emotional effect, then she continued.

"We will create a worldwide movement fueled primarily by viral videos that show people hugging. Not just everyday hugs between friends and loved ones, although there will be plenty of those, but hugs that bring enemies and even countries together to symbolize a renewed sense of empathy in the world, and a bridging of religious, ideological, and political divides.

"We will see notable Palestinians hugging Israelis, Sunnis hugging Shias, Hutus hugging Tutsis, Muslims hugging Hindus, victims hugging their persecutors, and so on and so forth. Some of this we'll seed, but much of it will be organic and all the more powerful for it.

"People will want to know who fueled this movement in the first place and our thought is that we attach it to a relatively unknown nonprofit group that is committed to tolerance and understanding of all types—religious, ethnic, social, and political.

"We have several groups in mind that we are considering. As the movement grows and our paid media efforts kick in, which

Massimo will detail shortly, we'll gradually seed a rumor that Alfredo Baptiste has bankrolled all this. At that moment, they'll turn their attention toward you, and that is when we'll introduce Sebastian to the world with a simple hug between the two of you," she concluded.

And then we waited for him to speak, and I could see the concern on their faces, but I wasn't concerned. I'd come to know Baptiste's looks and gestures and knew he was simply choosing the right words of praise.

And so it was no surprise when he looked up and calmly said, "I chose wisely when I allowed CREATIF to work on a small beer brand that no one had heard of twenty years ago, and I chose wisely when I asked Mal and this team to tackle this most unusual assignment. Ms. Bishop, your idea is quite brilliant, and I am putting our full resources behind funding the launch of," and he paused as Del interjected, "The Hug Challenge." He nodded and repeated, "Exactly. The Hug Challenge."

He continued, "I have one change I'd like to make to what you said, Ms. Bishop. When we ultimately reveal who has funded this movement, BAPTIST the company must be behind the curtain rather than just Baptiste the man. I have built this company into a global powerhouse that employs and creates wealth for millions of people around the world, and yet many still don't see it as a force for good. I believe an explicit association with what we are doing here can help to change that," said the great man.

Treading carefully, Oliver said, "Of course, Mr. Baptiste, you're aware of the fact that this movement and the promotion of Sebastian will be highly polarizing, to say the least. Would it not be prudent to position you as the endorser rather than BAPTIST? The impact on the share price alone could be quite unpredictable."

"Oliver, I appreciate and acknowledge your concern, and I recognize that any potential fallout that impacts the companies of BAPTIST also has an impact on your bottom line, but this is a path I'm committed to, and ultimately I believe we will reap our just rewards from this association," Baptiste concluded, with a slight nod indicating the discussion was now over.

The meeting continued for another hour as Del, Massimo, and Elliot outlined the various traditional PR, digital, and social media campaign elements that we envisioned launching, in the wake of The Hug Challenge. They proposed a global media spend which was equivalent to the annual GDP of a medium-size European nation, and yet Baptiste approved it with just the slight lifting of his chin, as if it were a mere trifle unworthy even of comment or a full hand gesture.

Once the meeting had wrapped up, Oliver proposed taking Baptiste and myself out to lunch, but he politely declined, explaining that he had various commitments that afternoon. He asked me to call him in a few days with updates on our plans to quickly seed The Hug Challenge and get the other campaign elements lined up. Finally, he promised to send Tish back to us at some point and, with that continuously knowing smile he wore on his face, he thanked us again and took off in the Bentley.

As we walked back to his office to congratulate the team, Oliver said, "Why do you think he wants to be overt about referencing BAPTIST's support rather than simply his own? Isn't he afraid of alienating his executive team, let alone the board? A public company can't afford to be seen to explicitly support a religious cause, especially in the person of an unknown and potentially polarizing figure like Sebastian, even if the CEO is Alfredo Baptiste, who basically walks on water in the international business community." And his logic was undeniable.

"I don't get it either, unless he's simply genuine in his desire to show that BAPTIST is a force for good and the hell with what people think. Either that, or for whatever reason, he's intentionally sending a message to the board that he can do and say whatever he pleases, and he's daring them to question him," I said.

"This makes your upcoming conversation with Vilas even more interesting. Perhaps you can learn something from him that sheds light on Baptiste's thinking in this instance, because it doesn't seem like his style. He's always been known as a collaborative leader, humble and reticent to do anything that smacks of flaunting his power and ego," said Oliver.

"Once we've opened this particular Pandora's box, Oliver, you know that anything could jump out, and we'll be unable to control where the narrative goes. My only solace is that Baptiste is one of the smartest people on the planet, and he must have a sense of where this will likely all shake out," I said.

"Well, I hope he knows what he's doing, because he's getting ready to fuck with a lot of people's lives for the sake of Sebastian, including ours," said Oliver.

15

KONG's New York offices were in a tall, innocuous-looking building in Midtown, on Fifty-Second and Ninth Street. My appointment was scheduled for two o'clock that afternoon, and I took a cab and arrived early, knowing how complex and time-consuming the check-in process can sometimes be at large corporations in Manhattan. Particularly those like KONG that were Chinese-owned, and where the paranoia could at times seem to be institutionalized.

Surprisingly, it turned out I had no trouble checking in. I was met in reception by Vilas' assistant, who shepherded me up to the thirty-fifth floor and settled me down to wait with a bottled water, Deer Park versus Veen, which was a bit of a comedown from what I'd grown used to at BAPTIST Tower.

As I was ten minutes early arriving, and Vilas was ten minutes late in seeing me, I felt I'd been hanging around for a while when I was finally shown into the office of Baptiste's former protégé.

Vilas got up to welcome me and shook my hand forcefully, ushering me to take a seat in a comfortable chair off to the right-hand side of his cavernous office. I noticed that he had an excellent view of Midtown, facing south down Eighth Avenue, but I wouldn't have swapped it for CREATIF's gorgeous views of the Hudson River.

There are two things that immediately strike you about Vincent Vilas upon meeting him in person. The first is his height; at around six feet five inches, he is an imposing figure, and I could imagine the fear that he must have inspired on the mound while you were waiting to try to hit his intimidating fastball. The second is his hands—they were absolutely huge, and when he went to shake mine, he enveloped it as if I were a child.

He was wearing a perfectly cut, medium blue pinstripe suit with a crisp white open-necked shirt, and his shoulder length hair was swept back neatly with a liberal amount of styling gel of some kind. Vilas was often seen on the pages of celebrity magazines, presumably because of his eligible bachelor status and his propensity to date stunning young models and actresses.

Meeting him in the flesh, while there was no doubt he was a good-looking man even though his complexion was somewhat potted—the apparent result of severe acne in his youth—my net impression was that his wealth was probably a significant factor in his being able to date all those famously gorgeous women.

He politely ushered me to sit down and, per his reputation, wasted little time with small talk, getting straight to business.

"Mr. Thomas, it's good to see you again. I understand that you are no longer with CREATIF, so it seems we've both made career changes since we last met. I recall that was in Cannes two years ago, when JetRider won a Gold Lion for your experiential marketing campaign, if my memory serves me correctly." I was impressed that he remembered when and where we had last met.

"I apologize, but I'm leaving momentarily for an extended period of business travel, and I only have about fifteen minutes to talk, so please tell me how I may help you," Vilas continued.

"I understand and appreciate you fitting this in on short notice," I said. "I am working on a confidential and rather sensitive consulting project for BAPTIST, about which I trust you'll understand that I'm unable to share many details, other than to say it's about protecting Mr. Baptiste's personal image and profile.

"I'm sure you know from your years spent with him, and your own esteemed position in the business community, that personal reputation matters greatly and must be defended at all cost."

"Well, I must say I'm intrigued now about what may have prompted BAPTIST to hire you in this capacity, but that aside, how can I be of any help as it relates to Alfredo's professional reputation?" Vilas asked. "It is well known that I viewed him and still view him as a mentor, and that I would never say anything less than positive about either the man or the company. I owe Alfredo Baptiste a great deal, and it was one of the most difficult decisions of my life leaving when I did."

"If I may ask, most people in the business community saw it as a foregone conclusion that you would eventually succeed him as Worldwide CEO, and so it was a shock to many when you left to take on what appeared in effect to be a parallel position at KONG to the one you occupied at BAPTIST. If it isn't too impertinent a question, could you tell me why you left?" I asked, recognizing that I may be close to crossing a line.

"I cannot imagine how that is relevant to your assignment, Mr. Thomas, but I will answer your question, because there is no secret about this. I had spent my entire career at BAPTIST, and I felt I needed to experience a different environment in order to progress. I will also admit that I wanted to prove to myself, and yes, egotistically to the world, that I could succeed without

Alfredo standing beside me and advising me," Vilas responded with unexpected candor.

"I see, and I must say that makes complete sense, but if I may press a little further, I'm also interested in the timing of your decision. You could have made this move at any time, as I'm sure you received similar offers on a regular basis, so why was this the right moment, particularly in light of the fact that Mr. Baptiste's wife had just passed away? I would imagine he would have strongly preferred that you had remained," I said, aware that I had now officially crossed that line.

He looked at me for a moment with predatory eyes, and I saw the fire that burned within him, as well as the arrogance. Here was a man who wasn't used to being questioned, who answered to no one and was only bound by the rules that he himself created. Also, the depth of his feeling for Baptiste and his ingrained sense of loyalty toward his mentor were written into his expression.

"Mr. Thomas, your question seems to imply that I abandoned Mr. Baptiste at a moment of personal difficulty for him, and I must say I resent the implication. If you knew anything about my relationship with Alfredo, you would understand that it was he who encouraged me to take this position, and I would never have done so had he not been entirely supportive of my decision," he fired back, with his temper barely held in check.

"I meant no offense by the question, Mr. Vilas. I am simply struggling to understand why your leaving BAPTIST at the time you did would be anything other than a personal setback for Mr. Baptiste, but I'm sure he had his reasons. I'm sure you both did," I said, leaving my obvious incredulity floating out there.

"Yes, we both had our reasons, neither of which have any impact on Mr. Baptiste's public profile, which to my mind remains impeccable. So if there isn't anything else, Mr. Thomas, I must be getting on," he said, without rising to the bait and with his composure now seemingly restored.

"Of course," I said, and went to stand up, but then paused for a moment and added, "There is one more unrelated thing I'm curious about, if I may? I've noted that KONG seems to be selling assets and apparently stockpiling cash at a time when other companies are on a buying spree. What do you know that they don't? Or are you perhaps planning to make a big acquisition sometime soon? My wife is convinced that you intend to invest heavily in the health sector, and I agreed I'd probe to see if I could learn something straight from the horse's mouth, so to speak," I said, this time quite expecting to be forcibly ejected.

Instead, he actually smiled, and said, "Why, Mr. Thomas, you'd have made a good investigative journalist if the career in advertising hadn't worked out! I'm sure your wife is very astute, but you know I can't possibly comment on that, as you might go out and buy shares in KONG, or possibly some other company you think we have in our sights, and then I could be accused of passing on privileged information. Anyway, I must rush now, my best to Mr. Grouse." And with that he opened the door and ushered me speedily out of his office.

As I exited through the lobby of the KONG building, I decided to walk for a while rather than immediately heading back to CREATIF. Frankly, I was surprised at myself, considering how much I'd chosen to press him, and concluded that I'd done so because I sensed he was lying to me about his reasons for leaving BAPTIST when he did.

What I didn't know was whether he was lying to cover his own embarrassment at the self-serving way he'd acted, or whether he was hiding something else. I guessed the former but feared the latter.

I pulled out my phone to call Oliver and gave him a quick summary of my conversation with Vilas, to which he replied, "Fascinating. And I will say, Mal, you've got some balls asking him directly about his motivations for leaving BAPTIST. No wonder he got pissed off at you."

I told him I planned to come back into the office to circle back with the team before heading off to North Carolina that evening, but our conversation was interrupted by an incoming call from a Miami number.

I told Oliver I had to pick up the other call and was surprised to find the great man himself on the line. "Mal, this is Alfredo," he said, as if I wouldn't have known his voice, "I've just had a rather unhappy Victor Vilas on the phone complaining that you came to see him and asked a series of random questions about why he left BAPTIST, under the veiled pretext of working on a public relations project for the company," he said.

I've always been fairly quick on my feet, so I admitted that I had been to see him out of curiosity. I said that I wanted to know whether his decision to leave had anything to do with Sebastian, and if so, whether we might have to run a defensive campaign in the event that he chose to leak sensitive information to the media before we were ready to make our own announcement.

"Well, that might have been smart, Mal, but if you were worried about that, why not just ask me? And indeed, why then did you not ask him about Sebastian directly?" He had me.

I was trying to think of a response when he chuckled and said, "It's all right, Mal. I understand why you really went to see Vilas. You wanted to know if he left BAPTIST because he thought the loss of Sylvia had affected my judgment and caused me to embrace

Sebastian. Even after everything you've seen, and the fact that Rahim has chosen to speak to you, I know you still doubt this is all real, Mal, and are afraid it's all the imaginings of a grieving old man."

I wasn't sure how to respond, but after a moment I said, "Alfredo, you were right when you said at the beginning that I would be the principal doubter in all of this and that only through the process of convincing myself would I ultimately be able to persuade others.

"It's true I went to see Vilas because I wanted to know if his departure from BAPTIST was connected to Sebastian. In truth, I now have personal experience of the loyalty that you engender in others, and I couldn't believe that he of all people would depart at such a difficult time for you, after you'd been his benefactor and mentor all these years. I'm sorry to have failed this test of faith, Alfredo," and I meant it.

"Mal, you were chosen for this in large part *because* of your nature. I can hardly now fault you for following it. I have always known you would arrive at a moment of true faith in your own way and in your own time. This changes nothing. Now, please go and tell your team at CREATIF that I am relying on them to do their best work, and I will speak to you soon, when we are ready to launch the campaign."

"Oh, and one other thing. It seems that Tish and Sebastian have become quite inseparable, so with your agreement, I shall not be sending her back to New York anytime soon," he said, and I heard him chuckle again as he rang off.

I didn't feel much like returning to CREATIF after that conversation, and I decided I needed to walk and think, and so I headed for Central Park. I found my way to the Boathouse Restaurant, where I ordered a drink and an appetizer, and I stayed there for an hour or so, taking some time for contemplation.

I needed to do a little soul searching to try and confront what I truly believed at this point. I knew that I hated the feeling that I had let Baptiste down by going behind his back to assuage my own doubts. And his understanding and magnanimity over the incident only strengthened my growing admiration and affection for the man rather than merely the corporate mogul, which was how I'd always viewed him.

I didn't want to feel that way again, and I was tired of denying what I knew I'd come to believe about Sebastian. At a basic human level, he was a sweet, simple man with a pure heart that, combined with his stunning good looks, drew people and animals to him like bees to honey. But beyond this mortal plane, I now believed in my heart that he was a vessel to share something of great importance with the world.

I'd also come to believe that Rahim was a higher being of some kind and the author of this message, but to accept that Sebastian was the Messiah reborn, the Son of Man, the Son of God! That was something my own belief system wouldn't allow me to accept, as I didn't recognize the existence of an all-knowing, all-controlling God in the biblical sense. But beyond that, the truth was that I was ready to put my doubts to the side and embrace what I'd seen, heard and felt.

In so doing, I was willing to commit myself fully to fueling a movement based on the philosophy that Rahim had outlined and channeled through the physical person of Sebastian—a movement driven to restore human empathy in a world that had become so brutally divided.

Armed with a renewed sense of clarity and restored purpose, I paid my bill and walked out of Central Park. I hailed a cab and headed back to CREATIF.

When I got there, I went straight to the small conference room, which the team had set up as their "war room" for Project

Judas. Upon seeing me come in, Oliver, Elliot, Massimo, and Del quickly joined me to get caught up on my conversation with Vilas, as well as my subsequent call with Baptiste.

I told them what I'd concluded about Sebastian, although I stopped short of telling them about Rahim. I told them about my MRI and the conclusion of the doctor that I was physically healthy, and yet spiritually open, which was as far as I felt comfortable going with Oliver in particular. I told them that I didn't trust Vilas or his motives, but that I didn't think that he and Baptiste were in cahoots over his departure from BAPTIST in any kind of sinister way.

Finally, I told them that I now believed in and trusted Baptiste fully, that I felt his motives in all of this were pure, and that I no longer believed his judgment to be suspect in the light of Sylvia's death.

In essence, I told them, and myself, that I was no longer the doubter I had been, and that I was *all in* on this extraordinary assignment and ready to be the messenger. We had a powerful and engaging idea at the center in the form of The Hug Challenge, as well as unlimited resources to spread the word to every corner of the planet.

As I looked around at each of them, I knew at that moment, whether or not they believed everything I said, that this usually cynical group was with *me*, including, miraculously, both Del and Oliver, and that emotionally, creatively and financially, we were now ready to roll.

16

We spent the rest of the day and well into the early hours of the morning, as it turned out, planning both the launch of the campaign as well as the role of the different media we planned to employ. I moved my flight to the following morning and let Mara know I'd be home a day later than planned. But it was worth it for the progress we made.

The first thing people would engage in would be The Hug Challenge, and we settled on a U.S.-based nonprofit organization called X LINES, which was a relatively unknown organization, coincidentally founded at The University of North Carolina at Chapel Hill, committed to "Lifting the ideological barriers that separate nations and religions around the globe."

X LINES was a loose acronym based on their leaders' mission statement that spoke to the need to redraw entrenched lines in the sand. Oliver knew their founder who in turn wanted access to our powerful client roster. Given the incredible amount of money being injected by BAPTIST, we were given carte blanche to frame and launch The Hug Challenge exactly as we saw fit, using the organization as our charitable vehicle.

Even though they didn't know at this stage precisely who or what would be funding the program, they assumed it was a consortium of different entities and individuals that BAPTIST had brought together. And although we didn't mislead them, we also didn't go out of our way to dissuade them of that impression, as letting them know at this stage that Baptiste was signing all the checks would have complicated matters.

Through our own extensive contacts and partner agencies in New York and via the CREATIF global network, we'd had preliminary conversations with a number of well-known figures in the entertainment, political, business, religious, and academic fields. We had arranged some amazing and extremely newsworthy early "huggers" to ensure the program would begin trending across all the major social platforms in a way seldom seen before and then quickly would be adopted by the mainstream media.

Del quipped that "It would take a talking cat playing the piano while the world's cutest baby tap danced in a tuxedo" to rival the share ability of The Hug Challenge videos.

Some of the earliest huggers included the now-adult children of a former Israeli prime minister and a Palestinian president, both noted peace campaigners in their own right. There was a pair of distinguished Rwandan leaders from the Hutu and Tutsi political and tribal divide. Two political leaders from the Shia and Sunni communities in Iraq pledged their involvement. And we also had a commitment from two senior figures within the Russian and Ukrainian administrations. I admitted to Oliver that even I was surprised that BAPTIST wielded such influence in global political circles.

It was CREATIF's media and entertainment contacts that came up big, however, when we got a commitment from Janis Angelo and Annie Jenson, the famously antagonistic Hollywood actresses, to hug, although I later discovered that they had actually been close friends for years and that their perceived rift was a pure invention of the media. For those early participants, the combination of the cause itself, combined with the opportunity to put themselves at the center of an intoxicating media frenzy, was a compelling draw. For those that followed, the momentum fueled by the early participants ensured they would jump on board.

Other pairs of entertainment huggers included pop idol Cleopatra and actor Kevin Costco, singers ML Brown and Jonny Fixx, talk show host and media megastar Joan Seward, and "darling of the right" newsman Sean Hanson, all of whom had been involved in very public rifts, as well as one of my awkward favorites, Genie Elan, the massively popular gay talk show host, and Strom Lingard, the right-wing "shock jock."

Within the business community, CREATIF's friends at Nasdaq were able to line up pairings like the traditionally competitive CEOs of Barnes & Noble and Amazon. The leaders of Google and Microsoft would also be seen embracing, as would the tech pioneers of Red Hat and Oracle.

But perhaps most extraordinary of all was the Pope and Ayatollah Katami. Having previously come close to meeting, they had finally agreed to embrace each other. Under a veil of absolute secrecy, Baptiste had brokered this one himself, and if anything was going to make the campaign tip, it would be this particularly significant and newsworthy hug.

We expected that as soon as the web began to explode with these images, in addition to posting videos, people would start making requests for notorious adversaries to hug one other. The U.S and Russian presidents, as well as the leaders of North and South Korea, could all expect to come under tremendous public pressure to "Hug It Out," which organically became the tagline and the mantra for the campaign, in tandem with the iconic Beatles anthem, "We Can Work It Out."

We expected all this to play out over a four- to eight-week period, and then we'd pick our moment to seed the news that BAPTIST was the real force behind The Hug Challenge. When the spotlight landed on Baptiste himself, we would then post the hug between Sebastian and Alfredo as a catalyst to spark a frenzy of interest in the handsome young man.

Only then did we intend to make the announcement about who Sebastian really was, and the details of how that would take place were still sketchy, as we wanted to first see how The Hug Challenge played out and whom we might want to involve in the big reveal.

The announcement itself would be the culmination of a massive PR and social media blitz, and we also planned to leverage existing and newly created sites to help frame and steer the narrative on our own terms. We lined up heavyweight media influencers to do various appearances, ensuring that no network, cable station or online channel was lacking A-list personalities with whom we had seeded our talking points.

The paid media effort was less a traditional media buy and more about driving interest in physical and online events where people would congregate to push our message of greater political, cultural, and religious empathy, all under the increasingly ubiquitous "Hug It Out" mantra.

We were engaged in conversations with leading figures in film, music and comedy to create massive events that became "Rock the Hug," "Hug the Stage," and "Hug Your Sides," with all the money raised then being matched by BAPTIST and its corporate partners.

Ultimately, all the money raised would be channeled into a newly formed charity, simply called "Sebastian," that was being dedicated to fueling empathy around the world in those areas where politics, religion or an entrenched conflict had created a seemingly intractable divide.

March Madness is when America goes nuts over college basketball, but in April of that year, the whole world went apoplectic over The Hug Challenge. The event launched on the first of April, and to set things in context, it had exceeded the Ice Bucket Challenge's total engagement numbers on Twitter, Facebook, Instagram, and Vine—in just a single day.

Over a comparable two-week period, the event raised slightly in excess of half a billion dollars. The single most viewed and shared video of the entire program was the hug between the Pope and the Ayatollah Katami, which caused unprecedented scenes as people ran into the streets to hug each other or stopped a passerby for an impromptu embrace.

Launching on April Fools' Day proved to be another of Del's masterstrokes. Because people thought it might be a hoax when several of the more high-profile hug videos first appeared, they shared them in greater numbers out of a sense of curiosity as much as in support for the cause. The Hug Challenge instantly became the highest-trending story online and across all social networks, and it stayed that way for almost three months around the globe.

The events driven by the film, music and comedy communities quickly eclipsed anything seen before. "Rock the Hug" concerts were held in Tokyo, Paris, Moscow, Cape Town, Rio, Los Angeles, and Chicago, and they became the single largest combined set of global music events in history. Viewed on computers, tablets, smartphones, and televisions, there were few places in the world where you couldn't view the concerts. "Rock the Hug" concerts took place on consecutive weekends throughout April and May and dwarfed previous global music events like *Live Aid* by comparison.

For two months, every talk show had an actor, director, producer or commentator appear that represented "Hug the Stage." Global celebrities like iconic director Steven Sorrell, Academy-Award winning actors Robert De Franco, Brad Jones, George Craft, Jennifer Phillips, Amy Aykburn, Dennis Denver, and even action star Curt Tarbor, appeared, which we found fascinating, given his very public Scientology beliefs.

They would dance onstage and display the signature self-hugging pose that Genie Elan had first begun, then at the end of the interview, they would turn to the audience and start the chant, "Hug It Out!"

Each of them had a variation of the same talking points we'd distributed, along the lines of, "This is a moment in history where the world has come together and said enough to political and religious division and conflict. It's time we rediscovered what unites us and demonstrate a renewed sense of empathy for each other."

The "Hug Your Sides" comedy events coincided with the "Rock the Hug" events but were held in different cities around the world, including Beijing, London, Prague, Nairobi, Buenos Aires, San Francisco, and New York. The greatest comedic talents on the planet, all appeared live at more than one event. *Saturday Night Live* was dominated for over a month by "Hug Your Sides" themed sketches, and when the concert came to New York, it partnered with *SNL* to create a live one-off special that became the most watched comedic event in history.

And while the entertainment frenzy was extraordinary enough, perhaps more incredible still was the political traction that started to be seen in regions around the world where some of the most intractable conflicts existed. Israel and Iran held meaningful talks, and the Israeli government also halted the building of settlements and engaged with Hamas for the first time after they had respected a mutual ceasefire for several weeks.

Uganda and their neighbors to the north of the country combined to encircle and destroy the grotesque Lord's Resistance Army. The African Union came together with the support of the United Nations to deal a series of devastating blows to the terrorist group Boko Haram in northeastern Nigeria, and, in partnership with the new government, finally freed, among many others, the last of the abducted children.

Equally extraordinary was the coalition that formed to destroy the militant group ISIS in Iraq and Syria. The air and land forces included military personnel from Iran, Israel, Jordan, Saudi Arabia, Japan, Turkey, Russia, China, and the United States, as well as reconciled forces from within Iran and Syria. And the collaboration continued as East and West united to solve the refugee crisis that ISIS had created across the region and throughout Europe and the rest of the world.

Ordinary people in the United States described the mood in the country as being akin to the feeling of togetherness that existed in the weeks after 9/11, except in this case there was no related desire for revenge, no sense of outrage, anger or fear.

There was simply a feeling of people coming together for the betterment of one another, and a growing excitement about what this global empathy movement, or GEM, as it was increasingly being referred to, was capable of achieving.

And yet, through all of these extraordinary events in the spring of that year, one thing was still missing, and one pivotal announcement still remained. In order to continue to perpetuate over the longer term, every movement that ends up changing the world has a single figurehead or a Chief Disciple.

The global empathy movement, GEM, had the participation of many of the most renowned figures in politics, religion, business, and entertainment, but it lacked a spiritual figurehead. So in late May, we agreed with Baptiste that it was time to give Sebastian to the world.

The hug between Sebastian and Baptiste was filmed at the water's edge in Marathon, and after much deliberation, it featured just the two of them. Instead of simply challenging a few friends to "Hug It Out," Alfredo challenged the world to adopt Sebastian, saying, "I ask you all to embrace Sebastian, the person who has saved me and who has been the inspiration for so much that has happened these past weeks."

Of course, an immediate media feeding frenzy that dwarfed even the coverage of the previous few weeks ensued. Seemingly everyone on the planet wanted to know who Sebastian was and what Baptiste had been referring to when he'd suggested that he had inspired everything.

At the height of the frenzy, a story was anonymously leaked to *The New York Times*, CNN, and Mashable that Baptiste had indeed been inspired to put BAPTIST's resources behind the entire Hug Challenge effort because of his *houseguest*. This only served to heighten the unprecedented level of interest in Sebastian and, as we intended, the speculation built up for weeks as Baptiste said nothing further.

Wild stories circulated about his identity, including one credible online magazine repeating the suggestion of an influential blogger that Sebastian was the new Messiah, although no other news outlet repeated it.

And then we scheduled the announcement. Three interviewers were invited to Baptiste's house in Marathon, and their arrival had all the pomp and reverence associated with the arrival of the Magi, or so it seemed.

Genie Elan and the now reconciled Joan Seward and Sean Hanson arrived together from Miami on Baptiste's helicopter, and after preparing themselves, they were led out to the main veranda, where the interview with Baptiste and Sebastian was scheduled to take place.

We'd chosen these individuals to conduct the interview in order to generate the largest possible audience. Joan Seward remained the world's biggest celebrity, talk show host, and media magnate, and her appeal crossed racial, political, and gender boundaries. Genie Elan had helped to fuel The Hug Challenge on her show more than any other personality and had brought in a younger audience as well as attracting the LGBT community. And as the most celebrated conservative newsman, Sean Hansen brought an older audience, a more right-leaning perspective, as well as serving to reinforce the event's "hard news" credentials.

It was a glorious morning in the Keys, and the backdrop of the water created the perfect setting for what had become an unprecedented global media event. Sebastian was dressed in a simple pair of slacks and a white shirt with his sleeves partially rolled up, and he sat next to Baptiste who was similarly dressed, although, as usual, he seemed to wear his clothes more formally.

Joan, Genie, and Sean were all impeccably dressed and each had a camera fixed on them personally, while another camera was focused on the three of them. Sebastian and Baptiste each had an individual camera and a shared camera for both of them as well. A final camera captured the collective scene.

They sat together in what felt, from a distance, like a casual scene of a group of friends conversing on the veranda over drinks. However, the informal setting stood at complete odds to the tension that resonated from the veranda. Oliver, Del, Tish, Massimo, Elliot, and I stood off to the side and reflected on the moment we'd been building and planning toward, and we took a collective deep breath.

It had been agreed in advance that Baptiste would make an opening statement and introduce Sebastian, while the interviewers were then allowed a total of five questions each. Such was the cordon of secrecy that we'd been able to maintain around Sebastian that the interviewers were told only minutes before we went live on air that he was in fact mute, and that they would therefore need to deliver their questions through Baptiste.

This *late-breaking news* caused an understandable and farcical degree of consternation and a flurry of intense discussions, with each interviewer sequentially threatening to leave, until their respective network bosses and backers told them politely to sit down, shut up, and get on with it.

As the live cameras rolled, Joan introduced the event, her fellow interviewers, as well as Baptiste and Sebastian. She then introduced Baptiste who made his opening remarks.

"Joan, Genie, and Sean, you are most welcome to my house, and I appreciate you all coming. Your viewers know all they need to know about me, I'm sure, but they don't know the young man sitting to my right, and it's him that I've asked you all here today to meet.

"Sebastian is my adopted son. He was born into poverty in the favelas of Rio de Janeiro, and through luck and the kindness of others, he found his way to me. Sebastian won't be speaking to you today because he is mute, and so I shall endeavor to speak for him, and relay his answers to the questions posed.

"Sebastian is the reason I decided to put the full resources of BAPTIST behind the worldwide phenomena that's become known as The Hug Challenge. He convinced me that our fragmented world must be brought together, and that we needed a renewed sense of empathy to help bridge our various political, cultural, and religious divides. Our friends at CREATIF, with the help of the good people at X LINES, then gave us the message and the medium to achieve this.

"We've all seen the results these past few weeks, as intractable conflicts have taken strides toward resolution, and intractable minds have been opened with the simplest of human gestures. We all owe Sebastian a debt of gratitude. He is the spiritual leader of this global empathy movement, or GEM, as we now refer to it.

"He is a modern Messiah, if you like, and I will continue to draw on his wisdom and guidance as we continue what we've started. 'Hug it Out,'" concluded Baptiste as he rose and embraced Sebastian, who smiled back at him warmly. At this point, everyone surrounding the set burst into spontaneous applause, and you could sense the power of that embrace grip the global audience watching on their various devices.

While each of the interviewers were clearly moved by Baptiste's remarks, as was everyone present that day, they quickly recovered and began asking their prepared questions, which ranged widely in nature from human interest to geopolitical, as might be expected from such an esteemed and eclectic triad.

After they had probed Baptiste on the details of Sebastian's upbringing and how he had come to be adopted by the great man, Sean asked incisively, "How would you characterize Sebastian's religious beliefs and affiliations, and has your own faith been shaped by him?"

"Sebastian has told me that he belongs to no single religion, although he sees great wisdom and commonality in each of them. He is a spiritual man who believes that our energy continues beyond this mortal plane. And yes, he has impacted my own beliefs about life after death.

"I will also say that he was a great comfort to me these past months after the death of my beloved wife, Sylvia," said Baptiste, which prompted several follow-up questions, none of which forced Baptiste to expand his answers beyond religious and spiritual generalities.

The interview continued with Genie asking several questions about Sebastian's stance on issues of social justice, to which Baptiste was able to reiterate their shared commitment to racial, gender, and sexual equality. Genie seemed delighted to hear that the British movie, *Pride*, which told the story of an unlikely bond between striking miners and gay rights activists in the 1980s, had become one of Sebastian's favorite films.

This prompted Genie playfully to ask if Sebastian liked to dance, and when he nodded and stood up beckoning her to join him, they began an impromptu tango. When the video of the thirty-second dance was later posted on Twitter, even after all the server precautions, it took down the site for almost an hour.

As time ran out, there was an opportunity for one final question, which it had been agreed in advance would go to Joan. Instead of posing her question to Baptiste, she looked directly at Sebastian and said, "Sebastian, Mr. Baptiste said earlier that he sees you as a modern Messiah. Did he mean that literally?"

I held my breath along with the rest of the approximately four billion people who were watching around the world. Sebastian gave her that knowing smile that would cause a dying man to stand up and follow him, and simply nodded at her.

And the world changed.

17

It was true that lots of people had engaged in The Hug Challenge purely for the fun of it, without having connected to or even having understood the underlying global empathy movement, and they continued to share their videos and like others that their friends were posting. The vast majority who had seen the interview and grasped the implication of Sebastian's gesture, however, reacted quite differently.

Many simply disengaged from The Hug Challenge on social platforms and stopped attending or tuning in to the events and effectively became invisible. Others continued their virtual support for the movement itself while distancing themselves from Sebastian and his extraordinary assertion. But the majority were highly vocal in their denouncement of Sebastian, and Baptiste by association.

Online media groups, commentators, and influential bloggers sensed the mood and led the way in wild speculation about Baptiste's motives for sponsoring Sebastian. The mainstream television and radio networks then quickly followed suit, piling on with their own conjecture and invention.

News outlets dispatched reporters to Rio en masse to gather anything they could on Sebastian's background and the events surrounding his adoption by Baptiste. Other journalists were sent to grill employees of BAPTIST, CREATIF, and X LINES, as well as anyone that had even the most tenuous of connection to those responsible for The Hug Challenge and the related campaign.

One supposedly reputable news magazine speculated that Sebastian was Baptiste's illegitimate son and went on to intimate that the strain and betrayal had contributed to Sylvia's death. This infuriated Baptiste to such an extent that he promptly increased BAPTIST's equity position in the magazine's corporate parent until he'd secured a majority stake and then forced the resignation of the magazine's editor. Baptiste's reputation in business had always been of someone who would take swift and decisive action when something needed to be handled, and his approach in relation to personal matters was no less incisive.

Another tabloid claimed to have it from a member of the Marathon household that Sebastian was Baptiste's lover, but people's entrenched public image of him as a virile man who was devoted to his wife meant this particular rumor didn't gain traction. It was also suggested that the body language between the two of them during the interview, and even during their original hug video, communicated a paternal bond rather than a relationship based on physical intimacy, or so we were informed by a parade of body language experts in the media.

Personally, the idea of Baptiste and Sebastian having an intimate sexual relationship was perhaps the most ludicrous in a long list of asinine news inventions that flowed like polluted water from the sea of international journalists covering the story.

The British newspaper, *The Daily Star*, printed a front-page story based on an interview with a renowned extraterrestrial investigator, who they seemed to be fashioning after the character of Agent Mulder from *The X-Files*. The headline of the story was, "Ten things that prove Sebastian is an alien!" These things included his overly perfect good looks, the fact that he hadn't mastered human speech, and apparently a glimpse the investigator claimed to have had of his pointed, snake-like tongue!

I had to laugh amid the media onslaught later when Sebastian was filmed from a distance while buying ice cream with Lula. He turned before getting into the car and took a pronounced lick of his ice cream, which was just enough for a not-so-well-hidden photographer to capture a shot of his perfectly well-rounded tongue.

Another story seemed to have been started by an influential Christian blogger, who'd suggested that Sebastian had been able to speak right up to the interview itself, when God had struck him dumb so that he couldn't utter the blasphemy that he would otherwise have spoken.

In a Fox News poll, some twenty-three percent of respondents believed this to be true, which the commentators noted was equal to the number who believed that the president wasn't born in the United States, as if to prove the consistent wisdom of this minority of their viewership.

Even Mara and I had reporters phoning to try and arrange interviews, and one even showed up at the house, but he was dispatched by Mara in a manner that ensured he wouldn't be back or likely be able to sit down again anytime soon.

Jess called to say that one of her deputy editors at *Wired* had blatantly hinted to her that it might be a good career move if she interviewed her own dad, to which, Jess being Jess, responded by going to the managing editor to clarify if this assignment was sanctioned by her, which of course it wasn't.

And while Jess made an enemy of the deputy editor in question, she put a stake in the ground about her own professional ethics and gained the respect of the managing editor at the same time.

Charlie was approached by a reporter while he was out snowboarding with friends, and he answered that he had met Sebastian, that yes he was mute, that he liked him, that he was charismatic, and that he had taught him how to snowboard.

From that brief exchange, the reporter, who was in the process of writing a story about the jet-set lifestyle that Sebastian had led since coming to live with Baptiste, then added a section on how Sugar Mountain was fast becoming the Aspen of the Blue Ridge Mountains, where the wealthy and elite led a hedonistic and often debauched lifestyle. When we all read that, everyone who knew the area was too busy cracking up to blame Charlie for talking to the reporter in the first place.

Tish in particular bore the brunt of the media's all-consuming fascination with Sebastian, as a paparazzi photographer managed to get a still shot of the two of them walking on the beach. They were strolling hand in hand, and the photographer had captured a moment where Tish was glancing at Sebastian with a look of undisguised adoration on her face.

This attractive addition to the soap opera cast and storyline created new momentum for a public that couldn't get enough of "The Miami Messiah," as many in the press had now dubbed Sebastian.

Tish's family, who lived outside Rochester, were bombarded by reporters, as were her old college friends from Syracuse. Bob Corker, NBC's leading sports journalist and commentator and a fellow Syracuse alum, broke the story about Tish having had a long-term crush on the New England Patriots' star quarterback. Given that many in the football community already thought that the Patriots' quarterback walked on water, it created a simplistic and superficial portrait of Tish's male preferences.

Worst of all for Tish, her former longtime boyfriend gave an interview to *People* magazine about how she had broken his heart and how he hadn't been able to understand why she had broken off their engagement until news of her relationship with Sebastian became public.

Tish still cared about him but, in reality, they hadn't become engaged because he'd never asked her. And they had broken up six months before she met Sebastian, after he'd slept with one of her best friends.

None of these facts would have suited the popular narrative of an opportunistic and ambitious young woman insinuating herself into the Baptiste household, so there was little point in Tish responding and trying to put forward a counter perspective.

The celebrities who had been so keen to be seen with their "Hug It Out" T-shirts, appearing on network and cable talk shows, or performing as part of "Rock the Hug" and "Hug Your Sides" events, chose to scatter like a school of minnows that sensed that the barracudas were on their way.

Strangely enough, only Joan Seward, whose question had unleashed the global media beast, appeared to publicly entertain the possibility that Sebastian might be who he claimed to be.

She was quoted as saying, "I felt something unusual being in his presence, even among all the cameras and the media circus. If I had to describe the feeling, I'd say it was a sense of peace and serenity, almost as if a state of grace surrounded him." I knew exactly what she was referring to, and I admired the fact that only she seemed to have the moxie to acknowledge what she'd felt.

Predictably, the religious as well as the political figures sought to quickly distance themselves from their very public and increasingly embarrassing hug videos. Both the Pope and Ayatollah Katami's spokespeople suggested that had the actual sponsors of the program, as well as their true agenda, been clear from the outset, they wouldn't have participated.

Similar comments followed from world leaders like the President, Chancellor Holtz and Prime Minister Bland, who had all been active participants in The Hug Challenge.

The journalists that had been dispatched to Rio to investigate Sebastian's upbringing had a tough time finding anything concrete to write about, as separating fact from fiction proved challenging, to say the least.

The moment they asked almost anyone in the favelas whether they knew Sebastian, they immediately claimed that they knew him well and, for a small amount of Brazilian real or, better yet, U.S. dollars, they would be prepared to reveal the true story behind Sebastian's early years.

As a result of these types of bogus transactions, stories appeared suggesting variously that Sebastian had been a drug dealer, a drug mule, as well as a prostitute. Conversely, there were also stories suggesting that Sebastian had had a cult-like following in his teenage years, based on the fact that he had performed several miracles.

These included apparently having made a crippled child walk, having restored the sight of an elderly man suffering from cataracts, and most bizarrely of all, having raised a goat from the dead with just the touch of his hand. Why the goat had been singled out for this life-restoring treatment, no one could say.

While all of this insane speculation or outright invention was focused on Sebastian and, by extension, those closest to him, Baptiste had plenty of troubles of his own.

BAPTIST's share price on Nasdaq fell dramatically, in one week losing a third of its value and causing the entire exchange, and with it the Dow Industrial Average, to plummet. During the financial crisis that led to the great recession of 2008, the term "too big to fail" was coined around financial sector companies like AIG that received government bailouts counted in the billions.

At the time of the now infamous interview and the resulting announcement of who Sebastian claimed to be, BAPTIST was the largest company in the world, three times larger in terms of market cap than any other American company, and one hundred times larger than AIG had been at the time it was considered "too big to fail."

And while the sheer scale of BAPTIST carried the potential to fundamentally undermine the U.S. financial sector, the breadth and diversity of their various businesses and the sectors they operated in could theoretically bring down the entire U.S. economy.

The sectors that really fueled America's economy were a mirror image of BAPTIST's organizational structure and its strength. BAPTIST Energy was America's largest producer of natural gas, had the biggest mining concern, and ran its largest oil refineries, while the company also owned what was effectively a controlling position in Exxon Mobil. BAPTIST's stake in companies like GM, Ford, and Boeing, as well as its ownership of JetRider, made it the largest American transportation company.

BAPTIST Tech operated the largest consumer electronics and telecommunications businesses in North America, while BAPTIST Health controlled more of the health care industry and infrastructure than any other company. At the same time, BAPTIST maintained a powerful position in pharmaceutical giants like Pfizer and Merck.

Other divisions of the company, like BAPTIST Financial and BAPTIST Education, held equally dominant positions through wholly owned subsidiaries or equity positions in their respective industries.

The companies of BAPTIST controlled what American consumers ate, drank, drove, switched on and off, injected, wore, and built. And yet, somehow, this public monolith that dwarfed everything beside it like Godzilla to a gecko, was under the Svengali-like control of a grieving man in his seventies who admitted to having recently undergone a spiritual epiphany and who had no anointed successor. Not surprisingly, therefore, the spotlight moved onto BAPTIST's board of directors.

The chairman of the BAPTIST board was the former chairman of the Joint Chiefs of Staff, General George Gregson. The general had met Baptiste many years ago when, as relatively young men, they had both found themselves on a U.S. delegation helping to broker a peace agreement after the military junta in Argentina had invaded the Falkland Islands, causing then-British Prime Minister Margaret Thatcher to send a task force to reclaim them.

After a relatively swift and decisive victory for the British forces, the two men at the center of the delegation had become close while brokering what proved to be a lasting, although still contentious, agreement. Ultimately, it had been the general and Baptiste who had taken the newly elected president of Argentina to one side, and played stick and carrot to perfection.

Having secured the peace on terms that delighted both James Baker's State Department and the Reagan White House, the two men cemented their friendship by getting royally drunk together and pledging support for one another in their respective careers in the years to come.

The general would secretly admit that he didn't know much about business, but he understood character and loyalty, and Baptiste had the former in spades and inspired the latter in equal measure.

A position on the BAPTIST board was the easiest and most lucrative game in town. They had the most respected business leader in America if not on the entire planet, they had a record of unprecedented growth and unequaled returns to shareholders, and they were obscenely profitable, uniquely diversified, and had a succession plan in place.

Then Sylvia, whom the general had also become close with, had died, Victor Vilas left the company for reasons that still eluded him, and Alfredo had embraced this boy from Rio and started a media firestorm that resulted in a catastrophic and as yet unchecked free fall in BAPTIST's stock price.

The deputy chairman of the board was Walt Pearson, the former president of the World Bank. Newer board members like Pearson didn't have the history with Baptiste that the general did, and Gregson didn't like what he was hearing from allies about conversations taking place among some members that were said to be seriously questioning Baptiste's leadership of the company.

The general had always believed that directness was the best policy, particularly in a crisis, and so he convened a special session of the board to which Baptiste wasn't invited. His intent was to air any concerns that might be simmering and get the board back on track and in support of his friend.

From the outset, it was apparent that the general had seriously miscalculated, as one board member after another rose to criticize Baptiste and talked in alarmist terms about the impact on the share price of "this wretched Messiah business."

Deputy Chairman Pearson rose and suggested that the board's decisions moving forward would have an impact that extended beyond the remit of the BAPTIST organization, and that, in effect, the stability of the U.S. economy and indeed the world's economy, now rested on their shoulders.

He concluded his remarks by asking that the general now call for a vote to suspend Alfredo Baptiste as CEO of BAPTIST effective immediately. Although he didn't suggest who should act as CEO in the interim, he left the board in no doubt that, if called upon, he himself would reluctantly take over the mantle for the good of the company and, of course, the country.

Predictably, his comments caused all hell to break loose, and the general fought for the next ten minutes to reestablish control, actually threatening to shoot the next board member that spoke out of turn, which is where having actually killed people in combat can come in handy when asserting your authority in a boardroom.

Finally, after more measured exchanges, as board members sought to leave the meeting without sustaining a bullet wound, it was agreed that Baptiste should be censored, which meant that he was no longer able to make public utterances in his capacity as CEO without first consulting the board.

The terms of the censorship also demanded that Baptiste disassociate the company from Sebastian and the global empathy movement or GEM. The final term sanctioned by the board stated that Baptiste must provide a succession plan by BAPTIST's next annual general meeting, which was scheduled for September 1, approximately three months in the future.

Lastly, the board agreed to make public the terms of Baptiste's censorship, a move that was bitterly opposed by the general and his minority of supporters, who suggested that this would serve to fatally undermine his capacity to lead the company in the future, which of course was Pearson's intent.

When the general called Baptiste to explain what had happened in the extraordinary session and offered to resign as board chairman, the great man appeared to be entirely stoic. As he later explained it to me, the board were like the three little pigs. "The wolf can huff and puff and even blow a couple of houses down, but in the end, I own the brick house, and the only way it will remain standing is with me in it."

And in the end, he was to be proven right. He was the only one that truly understood BAPTIST's strength and vulnerability. In the meantime, as the storm continued to rage around the man and the company, few were scrutinizing the seemingly disparate investor blocks that were quietly buying up large chunks of BAPTIST stock at historically low rates, gradually taking control in piecemeal fashion, from the traditional funds that had long viewed the company as the ultimate safe haven.

18

Ethan Pope had a difficult childhood in South Carolina. He never knew his mother, and he never felt like he had a permanent home, school, or the usual set of friends that most children take for granted growing up.

Ethan's father, Eldridge, was a revivalist minister, and they pitched their tent all over the South, from town to town and state to state, preaching the word of God. Ethan learned to read by studying his Bible every night, and he learned to hate when he and his father were run out of numerous towns for fleecing the congregation or because of some incident caused by the Apostle Eldridge's drunkenness and whoring.

It was in a whorehouse in Augusta, Georgia, a few miles and yet light years away from Augusta National, the hallowed home of golf's Masters Tournament, that Ethan lost his virginity at aged thirteen to a woman in her late forties that his father had paid to pluck the boy's cherry.

Eldridge saw nothing wrong in drinking and whoring, as the good Lord had given him these vices, and as long as he didn't overindulge himself and prayed for forgiveness afterward, he was sure that the path to everlasting salvation would remain open to him. After all, said Eldridge, "How can you expect to understand a sinner, if you haven't walked a good while in their shoes?"

And so he did walk a mile, and sometimes many miles, in sinners' shoes, and he took young Ethan along on the journey.

At the age of sixteen, while visiting his aunt and uncle in Columbia, South Carolina, Ethan met a girl in a convenience store and was immediately smitten. He asked her if she'd like to go for ice cream, and when she politely refused, he followed her home, broke into her house, and then proceeded to rape and murder her, and mutilate her body.

He was recognized based on an artist rendition and arrested several days later just outside of Gaffney. He was tried, convicted, and sentenced to thirty years in a maximum security prison at the Kirkland Correctional Institution in Columbia, but because of exemplary behavior, he was released after ten. In prison, he learned all about the harshest side of human nature, grew closer to God through his Bible reading, and came under the psychotic influence of his cellmate, Todd Byron.

By any measure, Byron was pathologically and criminally insane, having been incarcerated for life for successfully replicating some of the crimes of his hero Ted Kaczynski, better known as the Unabomber. Like Kaczynski, Bryon believed that technology and today's methods of web-based communication, including social media, were the scourge of mankind.

He successfully convinced the impressionable Ethan that these modern communication mediums were the devil's instrument, designed to lead us away from the simplicity and solitude of God's love. Byron's delusional philosophy was not only embraced by Ethan but fused together with the early teaching he'd received at the foot of his morally bankrupt father, creating a dangerous cocktail of bigoted, Luddite, and Christian fundamental beliefs.

Upon leaving Kirkland, Ethan felt he now knew who he was and what he believed in. All he required was a target to rail against, and when he saw Sebastian's interview and the now famous nod, his purpose in life became clear.

Taking a leaf out of the Unabomber's playbook, Ethan determined that he would deliver explosive devices to several of those involved in the satanic plot to use technology to elevate Sebastian, this false Messiah.

One parcel was sent to CREATIF's New York office, addressed to me. Another was sent to Natalie Brown, the president of X LINES, also at their New York headquarters. The third one, he delivered to Marathon and was addressed to Sebastian, and the final parcel was addressed to Gloria, Baptiste's personal assistant in Miami, at BAPTIST Tower.

Ethan's rudimentary bombs exploded once the parcel was opened. He had built them based on instructions he'd found on a jihadi website in some odious corner of the dark web.

Fortunately, Ethan wasn't the sharpest tool in the shed, and he decided to send the parcel to CREATIF and X LINES via express mail. Both were detected at the sorting office in New York before either could hurt anyone or do any damage.

The parcels that were bound for Marathon and Miami, however, he chose to deliver himself, first gaining entry into BAPTIST Tower while the less diligent weekend security staff were on duty and then gaining entry into the mailroom after creating a distraction by setting off the fire alarm. During the ensuing confusion, he was able to place the parcel in the incoming mail section, ready to be sent up to the executive floor where Gloria would open it on Monday morning, at the same time as the New York parcels were also due to arrive.

Ethan then traveled down to Marathon, where he stayed the weekend. On Monday morning, he walked the final parcel up to the gates of Baptiste's private residence, dressed in the USPS uniform he'd previously brought on eBay. Fidel, the security guard who controlled entry into Baptiste's property and knew the regular USPS driver, spoke with Ethan and refused to let the increasingly agitated young man enter.

As the discussion continued, based on some sixth sense, Fidel drew his weapon. At that point, Ethan ripped open the parcel, killing himself and the brave security guard instantly and seriously injuring a young maid named Rosa, who was approaching the gates en route to her morning shift at precisely the wrong moment.

Rosa would receive the best possible care for her partially severed ankle and dislocated knee, injuries received after a flying section of the twisted gate hit her in the left leg. Not only did Baptiste ensure she had time to recover and recuperate, he also arranged for child care coverage for her three young daughters and created a trust fund to ensure that neither Rosa nor her children need ever worry about money again. Of course, it was the smart thing to do rather than tempt a lawsuit, but it was also the right thing to do, which was why I thought Baptiste had done it.

At the same time as Fidel was losing his life in Marathon, on the sixty-seventh floor of BAPTIST Tower, Gloria was opening the parcel that was addressed to her. It exploded, killing her instantly and causing significant injury to Baptiste himself, who was in his office next door when he was hit by a volley of large glass shards.

He was airlifted to University of Miami Hospital, where he received in excess of seventy stiches to three separate wounds on his left leg, shoulder, and hip. The next day he was released, and his helicopter picked him up from the hospital roof and flew him back to Marathon to rest and recuperate, which was where I spoke to him by phone later that same day.

"Alfredo, I'm glad that you are all right, and I'm so sorry to hear the tragic news about Gloria and Fidel. I understand the bomber was also killed. How are you feeling, and how is Rosa doing?" I asked.

"Thank you for calling, Mal. Yesterday was an abomination. Gloria had been with me for over a decade. Her husband of thirty years is inconsolable. I didn't know Fidel, but by all accounts he acted very bravely. Their service to me will never be forgotten. We are making arrangements for their funerals and to ensure that their families want for nothing, not now nor in the future," he said. I noted a mixture of compassion and steel in his voice.

Baptiste continued, saying, "I am sore from the cuts, and that is one distinct disadvantage I've now learned of having one's interior office made almost entirely of glass. Young Rosa has come through surgery well, and the doctors assure me that she will make a full recovery, at least physically. The mental scars from something like this take longer to heal, I've found."

He paused for a moment, and then said, "Mal, I'm so grateful that the devices that this madman sent to your offices at CREATIF, as well as to X LINES, were detected before they could do any damage. I want you to know that I've come to view you as more than a partner in this venture we set in motion. I view you as a friend, and I hope you feel as I do, as I don't have that many people who I look upon in that way."

I thanked him warmly for his kind words, and in truth they meant a great deal to me. To be considered a friend of Alfredo Baptiste was something to be.

He continued, "Mal, I need to ask you a favor. Sebastian is quite distraught over what has happened and feels responsible for the deaths and the injuries resulting from this horrible attack. Tish has been a great comfort to him, but I wonder if you would consider coming down here to be with them both? Selfishly, I'd also like to discuss where things go from here with the campaign, as I must tell you that what has happened this past week, even before these atrocities, has strained to breaking point my belief in the basic goodness of people. So what do you say, Mal, will you come back to Marathon?"

In truth it was the last thing I wanted to do, but I didn't feel as though I could refuse him after what had just transpired. I agreed to fly down the next day, and while Mara was reluctant to let me go after the emotional trauma of realizing that someone just tried to kill her spouse, she agreed. In any event, I expected to be in Florida for no more than forty-eight hours.

It was the following afternoon when I landed in Marathon, and I noticed several other jets in the private hangar of the small airport. After being picked up by Lula and driven to the house, I saw that a temporary barrier had been erected to replace the twisted gates, while upward of thirty press vehicles were presently surrounding the complex.

When I walked into the house, one of the staff ushered me through to the veranda where Tish and Sebastian were sitting. They both jumped up and rushed to embrace me at more or less the same time. Sebastian looked genuinely relieved to see me, and Tish told me what they'd experienced when the bomb exploded.

She explained how they had been outside by the pool when they heard the deafening noise and had rushed to see what had caused the commotion. Tish told me, with barely disguised tears, how she had seen a look of questioning confusion on Sebastian's face as Rosa was being taken to the hospital and how he had tried to help Fidel and the other man before realizing there was nothing that could be done for either of them.

She looked at Sebastian, then turned to me and said, "He blames himself for all of this, Mal. You have to tell him it wasn't his fault, and that he couldn't have done anything. If it is anyone's fault, it's ours for agreeing to announce him to the world. Mal, I've come to know him and love him, and I tell you he isn't equipped to deal with all this ugliness. He doesn't understand any of it. Please tell him that it's not his fault and that it's going to be okay!"

But I couldn't tell him it was all going to be okay, because I knew it wasn't. If anything, it was going to get worse now before it got better. More religious zealots, fame seekers, and random wack jobs would be coming out of the woodwork. I couldn't tell them I thought we'd been lucky, that it could have been so much worse if a Timothy McVeigh-type monster with some military training and a truckload of explosives had attacked us, instead of this twisted moron.

At that moment, the police arrived in the person of Sheriff Adams from the Monroe County Sheriff's Office. The FBI were en route, but in the interim, local law enforcement was in charge. The sheriff introduced himself, and I explained who I was. He, of course, knew my name as one of Ethan Pope's intended victims. The sheriff told us what his office, in collaboration with the Miami-Dade and Columbia police departments, had learned about Ethan Pope.

He told us about Pope's upbringing, his incarceration and how, based on the near incoherent and non-grammatical ramblings on his Facebook page, they'd been able to piece together his plan and his overall agenda, such as it was. Preliminary forensic reports from the bombings in Florida and the unexploded parcels in New York confirmed that it was all has own work, and they suspected that he had acted alone.

In his final post, he'd referred to himself as the "Son of Ted," with apparent reference to Ted Kaczynski, and he'd written, "Today is jujment day for all you un-American non believers who have used Satan's wepons of mass perswazion to lead us into darkness, and promote the false Mesiah!"

All I could think of as I listened was how many more insane people like Pope were still out there, and how could we hope to keep Sebastian safe from them? I felt at that moment that Tish was right, and that we should never have introduced this beautiful young man to a world with so much anger and division. A world that spawned psychopaths like Ethan Pope—the self-proclaimed Son of Ted!

The sheriff explained that he had a few final procedural questions to ask Mr. Baptiste, and he left us to meet with him. My phone rang, and it was Oliver on the line, calling for an update on how everything and everyone was doing in Marathon, as well as to inform me that he'd had a formal request from Joan Seward, via her JOWN Network, for a follow-up interview with Baptiste and Sebastian. I told him she had to be joking after the last interview unleashed this media Armageddon, but he assured me she was deadly serious.

"Mal, Joan feels partly responsible for everything that has happened, recognizing that it was her final question that set off this firestorm. She wants to sit down with both of them and record an interview. JOWN is prepared to let us veto any segment before the airing that we consider inflammatory or likely to create more chaos. They'd also like Joan to do separate interviews to build out the television special with you and Tish, as well as with Rosa and Natalie Brown from X LINES.

"Mal, this isn't just anyone, this is Joan Seward, and she said this is personal for her. She said that she sensed something from being in Sebastian's presence, and she wants to give people the chance to see and feel it too. She said she wants to help us cut through all the nonsense and let people make up their own minds about who he is or isn't," he concluded.

I told him I wasn't sure it was a good idea at this point and that maybe, in the light of these attacks, the best thing might be to just make Sebastian disappear for a while. Oliver responded that he didn't think there was anywhere on the planet where he'd be able to disappear right now, and he had a point. We had done our work well.

I asked him how Del was, and he simply said, "She's here." I smiled, as I knew somehow they had started to work things out. I told him I'd discuss the Joan Seward interview with Baptiste and get back to him.

As I rang off, Lula appeared on the veranda and beckoned for me to follow him, and I assumed it was my turn for an audience with the great man. I followed Lula upstairs and through into Baptiste's private study, where he was lying on a large white sofa with a laptop resting on his knees and his reading glasses sitting on the end of his nose. He was dressed in a mauve smoking jacket, and I couldn't help but be put in mind of the founder of Playboy in his dotage.

He smiled and looked up as I entered, and he beckoned me to sit down, at which point Lula left us alone to talk.

"Thank you for coming, Mal. It's good to see you in person, and to know you were unharmed by these barbarous acts. You saw Sebastian, how does he seem to you?" he inquired.

"He seems both confused and troubled, Alfredo. We both know that he is an innocent, and too pure in spirit to be able to process this type of hatred and bigotry. I am hopeful that Rahim will come and help to comfort him," I said.

"That is the first time I've heard you speak of Rahim in a manner that suggests you believe him to be real. Is it possible that the doubting Mr. Thomas is finally in danger of finding his true faith?" he asked quizzically, and with the hint of a smile on his face.

"Yes, Alfredo. After I went behind your back and met with Vilas, I did some soul searching, and realized that I do believe in Rahim, I believe in the movement we're trying to launch around Sebastian, and I believe in you," I said, feeling some satisfaction in having come to a place where I could declare this unambiguously.

I expected to see that knowing smile of his appear, and so it did, but not before I thought I glimpsed another emotion momentarily. What I thought I saw at the moment was possibly a hint of guilt.

Then he spoke again, and said, "I'm so glad you are with me in this, Mal. I knew you would get there. And now that you are fully invested, there is one more thing I must ask of you." I nodded and waited for him to continue.

"Sebastian is the key to this global empathy movement that we've tried to fuel, and whether the idea at the center of it was his or not, he is the face of it. I'm not going to allow these setbacks to stop us from achieving what we set out to do, but we need to help Sebastian recover from this.

"After the bombings, Sebastian came to me and told me that he now believes his sister is still alive. He said that he'd had a dream and that he thought she was in danger. With so much resting on his shoulders, we need to find her. Or if she did in fact die in the favelas years ago, we need to know that in order to bring him some closure," he said.

Then Baptiste looked directly at me and said, "Mal, I need you to find this woman, Amelia, or at least discover whether she's alive or dead. You are the only one I feel I can trust completely to do this, and who understands the importance to Sebastian. Lula can be of practical help to you, but he doesn't possess the ability with people that is required. So will you do this for me, for Sebastian, Mal?"

"But Alfredo, you need an investigator for this. I'm an aging ad man, and after all, I wouldn't know where to start," I replied with a slight note of desperation creeping into my voice.

"You have underestimated yourself throughout this entire journey we've been on, Mal, and you underestimate yourself now. And to answer your question, yes, I do know where to start," he said, as he gave me a piece of paper, upon which was written an address that I noted was in Buenos Aires.

I looked up at him in confusion, but he continued, "This is the address that Aaron gave me when he came here to tell me about Sebastian. He said if I ever needed to find him again, or if something happened to Sebastian, I was to come to this address and ask for him, and he would contact me immediately."

"And so you want me to go to this address and find him, and through him to discover what happened to Amelia?" I sought to clarify.

"Yes," he said. "Will you do it?"

"Yes, I will," I answered simply, recognizing that my interview with Joan Seward would have to wait a while—and not exactly sure why I had agreed so quickly.

19

I've traveled all over the world in my career, yet strangely enough I'd never visited Buenos Aires before. So overcoming my fear of small planes, I was keen to see the city from the Bombardier 7000's panoramic window, and the view did not disappoint.

Buenos Aires is situated on the western shore of the estuary of the Rio de la Plata. It's the second largest metropolis in Latin America after Sao Paulo in Brazil, and the most visited city on the continent, largely because of its European style architecture and its relative safety for tourists in comparison to places like Rio and Mexico City.

If the city's architectural gems like the Barolo Tower and the Bencich Brothers Building don't provide enough of a draw, Buenos Aires has an abundance of theaters and art galleries, a vibrant nightlife, and lots of football, or soccer, as my American friends still insist on calling it.

Strolling past the Art Nouveau and Neoclassical-style buildings on the Avenida de Mayo, it was easy to imagine myself in Paris or Barcelona, as I discovered when I took a few moments to take in this magnificent city.

I lost myself for an hour in the elegant and highly affluent Recoleta district after Lula and I had agreed to stop for lunch, before making our way over to the Puerto Madero district. The recently rejuvenated docklands area of the city was where the address that Aaron had given Baptiste was located, in what we were to discover was a massive high-rise apartment complex alongside Dock 3.

To be honest, a recently built high-rise condominium wasn't exactly where I pictured this Aaron living, based on Baptiste's description of him as some kind of raggedy looking biblical sage who appeared to have just crawled out of the desert after a month of fasting.

I knew that Del had visited the city on a number of occasions, so I had called her from the plane to ask her for some recommendations of places to eat lunch. She had suggested we eat at La Cocina, which has the best empanadas in the city—and that's up against some pretty stiff competition. Del liked to joke that I loved empanadas because of my English heritage, and I had to admit that there were few foods that I didn't think could be improved by baking them in a small pie!

It was good to hear Del's familiar voice and catch up for a few minutes. She explained that they had stopped work on the campaign at the agency for the time being, until the dust settled, literally, in this case, from the bombings in Florida. "No one quite has the stomach to work on new ideas that have the potential to cause another bloody psychopath to go after Sebastian, or us, for that matter," she said. And she was right.

She told me to watch my back, not only because the letter bomb being addressed to me proved that I was a potential target, but also because she didn't trust Baptiste and didn't like me gallivanting around the world running errands for him. Mara would have agreed with her, and I wondered if they'd spoken after I'd called last night to tell her about this "last thing" I needed to do before coming back to the sanity and sanctuary of Boone and the Blue Ridge Mountains.

Mara was unhappy to say the least about my having agreed to do this. In truth, no one could have been more tolerant or understanding of my need to see this through, even though I knew she felt that none of this was worth putting my life, and our future, in jeopardy. I promised her I'd be careful and that this was absolutely the last time I'd say yes to "anything" without first running it by her. Although there was nothing but love in our goodbye, I hated the feeling that she wasn't completely with me in this.

Lula and I hadn't spoken a great deal on the flight over or since we'd arrived in Buenos Aires, but I tried to strike up a conversation over lunch, and he seemed pleasant and helpful as usual. I wonder now how I didn't sense anything sinister about him then, and I can only assume that either I wasn't really looking or he was an expert at hiding the darker side of his nature.

We talked over a plate of the most incredible empanadas, the mendocinas, which are filled with ground beef, onions, boiled egg, smoked paprika, oregano, cumin, and lots of other good stuff. It was as if a Cornish pasty got ideas of grandeur and traveled to the most exotic corners of the world, accumulating flavors the way people gather experiences. Lula had a healthy appetite and probably ate a half dozen on his own, and we discussed how to handle things when we visited the address.

We decided that I should enter the building alone, while Lula would stay close by in case I ran into any trouble or "resistance," as he put it. This cunning plan went out the window almost immediately when we discovered that there was a security guard in the lobby who insisted on knowing not only the address I was visiting but also who I was coming to see.

I was getting ready to retreat and regroup when Lula appeared and casually leaned over toward the guard, and then, with a maneuver I'd only ever seen Spock use in *Star Trek,* he rendered the man unconscious. In one apparently seamless movement before the guard fell to the floor, Lula was dragging him toward a closet I hadn't noticed previously, and within fifteen seconds, it was all over, and we were riding the elevator.

I said to him, "He'll be all right, won't he, Lula?" To which he replied, "He'll be fine. He'll wake up with a headache in an hour maybe." I asked him, "Where did you learn to do that?" He replied, "I've been lots of places with Mr. Baptiste, and picked up a number of useful skills." I nodded, as I was starting to get a clearer sense of what Baptiste had meant when he said Lula would be of "practical help" to me.

As we got off the elevator on the correct floor, I looked around and had the distinct feeling that the building had only been completed that morning, so new was the look and smell of everything. This impression was heightened by the fact that clear film appeared to still be covering several of the apartment doors.

I rang the doorbell and heard footsteps scurrying to open it. When the door opened, I was surprised to look down and see a little girl of no more than six years standing there, wearing a yellow dress and white rabbit slippers. She smiled at us and announced that her name was Camila. Then she asked me what my name was, and I told her.

Just then, an elderly woman appeared beside her, who I took to be her grandmother. The woman was wearing a loose-fitting powder blue tracksuit and a black apron with "I heart ARG" printed on it. She asked politely how she might help us. I explained that we were looking for a man called Aaron and that we needed to find him urgently, as we had an important message for him. The woman looked skeptical, so I gave her my card and asked her to have him call me.

I was getting ready to leave as she was shutting the door when I turned and added, "Tell him the message is about Sebastian." She looked at me again as if seeing me for the first time, then nodded without expression and shut the door.

We had just left the building through the lobby, where I noticed that the guard must be still sleeping off the effects of his Vulcan nerve pinch, when my phone rang and an elderly sounding man said, "Mr. Thomas, this is Aaron. I will meet you in one hour at the El Mercado café bar at the Hotel Faena, which is only a ten-minute walk from where you are now," and he hung up.

If I was surprised, based on Baptiste's description of him, that Aaron would live in the progressive docklands district in a modern condominium, I was equally surprised that he would choose to meet me at El Mercado, which appeared to be a trendy and somewhat eclectic cocktail bar. It seemed like the sort of place where people under the age of twenty-five would arrange to meet up with a date they were hoping to impress.

Lula took a table at the back of the bar, choosing not to be part of the discussion with Aaron. He seemed to have enough self-awareness to realize that he intimidated people, and I was pleased that he chose to leave the talking to me.

A man that I imagined to be about Aaron's age entered the café. He looked innocuous enough in a pair of jeans, sneakers, a blue plaid shirt, and brown cardigan. His hair was white and brushed back, and he sported an equally white beard that looked like it received a regular weekly trim. The color of his complexion was similar to my own, and if you had passed this man on the street, you likely wouldn't have given him a second glance.

We made eye contact, and he wandered over to me, stood beside the table, and said, "Are you Mr. Thomas?" To which I nodded and said, "And you must be Aaron. I've heard about you from Mr. Baptiste, and I'm pleased to meet you in person."

"Did Mr. Baptiste send you? Is Sebastian all right?" he asked. "I've been following the news these past weeks, and then I heard about the bombings that happened. I wanted to call, to reach out and make sure Sebastian was all right. But when I heard nothing on the news, I assumed he must be okay, and so there was no need to call."

I listened and then I asked him if he wanted something to drink, but he declined. He asked me if I had come alone, and I told him that I had a colleague with me, but that he was back at the hotel. I don't know why I lied, but something told me it would unsettle him if he knew Lula was lurking in the background, as it actually unsettled me.

Then I said to him, "Aaron, if I may, Mr. Baptiste has told me very few details about you or about the meeting you had with him, other than that you came to see him and told him about Sebastian, and where he might find him in Rio. I don't know what your connection is to Sebastian, or how are you involved in all this. Mr. Baptiste said you knew things about him that no one could know. Can you please shed some light on any of this for me?"

He laughed loudly for a moment, and then turned to me and said, "Mr. Baptiste likes to keep people in the dark, I think, and perhaps that's not a bad thing. But he has sent you here to talk to me, and so I will tell you what I told him, and I will tell you some things that I didn't tell him!"

"I can see from the way that you talk about Mr. Baptiste that you admire him and that you care for him, yes?" he asked. I told him that both of those things were true, and then he shocked me by saying, "Then you are a fool, Mr. Thomas."

He paused and then continued, "I went to see Baptiste and told him about Sebastian, because after his wife's death I suspected he might be vulnerable and looking for new meaning in his life. Baptiste's wealth is only exceeded by his ego, and for me to tell him that God had called him to take the Messiah under his protection and reveal him to the world suited his massively inflated sense of self-importance.

"Baptiste is an evil man who had done terrible things for which he needed to pay a price. I wanted to take from him the two things that he values most dearly—his money and his reputation—and Sebastian was the means of achieving that."

I shifted uneasily in my seat, but I didn't dare interrupt, as I feared Aaron might stop, and then I would never learn how he had planned to hurt Baptiste, or what he still intended. And so I didn't say a word, I simply let him continue.

"Now, let me tell you a story about this man you admire and who you probably think you know. Thirty years ago, Baptiste was a mere millionaire with successful companies in America and Brazil, but he wanted to expand his operations across Latin America, and specifically here in Argentina.

"In order to do so, he planned to take control of a small company based here in Buenos Aires that had managed to secure the exclusive manufacturing rights to a new type of computer processing chip. An American company called LET-IN had developed this chip, and it made any PC it was installed in several times faster.

"This was Baptiste's way to move his company into the technology sector as well as across the continent. But there was one problem, you see: the owner of this company didn't want to sell to Baptiste, or anyone else for that matter.

"And so Baptiste found another way to take over the company. He used his relationship with the new president of Argentina to

JEREMY D. HOLDEN

have the company investigated for a series of fabricated crimes they had supposedly committed, from tax evasion to operating without the appropriate government licenses.

"You see, Baptiste had been on an American delegation after the war over La Malvinas, and he helped our new president strengthen his position by securing concessions from the British. And in return for his help, the president made sure that the company Baptiste wanted to buy was so busy overcoming these legal hurdles that they could no longer operate effectively.

"In the end, they had no choice but to sell to BAPTIST, and your friend got his way, as he has so many times at the expense of other hardworking people," he paused for dramatic effect, and I let him continue without interruption.

"And so, Mr. Thomas, you are no doubt wondering how all of this is connected to me, as well as to little Sebastian. Well, you see, I worked for the family that owned the company that Baptiste stole. I was their servant, aide and friend. I did whatever they needed me to do, and I saw firsthand the harm that was done to them all.

"First, the husband, my friend, Sebastian Blumenthal, could not live with the shame or the pressure. You see, the legal hurdles that Baptiste created followed him, rather than his company, after the takeover.

"You will learn, I fear, that it isn't enough for Alfredo Baptiste to win a battle, he must crush the other man, destroy his family and his friends, and leave nothing but ruin in his wake. And he did his work well, as my friend Sebastian took his own life, and in so doing he left his wife and their two little children alone, penniless and vulnerable.

"Sophia Blumenthal was a beautiful, strong Brazilian woman. She had met Sebastian while she was working as an escort in an upscale hotel in Rio where he was staying while on a business trip. Eventually, he fell deeply in love with her, and after several subsequent visits, he asked her to marry him and come to live with him in Buenos Aires.

"Sebastian came from an old and established family in the city and, needless to say, they didn't approve of the marriage, and wanted nothing to do with either Sophia or the children after they were born. But Sebastian and Sophia didn't care, as they were very happy together, and he was successful in his own right.

"Sophia was passionate and proud, but when it came to her children, she was prepared to do whatever was needed to take care of them. After Sebastian committed suicide, she went to see his parents and asked for their help and protection, if not for her then for the children. But they rejected her and their own grand-children, may God forgive them," Aaron said, crossing himself.

"Since Sebastian's family wouldn't help her, she swallowed her pride and went to ask for help from the man who had been responsible for her husband's death, and their current plight. She went to see your friend, Baptiste. He agreed to help her and the children, but in return, he demanded she sleep with him and commit disgusting and depraved acts, that mongrel son of a bitch whore," he said, reddening with anger and wiping sweat from his forehead.

"I cannot tell you how repulsive I have found it over the years, reading interviews where he talked about his devotion to his wife, while all the while I knew what he did to Sophia behind his wife's back. Sophia was a beauty, but that isn't why he used her in that way. He wanted to show he could take everything from another man, like a Viking warrior or a Mongol invader. Your friend, Baptiste, is a brute and a monster, Mr. Thomas," he said, seemingly short of breath with the telling of his story.

I shook my head at what I'd heard, as in truth this was so far removed from the man I'd come to know, but still I asked him, "And what became of Sophia and her children?" and, of course, by then I thought I had guessed who her children were.

"Sophia had no choice, Mr. Thomas. She returned to Rio and to her old life as an escort, but her looks had faded a little with the passing of time, and in order to provide for the children, she went from being seen on men's arms to being under them," he said, and a look of great sorrow came across him as he continued.

"You see, I moved to Rio with the family and tried to protect them as best I could through all of it. I begged her not to take up that life again, but she felt she had to for the children. And perhaps you can guess what happened to this tragic woman, Mr. Thomas," he said, but I simply shook my head.

"She became sick and she died a couple of years later of what they now know was the AIDS virus, although we didn't understand what was wrong with her at the time. I took the children in, although I had very little to offer them. Amelia was twelve, and little Sebastian was just eight. Amelia was always strong like her mother, and Sebastian was a very quiet and sensitive little boy. After his mother died, I never heard him speak again to anyone except Amelia," he said.

"And what happened to the children, Aaron? How did they end up in the favelas? And do you know where Amelia is now?" I asked.

"That is the thing, Mr. Thomas. After a year or so, Amelia decided that she and Sebastian would be better off on their own, and so she took him and left. I looked for them, but I couldn't find them. I was told that they were living in the favelas with a group of orphaned street children, and that Amelia had taken up her mother's trade, God forbid, but I never found them. And then, perhaps two years ago, out of the blue, she came to see me," he said.

I was fascinated to hear the conclusion of his story and begged him to continue. "She was still such a beautiful child, like her mother, but there was a hardness to her that you see in those who have lived that life in the favelas. She told me that she had a plan to take revenge on the man who had ruined their life, and to make a better life for Sebastian at the same time.

"I was to go to Baptiste and tell him this story about Sebastian being the Messiah. She told me he would be vulnerable after his wife had died, leaving no children, and that I could use the knowledge I had about his liaison with her mother to convince him that I knew things that he thought no one else knew.

"I knew the type of ruthless man Baptiste was, and I never believed it would work, but to my amazement it did, and he came looking for Sebastian and took him back to America. Then he announced Sebastian's identity to the world, made himself look like a fool and crippled his precious company at the same time. Amelia had studied him, you see, and she knew it would work, and so it did," he concluded, with a sense of satisfaction.

"And what happened to Amelia, where is she now?" I asked.

He shook his head and said, "That I don't know, Mr. Thomas, but if I had to guess, I would say she is close by to Sebastian, watching over him as she always has!"

What he had told me was overwhelming. There was simply too much to process and respond to immediately. Everything he had said seemed to add up on one level, and yet it flew in the face of what I'd now come to believe over the past weeks and months and every instinct I now had about Alfredo Baptiste. He couldn't be this callous, ruthless man that Aaron described. Or could he?

Aaron read the struggle on my face and said, "You'll need time to think this through, Mr. Thomas. I understand that. But when you have, I believe you'll recognize the truth in what I've told you. What you do with this information is up to you now. I've done my job and paid my debt to Sophia and Sebastian, by first helping Amelia to set all this in motion, and now telling you what we did to Baptiste, and why we did it."

"Did you know that Amaliah, in Hebrew, or Amelia, as her name is written, means servant of God, Mr. Thomas? I believe she has done God's work in bringing shame and destruction upon that evil man," Aaron said.

"But what about Sebastian? What has she done to him by placing him in the center of all this? I've spent time with him, and he is an innocent, a tenderhearted soul. You cannot mean to suggest that he was part of Amelia's plan to avenge her family," I said incredulously.

"No, I have never believed that Sebastian knew about any of this, which is what made his behavior so convincing to Baptiste, I'm sure. Sebastian was always tenderhearted. I remember he had an imaginary friend, Rahim was what he called him I think, and Amelia would play along with it and never tease him. He worshipped her, and if Amelia told Sebastian that he was the Messiah, he would have believed her and blindly accepted it. He was quite lost without his sister, and she was devoted to him, and would do anything to protect him," said Aaron.

With that, he got up to leave. He offered me his hand, saying, "I wish you good luck, Mr. Thomas. And I fear that you'll need it in the days to come, when Baptiste realizes what has been done to him, and he comes seeking vengeance.

"The old woman and the little girl that you met at the apartment are not related to me. I simply paid them a little money to call me if anyone ever showed up at their address looking for me and mentioning Sebastian by name. I will be disappearing for good now, so you can tell your friend Baptiste not to bother looking for me. In any case, I've told you all that I know."

And with that, he turned and left the café. I swiveled my chair to look toward the back of the room and saw that Lula had also gone, although I didn't know if that was recently or if he'd left some time ago.

I wandered out and began to stroll along the Rio de la Plata riverbank to clear my head. If all of this had been a set up to ruin Baptiste's reputation and damage his company, then not only was Sebastian just a sweet, young man, but Rahim was a figment of his and, apparently my, imagination. My rational mind wanted me to accept that as fact, but my emotional psyche wasn't yet ready to, as it meant acknowledging that I'd deluded myself.

At this point, I only knew two things with any certainty. First, that I needed more time to process all this, and particularly that I needed Mara to help me think through things, and second, that I needed to confront Baptiste as well as warn him that Amelia might be close by and likely planning to attack him.

I would go back to Marathon and repeat what Aaron had told me, and I wanted to believe that I'd be able to recognize the truth when I saw how Baptiste responded.

At that moment, my thoughts were interrupted by my phone's vibrations, and when I answered, it was Lula on the other end. "Where are you, Mal? I went to the restroom, and you were both gone. Did you learn what you needed to from him, or do we need to plan to stay overnight?" he asked.

I told him I felt that I'd got what we needed, and that he could call Terry and ask him to get the plane ready for us to fly back that evening. I told him where I was, and about five minutes later he pulled up in a cab, and we headed back to the airport.

As we drove back through the Recoleta district, I noticed two "Policia Metropolitana" cars passed us heading in the other direction. As I was later to discover, they were answering an anonymous call relating to several people having seen a white-haired man floating face down in the Rio de la Plata, the River of Silver.

20

I found it curious that Lula didn't appear to want to know any of the details of what I'd discussed with Aaron, but I just concluded that he didn't consider it his business, and that what I'd learned should be relayed directly to Baptiste. I thought about calling him from the plane, but I decided that I needed to see him in person in order to measure his reaction when I shared with him all that I'd heard.

The return flight took about eight hours, and we arrived back in the early hours of the morning. Lula and I then drove to the house in somewhat of a sleep-deprived daze. I finally got to bed at around five in the morning, after being shown to my room by Gabriella, one of the housemaids who'd stayed awake for our benefit, and I barely managed to get undressed before falling asleep.

I slept until around two o'clock the following day, and by the time I'd showered and freshened up, it was late afternoon. I wandered downstairs and found Baptiste alone on the veranda, with his leg up, but overall looking much improved from when I'd left him just forty-eight hours earlier.

When he saw me, he said, "So you are awake at last, my friend. I was getting ready to send someone up to check on you. Lula said you didn't get in until around four this morning. I'm glad you were able to catch up on your sleep. Would you like something to drink or eat? I'm having a Bloody Mary, if I can tempt you."

"That sounds perfect," I said, thinking I'd need several in order to get through the ordeal of telling him all that Aaron had said. "I've always assumed the Bloody Mary was named after the Catholic Queen of England, Mary Tudor, whose brief reign unleashed a bloody assault on leading Protestants before she died and was replaced by the first Queen Elizabeth," I said in a fatuous attempt to avoid getting to the discussion in hand.

He humored me by saying that he also thought that was the origin of the drink's name, but that down here, so close to Key West where Hemingway had his home, "People like to talk about how the great writer had facilitated the fall of Hong Kong to the Japanese in 1941, simply by the strategic introduction of the Bloody Mary," he said.

We both laughed, and I asked where Lula, Sebastian, and Tish were, in part because I didn't want us to be interrupted. He explained that Lula was working on the boat, while Sebastian and Tish had just left to go on a bicycle ride across the Seven Mile Bridge, and so, in effect, we were alone.

I waited for my drink to arrive and then began by saying, "Alfredo, what I have to report after having met with this man, Aaron, is deeply troubling, I must warn you. And I will admit it was disturbing for me to hear." He nodded and I continued, starting at the beginning and doing my best to detail everything that Aaron had told me, including the man's suppositions and disdain for Baptiste himself.

As an experienced advertising researcher, I'm extremely accomplished when it comes to reading people and judging their reactions, right down to the smallest shift in their body language, and including the direction their eyes move when processing information. I studied him with a laser-like focus, and I must say his expression gave me absolutely nothing to get a read on. I had no idea how he was receiving this stunning indictment of his behavior, as well as of him as a man.

When I thought I'd told him everything, I noticed myself starting to feel hot and a little dizzy, which I assumed was due to the tension I'd felt in having related all of this, along with some delayed tiredness at being up most of the night. I took a deep breath and another gulp of my Bloody Mary, and I waited for him to respond. Indeed, I was desperate to hear him explain this away, and dispel Aaron's damning testimony. I wanted to hear a passionate and convincing defense of the man I'd come to like and admire.

When he looked at me, I detected a slight expression of sadness in his face, and then he answered, "Mal, it might surprise you to learn that I have been aware for some time of everything that Aaron told you last night." And he paused and looked at me, but I refused to respond with any word or gesture, as it was his turn to speak and to explain all this.

He continued, "I am not a monster, I am a businessman. I wanted to buy Blumenthal's company, and he wouldn't sell it to me; that much is true. So I used what leverage I had with the authorities in Argentina to create conditions that would increase the likelihood of him selling to me, which he then did, and I will say that we paid a fair price for his business.

"The fact that the government pursued him after the deal was done had nothing to do with me. It was because they found irregularities with his accounting and his government licenses. That was his doing and, in fact, it cost us money that we hadn't budgeted or anticipated to secure new licenses.

"It is also true that his wife came to see me after he had taken his own life and begged me to help her and her children. I have been truthful with you in the past, Mal, in saying that I betrayed Sylvia one time while I was in Argentina, and yes, this was the moment, but it did not happen in the depraved manner that Aaron describes.

"This woman, Sophia, offered herself to me, and she was beautiful. I was weak, and I broke my vows, and I've had to live with the shame of my indiscretion, but my conscience is clear as it relates to how I dealt with her and her children.

"There was a final payment that was to be made for the purchase of the business once the accountants and lawyers were satisfied. We justifiably withheld the funds once all the irregularities came to light, and my people recommended that we were no longer obliged to pay it. However, I ultimately insisted we do so in order to help secure her future and that of her children, after her weak and corrupt husband had killed himself," he concluded.

"So what happened to these additional funds then, if it's true what Aaron says that they became destitute?" I asked.

"All I know is that the money was paid over to her, Mal, and there was enough money to have ensured their future financial security," he replied. And I nodded, somewhat reassured that my view of him wasn't entirely mistaken, but there was still the big question to be asked.

"Thank you for your candor, Alfredo, and I'm truly relieved to hear your side of things, but there is still the question of Sebastian. Were you aware that he was the Blumenthal's son when you went looking for him and took him in? And if so, I can only presume that you knew he wasn't any kind Messiah from the outset.

"In which case, if you don't mind me asking, since I've spent the last six months trying to convince the world that he is, what the fuck has all this been about? And why did you send me to Buenos Aires to discover something you already knew about? Please do tell me," I said with undisguised scorn and rising anger.

He looked at me and gave me that slight knowing smile that I'd grown accustomed to. But this time I saw something else buried in his expression, and I sensed it was malice. It caused me to regret the tone I'd just used with him.

"I understand your anger, Mal. I used you and your people at CREATIF. However, you were paid handsomely for your services, and it was all necessary, I assure you, in order to achieve what I needed to, as you will discover momentarily.

"Perhaps unrealistically, I had hoped to be able to leave it at that, but I will tell you now what all of this has been about, and why it has been necessary to create this illusion," he said, and I stared at him, longing to finally learn how my friends and I had been manipulated, along with the rest of the world.

"When Aaron came to see me, I immediately suspected that this was some far-fetched scheme that had something to do with the Blumenthal affair. I always knew that business would come back to haunt me one day. I went along with it because I was curious to know what their intentions were, and I brought Sebastian back here in order to learn what I could from him concerning their motives.

"But it quickly became obvious that he was no more than an innocent simpleton and that someone else must be behind whatever this was. Having met Aaron, I doubted he had the wits to be the mastermind. And knowing the mother was dead, I suspected the sister must be the brains. So I played along and waited for her to reveal herself and her motives, and yet she never did," he said.

"I understand that, Alfredo," I said. "But none of what you have said explains why you needed me to convince the world that a boy you knew to be a 'mere simpleton' was the Messiah.

"It seems to have been going to extremes, to say the least, just to force Amelia to reveal herself, particularly as people have been killed in the process, your reputation has been tarnished, and your company is under serious duress," I responded. And if anything, I was more confused than ever about what possible motive he may have had for perpetrating this grand scale illusion.

"Vengeance, Mal! It is the only emotion that can surpass love in forging a person's destiny. I understand why Amelia may have committed her life to vengeance. As she saw it, she needed to avenge her parents. And she was happy to exploit her innocent brother, whom she no doubt loved, in order to achieve her purpose.

"Why she hasn't come forward yet, I don't know. But she will soon enough, I'm sure. And I look forward to having that conversation with her. I even applaud her for her elaborate efforts.

"As for Aaron, in order to get him to re-emerge, I needed someone I could trust, but who he wouldn't be suspicious of. He knew you were working for me, of course, but your manner is so unthreatening, Mal, and he'd never have revealed himself if I'd just sent Lula. And now that he has reemerged, thanks to you, he is no longer of any concern to us.

"You see, Mal, I understand what it means to devote your life to vengeance, to the exclusion of love, wealth, and power. I understand it because I've lived it," he said. I knew he was finally going to reveal his true purpose, and I was almost afraid to hear it. If anything, I felt more lightheaded, but I was determined to remain focused until he'd finished explaining.

He continued, "When Aaron told me his absurd story about Sebastian being the Messiah, it was all I could do to withhold my laughter, but then it occurred to me that perhaps he had provided the means to achieve my own goals. As I sat there listening to his nonsense, a plan formed in my head, along with an entire sequence of events that I could now set in motion. That was the real gift I received from God that day.

"But forgive me, my friend, as first you need to understand the motive in order for all of this to make sense. You see, my father was an advisor to former Cuban President Batista, and many have speculated that he was also an informer for the CIA. They were right, as it turns out, and he put his own life in danger on many occasions during the rebellion in order to keep Castro and his forces out of Havana.

"In return, he was promised safe passage and support in transferring his business interests to the U.S. in the unlikely event that the government was overthrown.

"But when Havana and the entire country fell, instead of receiving the support and protection of the American government, they left him and my brother to be taken and tortured by their enemies. I know this because my father called me from the airport where he had arrived to fly his plane to the U.S. mainland. His plane that was carrying important documents and family treasures wasn't there, you see, because it had already been flown out of Havana by a CIA operative before my father and brother arrived.

"My father told me this as he and my brother, Ricardo, waited for Castro's forces to come and take them to their deaths, and they knew it would be a cruel death. My father made me swear that I would seek vengeance on the Americans. He told me to find love but never to have children, as they would become

Americans, and that would weaken my resolve to do what I must in his name and in Ricardo's. We were still talking when they came for him, and I heard the shouts, the violence, and the gunshots.

"The American government, through their agents at the CIA, killed my father and my brother as surely as if they had pulled the trigger themselves. They did so because he knew too much about what the CIA had been doing to keep the rebels out of power those last months leading up to the fall of Havana. They thought their secrets would die with him, but I knew all that the CIA had done and what was promised to my family, and to others.

"I vowed to take from this odious country the only things that are truly valued, namely money and power. Although I received none of the support that my family was promised, and I had to build BAPTIST with nothing but my own sweat and ingenuity, somehow I managed to succeed.

"And yes, at times I had to be ruthless, as I was with Sebastian Blumenthal, but only the strong truly prosper in this godless country, and I had to be stronger than them all," he said, clearly now enjoying the freedom to tell another person of his true motives and what he had planned and worked so hard to achieve over the years.

I could feel dryness in my throat as well as the dizziness, and I knew my face was reddening as I looked down at my now empty glass. I knew then that there was something more than stress and tiredness affecting me, but somehow I had to hear this, so I remained silent as he continued.

"In a way, I did my job too well, Mal. I became the Miami Mystic, the man who could do no wrong when it came to growing BAPTIST and making investments. When I had built BAPTIST to a height and breadth that it had become the leader in every sphere of American industry and commerce, my plan had always been to find a way to have it fail absolutely. I wanted it to implode on itself like a star going supernova. Such would be the scale of the explosion that it would create a black hole in the U.S. economy that would suck everything into it.

"I wanted BAPTIST to fail in such a way that it destroyed the foundation of American industry and her financial markets. I wanted the government to feel the sense of hopelessness and vulnerability that I felt as I heard my brother's death scream," he paused and took a breath. I saw the madness in him, and I knew it would be nothing for him to kill me, as he'd killed so many others. And as I felt my consciousness slowly ebbing away, I feared that perhaps he'd already killed me.

He looked up at me and said, "It won't be long now, my friend, and you will feel no pain and simply drift into unconsciousness. But I want you to know that although it has to come to this, I have grown to like you very much and to admire your talents. I could not have chosen a better messenger than you, my doubting Thomas.

"I was surprised when you went to see Vilas, and for a while I thought you may have discovered more than you had, but still it showed courage and ingenuity, and I'm sorry that things should have to end like this, as I will miss your company." I had enough of my wits left to mouth the words, "You psychotic prick," which seemed to amuse him, and he continued.

"I also want you to know that this is something that I and I alone did for my family honor, without the support of any foreign government or power, although the Chinese will be the largest benefactor of America's economic collapse. Victor has been using KONG's resources through shadow companies and compliant hedge funds to buy up huge quantities of our cheap stock, which will ultimately enable him to possess what BAPTIST once owned.

"A Chinese company will control the pillars of the American industrial complex and dominate her financial sector, and although they will cry wolf and claim that the assets have been obtained illegally, it won't matter by then, because a new power will be rewriting the rules of international business," and he gave a satisfied—and sadistic—smile.

And with my last moments of consciousness, as I felt the darkness descending, I said, "I still don't understand ... Sebastian ... the movement ... why, and why now?"

"I'm sorry, Mal, you're fading, and I should have been more explicit. I needed people to know that the Miami Mystic had lost not only his touch but also his mind, or they would never have started unloading their BAPTIST stock in droves. And what better way to prove to people that you have become unhinged than to proclaim that you have found the Messiah and had a religious awakening!

"As for the timing, I didn't want to have to do this while Sylvia was alive. She understood my pain and my need for vengeance, but this was her adopted country nonetheless, and it would have hurt her deeply to see me inflict such harm and humiliation on it. When she passed away, I was free to act, but I didn't know how to inflict the necessarily devastating blow on my own self-image until Aaron came to see me and I learned about little Sebastian.

"If Amelia is alive, and we do get to meet and discuss the power of vengeance, I wonder if she will find it ironic that her quest to avenge her family ultimately gave me the means to avenge mine!"

Then he gave me a warm pitying look that said our time together was now over, and the last thing I heard was him say was, "Sleep well, my friend."

21

The engine of Baptiste's fishing boat slowed, and I could feel Lula gradually coming to a stop as he placed it into neutral. And there were those gargantuan feet coming toward me. I'd actually been conscious for around ten minutes and felt that in that time I'd made some progress in loosening the ropes that bound me. I found it strangely comforting to be wearing my old windbreaker, as it reminded me of simple conversations I'd had with Mara about trivial things.

I couldn't see his face in the glare, but I could see he had a wrench in his hand. So this was it then, my whole life wasn't flashing before my eyes, but I knew in that moment that I loved my Mara, Charlie, and Jess, and I felt a twinge of regret that I hadn't done more with my life or for each of them. But what I had done and the person I'd become, it was all for them. They were the loves of my life.

Lula stood above me and seemed mildly disappointed that I was conscious, and I said to him, "You don't have to do this, Lula, please don't do this." And he looked back at me, and I couldn't read his reaction, but then he replied, "I'm sorry, Mal."

At that point I felt and heard a rush of air as he brought the wrench down across the back of my head, and everything was darkness.

He must have eased me over the side of the boat, waited for me to sink, and then reengaged the engine and headed back to shore, certain in the knowledge that he had dispatched another potential witness to his master's vengeful agenda.

I'll describe what happened next as best I can, but you must understand that it had the detached vagary of a dream, and I felt nothing and heard nothing. I had simply arrived at a place of consciousness where I was aware of myself and the presence of others, and I had a feeling of absolute calm and peace. I didn't think I was dead. In truth, I wasn't capable of thought in the normal sense, and this is all just my conscious post-rationalization anyway.

In my seclusion in the warm darkness, I felt there were others there with me. And while they encircled me, and supported me, and loved me, there was one who loved me more who was closer still, and I knew it was Rahim.

We conversed like two elderly fishermen as they sat watching for a movement on their lines, or two little children telling bedtime stories to one another before lights out. We talked then, as I knew that we had talked for eternity, and it was blissful to commune with him again, and I sensed he felt the same way.

"Malachi, you have been so brave and so tenacious, and I am so happy that you are with me, and with us again, if only for a brief time," he said.

"Rahim, it is so comforting that you are here with me. I was afraid when he came toward me, and I knew that I would die, but I felt no pain, and then I was at peace and with you and my friends. But tell me, why do you say that I am only with you for a brief time? Was this what we planned, am I to go back now? And if so, how is that possible as he has surely killed me?" I asked my friend.

"Your body is suspended, Malachi, and your spirit is free to return to it when we have spoken and you are ready. The time we are talking will feel like minutes, but it will only be a moment, and no harm will come to your body, only the wound he inflicted as he rendered you unconscious will endure," Rahim said.

"Rahim, I was told that Sebastian wasn't the Messiah, and it made me think that you and our conversations were not real, and so I began to doubt again. Can you explain to me what has happened and what I should know that I may have forgotten?" I asked.

"Malachi, the pure spirit you knew as Sebastian hadn't existed in your plane of consciousness for a decade or more. He left and came across when he was still a child, but his bond with his sister was so great that he remained connected to her in your world, while he was also with us here," he said.

"I still do not understand," I said. "He has been with me these past few weeks and months, so how can you say he crossed over many years ago when his body still lives and breathes, Rahim?"

"It is not his body that lives and breathes, my friend. It is that of his sister's. It is Amelia. She took on his physical identity sometime after he died, and it is her that you have been with these past months. It is Amelia's body and soul, and while Sebastian has been with her, she wasn't able to sense his presence through all of her anger and bitterness, even though others could," he said.

. . .

And as I spoke with my spirit mate in that blissful state of grace, at the same time, in the physical plane of consciousness, there was shock, anger, and bitterness permeating from every corner of Baptiste's large brick house by the sea.

Tish and Sebastian had returned from cycling to discover Baptiste and Lula huddled on the veranda. And as they approached them, Tish could see a grave look on their faces, and she asked them, "What's wrong?"

"My dear," said Baptiste, "It seems there has been a terrible tragedy. Lula has just returned with the boat and Mal ... well, he is missing."

"I don't understand," said Tish. "What was Mal doing on a boat? He was sleeping when we left."

"When he woke soon after you left, we talked, and he said that after spending much of the past day or so on a plane, he wanted to get out on the water and do some fishing. So he and Lula went out together on the boat. I wanted to join them, but my wounds are still too tender.

"Lula radioed me from the boat to say that they had been heading to a fishing spot a few miles out on the Atlantic side, when he turned and looked behind him and realized that Mal wasn't there anymore.

"It seems that he must have fallen overboard. Lula said there was quite heavy chop out there, and he may have lost his footing, hit his head, and tumbled overboard. Lula immediately contacted me, and I called the Coast Guard, and he then spent an hour or more circling the area where he thought Mal may have fallen overboard until they arrived to search for him. And I can hardly bring myself to say this, Tish, as I feel so responsible, but it appears that Mal is lost to us," Baptiste concluded.

Sebastian looked to be in a state of shock, and Tish turned to him as if readying herself to speak, but then she turned back to Baptiste and Lula with a sudden look of recognition and said, "No, I don't believe you. I don't believe any of this. Why would he immediately go fishing after having been away for two days? This doesn't make sense, and in any case, Mal has always been a cautious man. He would have held on to the sides of the boat. This just isn't possible, and what will we say to Mara? They were totally inseparable. They were more in love than any couple I've ever met.

"This can't fucking be happening. Lula has done something to hurt Mal. What have you done to him, you bastard? I need to call Oliver, and you need to call the sheriff, Alfredo. Something is wrong here, I know it," Tish screamed, as her temper flared, driven by a rising sense of confusion and panic.

"You must calm down, my dear," said Baptiste, "Lula has done nothing other than to search for Mal. He was equally devastated when he got back, I assure you. But this is just a terrible accident.

"Lula, please take Tish upstairs to lie down. She is understandably overwrought. We will wake you when the sheriff arrives, but for now, you must be calm and not upset yourself, or Sebastian, for that matter," said Baptiste.

"I'm not fucking going anywhere, least of all with him," she said, pointing at Lula. "I'm telling you something is wrong here. Sebastian, we need to leave now. I'm going to get the sheriff," said Tish, with a look that said she would fight anyone who tried to stop her.

"I told you, Tish, the sheriff is already on his way. Please calm yourself. Becoming hysterical is not helping anyone. Lula, take her upstairs," said Baptiste, and the big man moved toward Tish and rather forcibly took her by the arm and attempted to pull her toward the house.

Tish pulled back on him and said, "No, leave me alone. Sebastian, help me, I'm afraid he's going to hurt me. I don't want to go with him."

Then, as Lula continued to drag Tish away, a woman's voice spoke up loudly and with authority, and said "Take your hands off her, now!"

Tish, Lula, and Baptiste looked from one to another, confused for a moment, until all eyes settled on Sebastian, who then spoke again in the woman's voice. "I said take your hands off her now, Lula, and back the fuck away."

Such was Lula's shock that he immediately unhanded Tish and stepped back toward Baptiste, even before he realized that Sebastian had a small ankle pistol in his hand and pointed at them.

Without turning to look at her, Sebastian said, "Tish, come to me, now." And in a state of utter shock at what she was seeing and hearing, she slowly walked over to his side.

At that moment, the infamous knowing grin crept across Baptiste's face as he began a slow clapping sound while staring at Sebastian. "Bravo, Amelia, bravo," he said. "I knew you would reemerge soon enough, but this, this is incredible. I had no sense of it, no one did.

"You are a talented and resourceful woman. You had us all fooled, you even had my doubting friend Mal believe he was conversing with Rahim, the imaginary spirit guide. Truly a magnificent performance. Tell me, when exactly did you assume your brother's identity?"

"Be quiet, old man. I've heard enough from you. People believe what they want to believe, especially if you are silent and allow them to create their own

reality. Rahim was a figment of my dear brother's innocent imagination, but it suited my purpose to suggest that Sebastian, the Messiah, was naturally in contact with the spirit world.

"But now, finally, it's my turn to talk. Lula, if I see you make any kind of movement, Baptiste dies. Now, lie down flat on the floor with your hands behind you back," said Amelia.

"How does it feel, Alfredo, to be helpless and vulnerable? I've wanted you to feel that way for such a long time. Since you caused the death of my father, since you raped my mother, since I was forced into prostitution, since my sweet innocent brother died in my arms from dysentery. I've wanted you to feel an ocean of pain and suffering as you lost your wife, your company, your precious fucking reputation, and now your life," she said to him.

"You would kill me just like that, Amelia? No exquisite torture, no opportunity to savor the moment of vengeance you've craved for so long?" asked Baptiste.

"No, Baptiste, I've taken my pleasure watching you being manipulated these past months, watching your fortune sink ever lower. But now I'm tired of toying with you, and it's time to kill the monster," she stated, as a matter of fact.

"As I said, Amelia, I applaud you, but all you've done is allow me to avenge my father and my brother. I didn't know that you were masquerading as Sebastian, it's true, but I guessed your plan and I exploited it for my own purposes. You see, I wanted my reputation and my company destroyed, and this country with it, so if you plan to shoot me, go ahead. But do so knowing that because of you, I'll die content at having fulfilled my purpose and my vow to my father," he said.

Amelia had a look of concern on her face for the first time, but she composed herself quickly and said, "Enough of your mind games and manipulation, Baptiste. I'll look for you in hell," and as she raised the pistol to shoot, Tish shouted, "No, Sebastian!" distracting her for a split second and allowing Lula to launch himself at Amelia.

The gun fired as Lula landed on top of Amelia. As Tish reeled back, she saw Baptiste topple and then fall forward off the sofa while Lula lifted himself off Amelia and scrambled back to where Baptiste lay dying from the bullet that had passed through his throat and lodged in his spine.

Tish looked down at Sebastian, the man she had come to love, and saw a knife protruding from the chest of the sister who had assumed his identity. Amelia was dead.

Amelia's arm was outstretched beside her, and the small pistol was still in her hand. Tish knelt down to pick it up, and then pointed it at Lula who was too busy whimpering and stroking the hair of the man he had spent his life attending, to notice. But Baptiste no longer felt anything, as he had gone to be reunited with Sylvia, his father, and his brother.

When the shot was fired, members of the household staff had rushed into the courtyard only to witness the death of their employer. Gabrielle, one of the maids, eased her way slowly toward Tish and gently implored her to put the gun down, but she continued to point it at the inconsolable figure of Lula, who now had Baptiste's head in his lap and was patting it gently. With her gaze maniacally shifting from Amelia to Lula, she shouted at Gabrielle to call the sheriff, and the maid ran off to do so.

It took less than five minutes for Sheriff Adams to arrive, as he was already en route after being informed that I was missing and that the Coast Guard was busy searching for me while all this was happening.

He managed to get Tish to give up the pistol without any further bloodshed, and while his deputies secured the crime scene in preparation for the forensic unit to arrive, he began interviewing everyone individually, beginning with Tish and followed by

Lula, who had had to be forcibly removed from the stricken body of his patron.

Tish related everything that had been said and done, and then Lula largely confirmed the events, although the telling of his own actions were slanted toward his attack on Amelia having been an attempt to save Baptiste's life. Sheriff Adams was getting ready to move onto interviewing the household staff when something miraculous happened, according to Tish's telling of it.

I walked in.

I was accompanied by Captain Williams of the Islamorada-based Coast Guard vessel that had picked me up about two miles from the Marathon Key inlet. As I came into the room where Sheriff Adams was wrapping up his interview with Lula, I stared directly at the big-footed murdering bastard and watched with glee as his eyes tried to process the impossible. At that point, Captain Williams pointed at him and said, "Sheriff Adams, arrest that man for the attempted murder of Mr. Thomas here."

I continued to stare at Lula, who was still trying to process what was happening when Tish ran into the room, saw me, and screamed, "Mal! You're alive!"

...

I believed that Rahim and I had spoken for what seemed like hours, and yet in this plane of consciousness, it was mere seconds. He told me what would be happening back at the house and that both Baptiste and Amelia's game was almost played out.

He told me I must return now, not only for my beloved Mara, Charlie, and Jess, but also because there was work for me to do as a messenger. He told me I needed to write this story, and that when people read it they would realize who Sebastian was and come to rediscover the power of empathy.

He told me that a new spiritual movement would arise from these teachings, and that I would be remembered as an important messenger by future generations, as they reflect on a world where people are driven to discover what unites them rather than what divides them.

He told me that our channel would remain open now, and that he would be with me in all that I needed to do. And finally, he told me to open my eyes. And when I did, I saw that I was floating on top of the water with my face looking into the bluest of skies and with the subtle spray of the warm revitalizing waters of the Keys lapping at the edge of my face.

The back of my head was pounding, but the ropes that had tethered me to the weights that Lula had attached had seemingly come undone, and I felt more alive in that moment than I ever felt before or since.

I could just see a glimmer on the horizon to my right, which I knew instinctively, was the Seven Mile Bridge, and emerging through it, I thought I saw a boat. I rolled myself over and prepared myself for the long, slow swim toward the shore, unless the boat spotted me first. I could feel an air pocket in the back of my trusted windbreaker giving me added buoyancy, and I made a promise never to replace this old thing however much Mara nagged me to do so.

Ahead of me, every so often, I saw a single bottlenose dolphin rise, and I remember wondering if it had helped to free me of Lula's ropes. It was keeping its distance yet shadowing me, as if wanting to ensure I made it back safely, able to tell my story.

22

After the sheriff had received my full statement, which took several hours given all that had happened, I told him that I planned to check into a hotel in Marathon, as I needed to get away from this house for a while. The sheriff also arranged for an EMT to check me over, as I'd insisted that the Coast Guard bring me straight to the house instead of the hospital, and I still had an almighty headache. The EMT confirmed that I had a large lump on the back of my head, and that I probably had a mild concussion and needed to get an X-ray at the earliest opportunity, which I committed to do.

I called the Holiday Inn around the corner and booked two rooms for Tish and myself, although it turned out that I only needed one, as Tish refused to leave my side for the rest of that day and during the night. I knew Mara would understand. After all, she was traumatized and almost young enough to be my daughter. Once we got checked in, I was finally able to make a few calls.

First, I called my Mara and told her what had unfolded. I could hear her going through a roller coaster of emotions as I told her about the past several days, from fear at how close she'd come to losing me, to fury at Baptiste and Amelia for bringing so many innocents into their game of vengeance, to finally a desire for violent revenge against Lula for giving me the large and increasingly tender lump on the back of my head. That and trying to murder me in the process, of course.

I could tell she couldn't yet quiet absorb all that I was saying about Rahim, but there would be time for that and for her to come to benefit from his wisdom as I had. But for now it was enough for her to know that I believed that he had saved me, both physically as well as spiritually.

I told her I would need to stay in Marathon for one more day and night at the request of Sheriff Adams, who told me that given Baptiste's profile and his alleged crimes against the U.S. government, the FBI were en route—and would want to interview Tish and me—along with a whole bunch of other government types who would soon be arriving in their private jets and black Suburbans.

Mara told me she loved me "like the wind," which was our way of saying everything that needed to be said. And I thanked Rahim at that moment, for sending me back, and for giving me the chance to spend the rest of my life showing this woman and our children how desperately I loved them, and how little my life meant without them.

The next person I called was Oliver, and I asked him to try and conference Del onto our call so I could tell them both in person all that had happened. Listening to their reaction reminded me of why I still loved these odd characters so dearly, and hearing their exchanges with each other while I told my story, I knew that their own prickly sibling relationship was well on the mend.

"So let me get this straight, Sebastian was a woman, his sister Amelia, in fact. Is that what you're telling me, Mal, because I've got to say I did not see that one coming," said Oliver.

"Oliver, you really are the world's largest tool, aren't you? Mal, our dearest friend, was knocked unconscious with a wrench, weighted down, thrown into the sea like a bag of chum, and left for dead by the serial killer sidekick of a megalomaniac bent on the destruction of America.

"Meanwhile, our little Tish witnesses a double homicide, is dragged away and almost stabbed to death herself, and all while she's having to deal with the apparent drowning of her boss and mentor, not to mention the fact that the man she's fallen in love with turns out to be a woman!

"And all you have to say is you didn't see the whole Sebastian and Amelia thing coming," said Del, pausing for dramatic effect. At which point I was the first one to bust out laughing, as the tension of the last forty-eight hours found its first release.

I appreciated Oliver finding his edit button and not commenting on the fact that the death of Baptiste was unlikely to be good for CREATIF's bottom line, or that he wasn't sure at that moment who to call to ensure we still got paid for our services.

Because he'd managed to contain himself, I threw him a bone and told him he needed to contact the deputy chairman of the BAPTIST board, Walt Pearson, who I fully expected to be voted interim CEO while the company looked for a suitable replacement from within or, more likely, given the circumstances, from outside the organization.

I imagined him being desperate to get me off the phone so that he could talk to Pearson and start to repair the situation for CREATIF. And that laser-like focus, I realized, was what made Oliver the best at what he did.

I asked Del if she could fly down to Miami to come and collect Tish and bring her back to New York, as I would be flying home to North Carolina. And we agreed to meet at the airport in the morning of the day after tomorrow. Then she dropped off the call because she had to review some creative work that her teams had been developing for a meeting first thing tomorrow.

After she left the call, I said to Oliver, "Sounds like our Ms. Bishop is back on board at CREATIF, and I couldn't be happier for her, or for you, Oliver. You need her, and that's where she is supposed to be. Your life is too simple and too dull when she isn't there to take the piss out of you and to challenge your basic morality every day."

"I know it, although it pains me to say so. But what about you, won't you consider putting the full band back together, Mal? We need you here, and maybe you still need us," Oliver said.

"Listen, you inbred git, you know deep down I love you guys, but I can't come back. I've moved on, and there are things resulting from this whole experience that I need to do now. And I also recognize that Mara, Charlie, and Jess need to be my main focus now.

And in any case, you have Massimo, who is much smarter than me, so you don't need me all the time, anyway," I said. And I felt a sense of relief that the distance that had existed between us had now completely fallen away.

"All right, but I won't take no for an answer, you pompous English tosser. Eventually I'll get you back at CREATIF. Travel safe, and try not to provoke anyone else into trying to drown you, at least for a week or so."

"Why do you think I'm heading back up to the mountains, you buffoon? It's safer up there," and I hit the off button.

I didn't get a lot of sleep in the trundle bed, having given Tish the king bed, and I was afraid to go and sleep in the room she'd vacated in case she woke up and freaked out because I wasn't there. I also didn't want to let her out of my sight, as I was concerned that the press was eventually going to locate us, and I wanted to be able to keep them away from her until we got to Miami, where Del would take over my duties as her "minder."

Once we'd both freshened up the following morning, FBI agents were waiting at the hotel to take us back to the house where we were introduced to Special Agent Chloe Swift. I almost guffawed when she said her name, given the awkward similarity to Clarice Starling of *The Silence of the Lambs* fame. I made a mental note to work the phrase, "A nice chianti and some fava beans," into the interview, and I was buoyed to see that my sense of humor was starting to return.

Special Agent Swift was excellent as it turned out, in that she'd taken the time to be fully briefed by Sheriff Adams and didn't feel the need to have us go over everything again in excruciating, repetitive detail. Instead, she focused the discussion on one thing, or rather one person, Victor Vilas.

Tish knew almost nothing about him and his role in all this other than what she had gleaned from me, and so Special Agent Swift quickly dismissed her and had one of her subordinates talk with her, sensing her discomfort at being separated from me. Swift had a heart and she was equally smart, realizing she had a better chance of getting something meaningful out of me if I was motivated to speak with her.

"To what extent to do you think that Vilas was a willing partner in Baptiste's plan to destroy his company and through it to undermine the United States, Mr. Thomas," she asked me?

"Well, Agent Swift, I can only tell you what I think versus what I know. Baptiste was a man who created incredible loyalty. No one benefited more from his patronage than Vilas, who he viewed as the son he never had. I don't believe Vilas would have left BAPTIST if Alfredo hadn't told him to.

"So, yes, I think Vilas knew everything that Baptiste was planning, and that's why they had been storing up cash and creating partnerships with hedge funds in order to vacuum up cheap BAPTIST stock when things started to free fall. Now, whether his motivation was to hurt the U.S., I rather doubt to be honest. He never struck me as a particularly moral man when I'd met him, and I think he enjoys his playboy lifestyle.

"My guess, and that's all it is, was that he owed Baptiste everything, and so even though he might have thought this whole scheme was nuts, he'd have gone along with it out of loyalty. That, of course, and the not insignificant fact that as CEO of KONG, he'd potentially net billions from the acquisition of cheap BAPTIST assets," I concluded.

"Thank you, Mr. Thomas. Your country owes you a debt of gratitude for all that you've been through and for your crucial part in exposing Mr. Baptiste's treasonous intentions. I say that of course because he had been a citizen of the country he tried so hard to sabotage for over forty years and had been able to build his extraordinary fortune because of our way of life. It's incredible and tragic how he managed to carry that hatred with him for all those years," she said.

"What do you think will happen to all *this* now, Agent Swift?" I asked with a sweep of my hands encompassing the whole estate, and beyond that, his other properties, as well as the BAPTIST corporation itself.

"I honestly don't know, Mr. Thomas, but since he had no heir, and most of the people he might have left his fortune to are likely to become ineligible because of their roles in aiding and abetting his crimes, my guess is that it will end up in the hands of the U.S. government, which would be kind of ironic, don't you think?"

After a lifetime of building something up only to then destroy it in order to satisfy a quest for vengeance, and to then see it all go to the government of the country you set out to decimate, seemed beyond ironic. It was actually quite perfect!

And although it took the best part of a decade to sort it all out, Agent Swift's predictions were proved right in the end. The U.S. government ultimately stepped in and secured BAPTIST's financial and industrial assets. The company was broken up into broad business segments, some of which were then acquired by North American corporations, while others continued to operate under former BAPTIST management teams with new corporate personas like "BHC," which stood for BAPTIST Healthcare Corporation.

One of the factors that it was said enabled the U.S. government to ultimately resolve the corporate limbo surrounding BAPTIST, was a deal that was brokered behind the scenes between China and America. It related to what the latter considered to be the illegal acquisition of shares in a private company by a foreign government, with KONG having been shown to be a loosely veiled subsidiary of the Chinese government.

In order to avoid a very public spat while allowing both sides to save face, it was agreed that a number of BAPTIST's former assets, now under the effective control of the Chinese government, would be sold off. In addition, KONG would make previously "untouchable" blocks of its stock available for public acquisition internationally.

While both governments fared reasonably well, the same could not be said for either Vilas or Lula. Vilas was convicted of insider trading and attempting to defraud the U.S. government and received a twenty-year sentence, with a mandate that he serve at least ten of them in a federal prison.

Lula was convicted of the murder of Aaron as well as the attempted murder of yours truly, although he escaped conviction for the killing of Amelia, as the jury believed he had acted in the capacity of a bodyguard in order to save his employer. Ironically, he ended up serving his combined thirty-year sentence at the Kirkland Correctional Institution, where Ethan Pope had adopted his delusional agenda. Lula never got to fish again, as he died five years later of pancreatic cancer while still in prison.

And I'm happy to say that my dear friends prospered in the years that followed. Tish met and fell in love with a guy and decided to consummate things early on to make sure there were no "unexpected surprises" later in their relationship.

Massimo ultimately became CEO of CREATIF New York when that position became available and promoted Elliot to agency president.

The success of The Hug Challenge, even in light of the scandal that engulfed BAPTIST, established Del once and for all as perhaps the greatest creative force of her generation within the U.S. advertising industry. She eventually accepted the position of worldwide chief creative officer at CREATIF and moved to Paris, where she fell in love again, and again, and again. The position was offered to her by CREATIF's new worldwide CEO, a certain Oliver Melville Grouse III!

While BAPTIST and the man that created it were irreparably tarnished, the global movement for empathy, GEM, took on a life of its own after my book of the same name was published and became the basis for a spiritual awakening that has gripped America and many parts of the world, it seems.

I have Joan Seward to thank in part for the extraordinary global success of my book, after she chose to re-establish her book club and then create a television special in order to champion it. It has brought renewed understanding and tolerance to those cultures and societies where the divisions have appeared to be most intractable.

Mara and I went to see Dr. Badarwi again soon after returning home to ensure that the blow I'd received on the back of my head from Lula hadn't created any further damage to my much abused skull. We sat there with a look of amazement as she explained that Lula had struck me on the exact point of my original head injury, creating a dent in the titanium plate itself.

"What's even more fascinating is the fact that it's clear from this latest X-ray and scan that your skull had effectively grown a new layer of bone under the plate itself over the years. If you hadn't had this double layer of protection at the exact point where you were struck, the blow probably would have killed you, Mr. Thomas. You've been extraordinarily lucky, it seems," she said.

Although she's never said as much, I know Mara suspects that everything that happened on the boat that resulted in my survival can be explained logically. Certainly that is how Del sees it. The fact I might have already loosened the ropes when I went into the water, that my old windbreaker could have created enough buoyancy to keep my head above the water, and that Lula struck me on the exact point of my old head injury where an extra layer of protection now miraculously existed, allowed me to survive the blow to my skull.

Whether you believe that this unlikely set of circumstances was what kept me alive, or whether you believe that it was Rahim who saved me, is up to you. I know what I believe, and in any event, to my mind both explanations still constitute a miracle.

Rahim told me that everything that has ultimately transpired would happen if I told the truth and told it all in the book, especially the doubts that had plagued me as events unfolded. It seems that people are better able to find their way to the truth, if they know that like them, their messenger also had to sail through a sea of doubt.

ACKNOWLEDGMENTS

I first need to thank my wife, my love, my companion, my best friend as well as my business partner, Natalie Holden, for always being my greatest source of advice and inspiration.

Alongside Natalie, I must acknowledge Scott Scaggs, our business partner at Clean Design, and the core team that supported me on the book, including Wesley Hyatt, Debbie Vandiford, Lindsay Hamilton, Elise Karsten, and Jenny Storey. And a big shout out to all the fantastic people at our agency that contributed their time and ideas in relation to the content, presentation, and promotion of this book.

I'd like to thank Wright Tilley and the members of the Watauga County and Boone Tourism Boards for their insights in relation to the sections of the book that are set in the spectacular Blue Ridge Mountains of North Carolina.

Specifically, I'd like to thank the staff of the Gideon Ridge Inn in Blowing Rock, North Carolina, for always treating Natalie and me like royalty during our inspirational stays at your beautiful facility.

In a similar vein, I'd like to thank Dean Susan King and the staff and faculty at the University of North Carolina School of Journalism, as well as Michael Schinelli at UNC's Kenan Flagler School of Business, for their input as well as encouragement.

I want to acknowledge Laurie Paolicelli and her team at Chapel Hill and Orange County Tourism for helping to highlight the many attractions that this wonderful area has to offer.

I'd be remiss in not thanking the hundreds of folks who work at Publicis Kaplan Thaler in New York and at Publicis around the world for the inspiration that led to my inventing CREATIF, where Mal, Del, and OMG spent their careers.

And down in Marathon Key, I'd like to thank Captain T.J. Yzenas for all the wonderful fishing experiences and tips that found their way into the book.

I want to thank my old school friend, Matthew Hickman, for his invaluable guidance concerning business and investing in the Latin American region, as well as Dr. Chester Phillips for being my trusted medical consultant.

I must also thank all the great friends and colleagues I've crossed paths with over the years at agencies like Michael Peters, The Design Bridge, Howard Merrell and Partners, and McKinney, who've shared great times and stories with me that became the catalyst for the events in the book.

I'd like to thank Kevin Grealey for doing a masterful job of copy proofing the book, as well as Cynthia Zigmund, my trusted agent and editor, for making this, my second book, a reality.

Lastly I'd like to thank my mother, Dee Holden, who we love dearly and miss every day, for instilling a love of writing in me, and for inspiring me to cope with whatever life has thrown my way.

ABOUT THE AUTHOR

Jeremy Holden is an award-winning creative professional and accomplished author with ties to both sides of the Atlantic. He received a degree in graphic design from Ravensbourne College and studied law at the University of the West of England, giving him a distinctive right- and left-brain approach to business and life, including his writing. In 1995, Jeremy moved to the United States, where he met his wife, Natalie, and became a citizen.

Jeremy has worked for some of the best known advertising agencies in the world, including Publicis Worldwide, where he was responsible for strategy for New York. During his tenure in the industry, he has earned many of the industry's top honors, including the prestigious "Gold Effie," the advertising industry's Golden Globe.

Jeremy has counseled some of the world's most recognized names and brands, including Citigroup, Proctor & Gamble, Audi of America, Nasdaq, and many others. His experiences are integrated into, and integral to, *Sea of Doubt*.

Jeremy's first nonfiction book, *Second That Emotion: How Decisions, Trends, and Movements Are Shaped* (Prometheus Books, 2012), explores how movements are created in the political, cultural and commercial realms. The book received wide-ranging media coverage including *Fast Company*, The Huffington Post, CNN, and NPR.

Jeremy currently lives and works in Raleigh, North Carolina, where he runs Clean Design, a successful brand communications agency, along with his partners Natalie and Scott. He also teaches at the University of North Carolina at Chapel Hill in the School of Media and Journalism. A popular speaker and facilitator, Jeremy has run workshops with fellow authors Malcolm Gladwell and Professor Dan Ariely.

Jeremy is father to two overachieving children, Lily and Sam, and enjoys spoiling his dogs, Stella and Wally.